"GRIPPING."
—St. Petersburg Times

"A solid thriller beginning to end. . . . The macho cop-talk humor, the profiling details, and telling little asides—all build to give this book a richer feel than your average bang-bang thriller."

—Detroit News

"A rapid-fire pace . . . He knows how to create suspense . . . You'll find yourself rooting for Devlin . . . through many a tense moment."

—The Denver Post

"A turbo-charged tale with crackling dialogue, authentic characters, and a deftly innovative plot."

—Lansing State Journal

"The action is fast and furious. . . . An exciting and entertaining thriller."

—Sullivan County Democrat

"Lindsay is a sharp, skillful writer whose FBI has a realistic feel. His action scenes are edge-of-your-seat suspense, fueled by split-second timing and sparked by the reckless and likable personality of his protagonist. Top-notch storytelling."

—The Herald (Portsmouth, NH)

By Paul Lindsay
Published by Fawcett Gold Medal:

WITNESS TO THE TRUTH
CODE NAME: GENTKILL
FREEDOM TO KILL

FREEDOM TO KILL

A NOVEL OF THE FBI

Paul Lindsay

FAWCETT GOLD MEDAL • NEW YORK

A Fawcett Gold Medal Book
Published by The Ballantine Publishing Group
Copyright © 1997 by Paul Lindsay

All rights reserved under International and Pan-American Copyright Conventions. Published in the United States by The Ballantine Publishing Group, a division of Random House, Inc., New York, and simultaneously in Canada by Random House of Canada Limited, Toronto. Originally published by Villard Books, a division of Random House, Inc., in 1997.

Freedom to Kill is a work of fiction. The characters and dialogue are products of the author's imagination and do not portray actual persons or events.

http://www.randomhouse.com

Library of Congress Catalog Card Number: 97-97190

ISBN 0-449-14994-3

Manufactured in the United States of America

First Ballantine Books Edition: July 1998

10 9 8 7 6 5 4 3 2

For my children,
Larisa and Erik

Man is condemned to be free.
          —*Jean-Paul Sartre*

||| ACKNOWLEDGMENTS |||

Thanks to:

Gregg Schwarz for his unique perspective on Washington, D.C., without which this book would not have been possible and, while disguised as Captain Bucko, for saving the world on countless occasions from boredom. *Burn it down to the lug nuts, Captain!*

Bill Hagmaier for his insights into cases past, which in turn have inspired many of the villainous moments of these pages, and for his endless work to recover the missing children of this country.

My daughter, Larisa, for her exhaustive work during this effort and for taking our clan, in my lifetime, from sixth-grade dropouts to Phi Beta Kappa.

Leona Nevler for her always gracious support, and for reminding us all that there is still elegance inside and outside the boundaries of fiction.

David Rosenthal for his flawless ear, exquisite patience, and, above all, his maddening contempt for mediocrity.

Esther Newberg for her indestructible loyalty and concussive honesty, and for continuing to bring the wolves to my door, which, hopefully, is what this life is all about.

III CHAPTER 1 III

With the practiced invisibility that government agencies were so good at during a time of crisis, the U.S. Centers for Disease Control had spent the previous twenty-four hours quietly but frantically searching for Nate Walker, one of its research assistants, and the two vials of deadly African Lassa virus that had disappeared with him.

The last place anyone expected to find either was Disney World.

The missing researcher sat slouched, frozen in a wheelchair, unable to raise or lower his half-masted eyelids. Walker guessed he had been given a massive dose of some sort of animal tranquilizer. Uncontrollably, his head canted to the right and his neck strained to an unnatural length. He could feel the saliva cool the lower corner of his mouth. The man he knew as William Blake pushed him slowly through the world's busiest amusement park, whistling luxuriously. Through the warm, gray fatigue that had settled over his senses, Walker recognized the heroic strains of Wagner's *Ride of the Valkyries*.

One of the Seven Dwarfs—Dopey, he thought—walked up to him and waved kindheartedly. Walker gazed blankly at the mammoth head painted in trustworthy cartoon colors. It wore an expression as immovable as his own. He sensed the person inside was staring back, trying to guess what illness had left

1

him so pathetically helpless. He wanted to scream a warning: Greed, goddamnit—GREED!

Somewhere from within the deep, atrophied well of his conscience, Walker heard an echo of self-mocking laughter: *It was all going to be so easy.* And now, looking back into the closing oval of his life, he understood the lesson he had chosen to ignore: *It had been too easy.*

A month earlier, he had met William Blake while attending a communicable diseases seminar in Washington, D.C. At the end of one of the tedious daylong sessions, he was sitting in the hotel bar finishing a second double vodka when Blake sat down, introduced himself, and bought a third. As the evening wore on, Blake graciously insisted on buying every round. Walker guessed the source of the generosity was some corpulent expense account somewhere. And that was fine with him, because he had been charging all his meals and drinks to his room, hoping that when he checked out, some computerized miracle would cause his bloated credit card to be accepted.

At his first moment of consciousness the next morning, despite vodka's ability to slur conversation and conscience, Walker remembered Blake telling him he represented a Middle Eastern country whose intelligence sources had discovered that one of its neighboring enemies had obtained some Lassa virus and was attempting to develop a biological warfare strain. They were desperate to obtain their own samples to start defensive research. A quarter of a million dollars had been mentioned, and Walker thought he had agreed to help. He jumped out of bed and checked his suit coat. There were fifty hundred-dollar bills in the pocket.

A week later, he started receiving a series of calls from Blake. And then yesterday or the day before—he couldn't remember now—he was instructed to bring two vials of the Biosafety Level 4 agent to a little-used medical laboratory in the Atlanta area, where Middle Eastern technicians would, with all the necessary biohazard precautions, shave off minute samples of the contaminated tissue. Then Walker would be able to return them to the CDC undetected. The remaining $245,000 would be there waiting.

But the only thing waiting was Blake, a gun in one hand and a syringe in the other.

Dopey was gone now, and Blake was wheeling the research assistant into a rest room. Once they were in the roomy handicapped stall, Blake locked the door and, after turning Walker around to face him, pulled on a pair of surgical gloves. Gently, he raised Walker's head until he could see his prisoner's targetless eyes. "You are indeed fortunate. So seldom in this nation of homicidal mismanagement does one's death serve such historic purpose. Yours will announce the beginning of the end for the Land of the Free."

Carefully, he lowered Walker's head and unbuttoned the man's shirt. Taking out a slender, double-edged combat knife, he cut a shallow six-inch-long incision just above Walker's belt line. Because of Walker's chemically lowered heart rate, the wound bled slowly. Blake rebuttoned the shirt.

From behind the wheelchair, he took the small plastic cooler that Walker had used to transport the deadly samples from the CDC. Filled with dry ice, it held two white plastic vials marked LASSA OB-5. He studied the containers appreciatively and said, "One for me . . ." putting one back in the cooler, ". . . and one for you." Blake uncapped the frozen vial and dropped it down the front of Walker's shirt.

Walker felt a white-hot terror fall through him. In an hour or so, the diseased tissue would thaw, and he would become infected with the hemorrhagic fever. An extensive breakdown of tissue and organs would follow, causing blood to ooze from every one of his body's openings.

But he knew something Blake apparently did not: Statistically, the Lassa virus, unlike the Ebola, was fatal only about

3 percent of the time. Although he was in for a biological nightmare, he had a 97 percent chance of survival.

Blake turned the wheelchair around and, from behind, slowly slid his left hand around Walker's neck until his middle finger found the carotid artery. He timed its thick, lazy rhythm. "Oh, I know you think that you have an excellent chance of living through this . . ." he said, and felt Walker's pulse quicken. He smiled. ". . . but since you know what I look like . . ." There was another surge in Walker's heart rate. Blake smiled again. "Good, you understand."

Walker's fear struggled desperately against the tranquilizer, but finally, the only defense he could summon was a single tear that slowly crawled down his cheek.

With the patience and discrimination of a diamond cutter searching for the most advantageous entry point, Blake studied the juncture between the back of Walker's neck and his skull. Then carefully, with his right hand, he pushed the razor-edged blade of his knife deep under the base of the skull, severing the technician's brain stem. He continued to hold the finger of his left hand on Walker's carotid artery for another twenty seconds, waiting for the next beat. It never came. He turned up Walker's shirt collar to cover the wound, unlocked the stall door, and removed his rubber gloves. "Well, Nate, let's take you out among the great unwashed so you can spread your particular brand of sunshine and I can start showing America just how irresolute and powerless it really is."

III CHAPTER 2 III

Mike Devlin sat watching the Downriver Gun Shop. The entire FBI bank-robbery squad was nearby but out of sight, letting him take the eye. They were waiting for the "Jacktown Ski Team," a Detroit-area bank-robbery gang. The use of such nicknames, necessary only when criminals were able to maintain their anonymity, was distasteful to the Bureau because it was a glaring reminder that the part-time felons were being more successful than the full-time agents.

While most bank robberies were committed by close-your-eyes-and-floor-it amateurs, the Ski Team brought a cold, brutal professionalism in through the front door with them. Their method was always the same: They wore ski masks, jumpsuits, and gloves, were never inside for more than five minutes, and always cleaned out the vault. The nickname was derived from their clothing, plus some vague informant information identifying everyone in the group as having done time at Jackson prison, nostalgically referred to by its alumni as Jacktown.

The targets they chose were always in some sleepy Detroit suburb that, because of commerce in the area, kept a couple hundred thousand dollars in the vault. The small towns were also attractive because they would have only one or two single-officer cars that could respond to the robbery. And these officers were far more practiced in handling barking-dog complaints than stopping armed felons.

The gang had already netted over a million dollars, and until a week ago, the FBI had no idea who they were. But then the subject of a Bureau drug case decided to transfer some of his impending prison time to the ski mask crew by informing on them. He did not have a lot of details, but he had sold the gang's leader, Frank Butler, the guns that had been used in four of their previous robberies. He also knew that just before every job, they met at the Downriver Gun Shop. It was run by an individual who had served time at Jackson with both Butler and the informant. The only people Butler trusted were those he had known in prison, and the gun shop's manager was paid a thousand dollars to keep the business closed while the gang made last-minute plans and test-fired the guns they always left behind in their stolen getaway car.

For the past week, the bank-robbery agents had taken turns surveilling the shop, waiting for the gang's van to show up. Today was Devlin's turn, and as he was lifting the lid off his first cup of coffee, it pulled up. According to the informant, the vehicle's presence at the gun store meant that, in all likelihood, the crew was about to rob another bank, their ninth in the last five months. The rest of Devlin's squad had responded quickly and now sat waiting, nervously checking their handguns and M-16's.

The basement of the gun shop housed a small target range. The four members of the Ski Team were there alone. Frank Butler leaned against one of the shooting-booth walls and let his blazing eyes measure Benny Wilson, the gang's new getaway driver. Having witnessed Butler's self-validating need for violence on several occasions in prison, Wilson shifted uneasily in his chair and spoke with forced nonchalance, attempting to interrupt whatever paranoid delusions might be growing behind those shrinking, retaliatory pupils. "Tommy says you been doin' real good."

Although Butler was convinced Wilson was more afraid of him than of any problem his crew might run into during the holdup, he continued to stare at him for another fifteen seconds. Wilson tried a number of different positions for his hands but could not find a comfortable place for them. Butler noticed that he could, by moving his head slightly, make Wilson nervously shift his hands and feet. It was as though he had him on strings. He really missed the intimidation of prison life, the sweet smell of fear. On the outside, it was far less useful.

Butler let his knotted eyebrows relax, which was as close as his face ever came to a smile. "Yeah," he answered condescendingly, "because we're the best at what we do. Hitting the tellers and coming away with twenty or thirty grand is a punk's move. The vault is what pays the freight to Vegas."

Wilson said, "You guys like Vegas, huh? Afraid I'm not much of a gambler."

"What about all those *nasty hookers*? Or don't you have a dick, either?" The other two men laughed.

Wilson forced himself to laugh. "No, no, I like women fine. It's just—"

Not seeming to hear him, Butler went on. "Last time, I had one tell me what a *big* dick I had."

"What she said was"—Tommy Nolo smiled—"what a big dick you had—for a white boy."

Butler gave a short, joyless grunt that served as his laugh. When he had been released into the general population at the State Prison of Southern Michigan at the age of eighteen, he decided he needed to do two things to survive his fifteen-year armed robbery sentence: lift weights every day and constantly think violent thoughts. The results could not be argued with. Nolo had once likened Butler's unabated hatred to driving a car with the accelerator locked to the floor, using only the brake to control the speed. It was always at full throttle, and the least little nudge was all the gang leader needed to remove all restraint and become homicidal.

Nolo was the only person Butler would allow to kid him. They had been rap partners for eight years in Jackson. During their first year together, Nolo had demonstrated his loyalty to Butler by taking a Black Muslim shank meant for him. While Nolo was recovering in the prison hospital, Butler returned the courtesy by isolating the Muslim and then taking a full twenty minutes to methodically beat him to death with a mop handle.

Although Wilson feared Butler, he admired his reckless confidence. There was something appealing about an individual who took great chances to live the way he wanted to. Wilson knew he wasn't equally courageous, but at this moment, that kind of life seemed within his grasp. With as much confidence as he could manufacture, he said, "Let's do it!"

But Butler could see the tiniest flickering of reluctance in his eyes. His words were now quiet, measured, dangerous. "You're only here because our driver had his parole violated, so understand something, and understand it good. This is our business. When we go in that bank, our lives are on the line. This *ain't* no fucking rodeo, so we don't need any cowboys, or clowns."

"You know I'm a good wheel, and that's what you need, isn't it?"

"What I *need* is a guy who'll stand up when everyone else's assholes are slamming shut. And I'm not sure that's you."

Prison had taught Wilson how to keep fear out of his voice, but now he intentionally let it creep into his words, because he knew Butler needed its reassurance. "Frankie, you know me; I'm stand-up."

"If you're not and we go back to the joint, guess what my first piece of business is going to be?"

"It's just that I never did a stickup before."

"And that's exactly what's starting to worry me."

Wilson's eyes darted around the range. His lungs were taking in more oxygen than he needed. For the first time, he noticed the smell of cordite from previous target shooters. It reminded him of the deadly reason they were there. He had made a mistake. He was only a car thief, one of those criminal occupations that were usually the end result, as was his case, of a drug habit. But these guys were hard-core, puberty-to-postmortem felons, who believed that bank robbers were the warrior class of society. Wilson looked down at the four weapons on the bench and realized he had no way out. He chanced a look at Butler, whose eyes bore into him. Defensively, he blurted out, "Since I don't go inside, do I have to wear a mask? I can't stand the itching."

In a blur, Butler stood up and knocked him over the back of a folding chair he was sitting on. "Goddamnit, you'd better start thinking. What do you think? There are no witnesses in the parking lot?"

Wilson was barely aware of what Butler was saying. As he struggled to his feet, a school of flashing white disks swam crookedly before him. His survival instincts took over. "Sorry, Frankie, I wasn't thinking."

Butler turned and stared hypnotically downrange at the four black silhouette targets that hung from metal clamps. After a few seconds, he turned back to Wilson. He had made two decisions. The bank, because of the armored car delivery, had to be hit today, so he would use this driver. And because of Wilson's obvious weakness, if anything went wrong during the robbery, the first thing he would do was shoot him through the head. Calmly, he said, "Tell me again what you're doing while we're in the bank."

"Listening to the scanner."

"That's right. When we're inside, you're our lifeline. You

stay in the car and listen. You hear anything that sounds like
we have a problem, you call us on the walkie-talkies. If the
cops pull in, you got to open fire on them until we can get to
the car." Butler looked at him hard. "Think you can do that?"

"Hey, Frankie, I want to get out of that lot, too."

"Just make sure we're in the car when you do." Butler
picked up one of the weapons from the bench, a .45-caliber
automatic, and threw it into Wilson's lap. "Convince me you
know how to use that." The car thief knew the basic procedure
for loading and firing an automatic handgun, but he was also
aware that Butler would not allow any more mistakes. His
fingers felt thick and confused as he pushed the fat bullets
into the spring-loaded magazine. Finally the clip was full and
Wilson anxiously slammed it into the weapon. With a mixture
of bravado and relief, he pulled the slide to the rear and let it
go home, chambering the first round. He held it out to Butler
in an open palm as if offering an instructor a completed project.
"That's fine," Butler said sarcastically, "but I meant actually
shooting it at something." Wilson turned toward the target. He
picked up a set of ear protectors and started putting them on.
"Shoot without them," Butler ordered. "You'll need to get used
to the noise." As Wilson lined up the .45's sights on the paper
outline of a human being, Butler gave him one last instruction.
"If the shooting starts, the first thing you do is shoot as many
civilians as you can. That really keeps the cops busy." The other
gang members laughed in agreement. Wilson held his breath,
trying to get the gun's front sight to stop shaking.

A half hour later, Butler came out of the front door of the gun
shop and scanned the street. He spotted Devlin's car a block
away and studied it for a split second. Because of the distance,
he couldn't see the driver, so he disregarded it as a threat.

Sitting low in the seat, Devlin watched Butler through bin-
oculars. As soon as the bank robber had walked out, Devlin

did not need the old prison photo rubber-banded to the visor to know who he was looking at. Butler moved with the agility and sovereignty of a middleweight contender. His skin, though tan, still held that underlying gray pallor that long-term convicts never seem able to eradicate. He turned back to the door and motioned for the others.

Quickly, the remaining three gang members walked to the van, loaded two heavy bags into it, and got in. Devlin picked up the mike. "Fire 'em up. We've got the four targets loaded into the chopper." The van backed out onto the street and headed west. "We're away, nine bound on the main. Can someone get up here and take the eye? Number one gave me the hard eyes when he first came out."

"Four-one, Four-six is on the way. Can you hold him for another minute?"

"Yeah, but you'd better hurry; the driver's got his foot down." The van sped along the street, and Devlin watched it turn off for the northbound I-75 on-ramp. "They're twelve on the ditch."

Four-six flashed past Devlin. "You can pull back on the stick, Mike. I've got him."

Devlin decelerated and more bank-robbery squad cars sped by him. The van was doing ten miles an hour over the speed limit, which on Detroit's expressways was considered inconspicuous.

Butler rode in the front passenger seat and adjusted the sideview mirror so he could watch the traffic behind him. He looked over at Wilson, who was watching only the cars in front of him. "You fucking moron, don't you see we're being followed?"

Panicked, Wilson looked in his mirror. "Where?"

Butler did not answer immediately as he continued to study the pattern of traffic behind him. "The dark blue Lumina and the gray Grand Am."

"Should I lose them?"

Butler ignored the question. "Tommy, you got the guns stashed?"

"Yeah, the bags are zipped up and under the seat. They'll need a search warrant to get them."

"They can't have any paper or they'd have popped us when we came out. They're just following us, hoping we're on a score. Some motherfucker dimed us."

With a hint of relief, Wilson said, "Maybe we can try it again when things cool off."

Butler stared at him in disgust, and then realized they were slowing down for an accident that was clogging all four lanes. "Quick, get to the shoulder!"

Without thinking, Wilson responded, pulling hard to the right, narrowly missing the braking cars in the three right-hand lanes. Butler watched the surveilling cars disappear into the halting traffic jam. As soon as the van hit the shoulder, he said, "Punch it!" Wilson drove at sixty miles an hour along the edge of the highway. A quarter of a mile up, they passed the accident, a jackknifed semi. Once around it, they sped up the expressway alone. Butler said, "Okay, let's go to work."

Forty-five minutes later, a stolen four-door sedan that had been stashed a mile away pulled up abruptly to the front door of the White Lake Savings and Trust. Three men dressed in dark blue jumpsuits and black ski masks exited. Two were carrying sawed-off carbines, and the third, Butler, carried a 9-millimeter automatic. Wilson, dressed identically, remained nervously behind the wheel and turned up the volume on the police scanner, his .45 on the seat next to him.

As soon as the three men were through the front door, Butler, in a controlled scream, said, "Everyone on the floor!" Then, as if choreographed, all three of them chambered rounds into their weapons to punctuate the command. In response, a murmur of panic was followed by the subdued sounds of a dozen bodies hitting the floor.

A week before, Butler had sat outside the bank until the armored car made its weekly drop-off. He walked in just as the branch manager was signing for the shipment. After one of the tellers changed a hundred-dollar bill for Butler, he left.

Now, he quickly scanned the people on the floor and spotted the manager lying next to a desk. Butler yanked him to his feet and glanced at the other two gang members to ensure they were controlling the customers and employees.

The heavy vault door was open, but a locked stainless steel gate prevented final entry to the stacks of banded currency. Effortlessly, Butler flung the manager against the wall next to the vault and jammed the barrel of his automatic into the banker's left eye. With frightening calm, he said, "You get paid to make decisions. Here's an easy one: The only way I'm leaving here without the money in that vault is if you and two of your customers are lying dead on the floor." Keeping one hand on the manager's throat, Butler turned around and pointed his gun at the nearest person. "Five, four, three—" The manager dug both his hands into his pockets looking for the gate key. Before he could pull it out, all three of the holdup men heard something that made them freeze.

It was the voice in their radio earpieces. Slightly distorted by panic, it reported, "Scanner says there's a silent alarm! We've got cops inbound!"

Although the bank robbers had never been caught inside before, they knew exactly what to do. Without a word, they all broke for the door. Once outside, they could see the driver's masked head snapping anxiously from the bank door to the entrance to the parking lot. The getaway car's engine was revving, begging to leave.

The three men piled in, and before the doors could slam shut, the car's tires started screaming. As soon as the sedan cleared the parking lot, the sound of a police siren tore through the air. Butler looked back and saw that a White Lake squad car was in close pursuit. "Keep your masks on. He's close enough to identify us." He turned to the driver. "This is what you're supposed to be so good at—lose this motherfucker!" Butler was surprised at the look of confidence in the driver's eyes. The man didn't say a word but, instead, let the car's suddenly increasing speed answer the challenge.

The getaway car slid through a turn at fifty miles an hour and then accelerated to eighty-five, but the police car stayed with it.

"Shit! He's still on us," Tommy Nolo yelled from the rear seat.

Butler rolled down his window and said, "Hold the car steady; I'll take him out." He turned around and kneeled on the seat, pushing his upper body through the window. Just as he was about to take a shot at the pursuing vehicle, the getaway car took a hard left and Butler had to use his considerable strength to keep from being thrown out the window. They had turned into an all-but-deserted construction materials yard. Insanely, Butler pressed his gun under the driver's jaw. "What the fuck are you doing?" he screamed.

Tommy Nolo jabbed the barrel of his carbine into the back of the driver's head. "Frankie, kill this motherfucker if he swerves this car again. We'll take care of the cop."

As the two men in the backseat rolled down their windows and started to lean out with their carbines, Butler looked closely at the driver and realized he had not said a word since leaving the bank. "Say something, goddamnit!"

The driver turned to him and said, "You should buckle up."

For a moment, the seemingly inappropriate statement confused Butler. "Buckle up?" But then he realized that the voice was not Benny Wilson's. He reached over, ripped the ski mask

off, and froze in astonishment as he looked into the face of a
man he had never seen before.

Mike Devlin smiled back defiantly. Before Butler could
react, Devlin jammed on the brakes and cut the wheel hard,
causing the sedan to spin out in a circle and slam into a
twenty-foot-high dune of construction sand. Both of the men
leaning out the back windows were thrown out of the car, and
Butler's head shattered the windshield, temporarily stunning
him. Devlin ripped the gun from his hand and said, "Yeah,
Frankie, it's the law."

III CHAPTER 3 III

Assistant Special Agent in Charge Eric Bolding's secretary
told Devlin he could go right in. When he walked into the
small office, Bolding rose and offered his hand. Devlin's squad
supervisor, Jim Harrison, was already sitting on a couch in
front of the ASAC's desk. Bolding said, "Jim's been filling me
in on yesterday's arrests. Helluva job."

Since the entire squad had been involved and he was the
only one summoned, Devlin suspected this was not going to
be the congratulatory session the ASAC was presenting. "But?"

Coming around his desk, Bolding ignored Devlin's wari-
ness. "Have a seat, Mike." He pulled up an armchair, and
Devlin sat on the couch between him and Harrison. "There are
a few details that aren't clear." Devlin was now certain he had

a problem. When management asked for "details," they usually meant *self-incriminating* details. "After you lost the gang in traffic, how did you find them again?"

"Are you sure you want to know?" Devlin asked, his tone deliberately ominous. Within the Bureau, that question held a standard submessage: If you value your career, you don't want to know. When properly used, the query had been known to clear FBI managers from a room faster than a package from the Unabomber.

"You're going to have to trust me for a few minutes until I can find out exactly what happened. Believe me, no one is here to hurt you."

Bolding had been warned, and he still wanted an answer. Devlin was reluctant to give it because admitting what had been done, although it was just rule-bending in his eyes, could be interpreted by the Department of Justice as a misprision of a felony. He turned to Jim Harrison, who had stood by him through similar situations in the past, and by the look in his eyes, Devlin knew he could trust the ASAC's assurances. "After I spotted the van at the gun shop but before the troops arrived, I put a tracking beeper on it."

Bolding said, "I guess we can assume you didn't have a court order for it."

Again Devlin asked, "Are you sure you want to know?" He made the warning in his voice a little stronger. He was offering a loophole: If officialdom did not know for sure that the beeper was unauthorized, the most they could be accused of was poor personnel management, hardly a felony within the United States government.

"Okay, we'll leave that question unanswered for now. Tell me what happened at the bank."

"When we got there, three of the gang were already inside. The driver was so busy with the scanner he never saw us."

"Didn't they have our frequency?"

"I don't know, but it wouldn't have mattered, because we had the scramblers on. Anyway, the decision was made to grab the driver. But we knew if we waited and confronted the rest of them when they came out, they'd run back inside and turn it into one of those hostage standoffs that would be used as a New Agent Training horror story for the next hundred years. So someone came up with the idea that one of us should put on the driver's mask and jumpsuit and take the rest of the gang to an isolated area, where they could be arrested without endangering civilians. I—"

Harrison interrupted. "Exactly whose idea was that, Mike?"

Devlin hesitated a moment and then said, "Well . . . I guess it was mine."

Harrison gave the ASAC a glance that seemed to confirm some previously discussed suspicions. Bolding said, "Go ahead."

From the body language passing between his two bosses, Devlin sensed he was getting in deeper. He smiled his surrender. "What exactly is it you would like me to confess to?"

Bolding gave an honest laugh. "Come on, Mike. We asked you to trust us."

"Okay. I was the driver's size, so I volunteered. I put on his jumpsuit and mask, got on their walkie-talkie, and told them an alarm had been tripped. They came running out, got into the car, and I drove them to where we made the arrests."

Bolding said, "Tell me about the police officer who was chasing the getaway car."

"As soon as we saw them getting out of the van at the switch site and going to the getaway car in those jumpsuits, we knew they were going to hit close by. So we used a cellular to call the locals and tell them what we needed. That cop did a nice piece of driving."

"Yes, we've interviewed him. He said you probably saved his life the way you kept the bank robbers from getting a shot off. In fact, he said he thought you must be"—Bolding smiled to soften the word— "crazy."

Devlin still did not know where the ASAC was heading, but experience had taught him that a compliment during this kind of questioning, if that's what the cop's words were intended to be, should be treated with suspicion. Noncommittally, he shrugged his shoulders.

"Just a couple more questions. When you volunteered to be the driver, did that seem like a dangerous thing to do?"

"I really didn't have the time to analyze it."

"Please take the time now. Do you think what you did was dangerous?"

"I suppose it might have been. But at the time, it seemed to be the only way to take those three into custody without anyone getting hurt."

Harrison said, "Anyone but you."

Devlin reached into his suit jacket and pulled out his identification, opened it, and read, " 'Michael Devlin, whose signature and photograph appear hereon, is a regularly appointed special agent of the Federal Bureau of Investigation and, as such, is charged with the duty of investigating violations of the laws of the United States.' " He looked up and smiled. "That's just my luck. I got the one set of credentials that doesn't allow me to refuse to do something because it might be dangerous."

"Mike, I know doing dangerous things is part of what we get paid for, but it seems like you have this *need* to involve yourself in these situations."

Two years earlier, Devlin, on his way home, had been covering a lead on Detroit's lower east side. He spotted smoke coming out of an apartment building's third-floor window. He radioed for police and fire before he ran to the building. At the same time, a tall black middle-aged man had also seen the smoke and got out of his car. They exchanged glances of understanding and hurried inside. Devlin took the doors on the right; the other man, the left. Hastily, they pounded on them, and as soon as someone answered, they warned them and moved on. The farther up they went, the thicker the smoke became. Ten minutes later, after everyone had been warned, the two men found themselves back outside. Only a few of the tenants had left their apartments for the safety of the street. The man looked around in disgust and said, "Fucking dope fiends. Don't even have the sense to git outta the building."

Devlin knew he was right. It was one of those decaying structures that would be boarded up within months. No maintenance had been done in years, and the only level of human existence capable of surviving within was that of the drug addict. They were a building's death knell, its final cancer, and they brought with them an unconditional distrust of everything. Devlin had been in a hundred of these dwellings and had been told a thousand lies. Most of the junkies didn't have to lie, but it was the first rule of their self-preservation: See a badge, tell a lie. It was their obligation, their fraternal duty.

The doors Devlin had gone to were answered by lethargic suspicious faces. He was obviously a cop and not to be believed, even if he was yelling "Fire!"

As Devlin and the other man heard the sirens approaching, they looked at each other, searching for something to say that would give what they had done some meaning, but finally they could exchange only cynical smiles and drive off without another word.

Devlin had not intended to tell his wife about the incident, but as soon as he came through the door, she smelled the smoke on his clothes. He told her only that there had been a fire and he had gone inside to warn the occupants.

She led him upstairs to the bathroom and took all his clothes off. After stripping herself, she pulled him into the shower and let the hot water wash away the fire's stench. Then she washed the last of it out of his hair. "If you run into every

burning building you see, sooner or later I'm afraid there will
be one you won't come out of."

"Which ones do I ignore?"

"The ones you can't run out of."

Now, Devlin looked at the ASAC unemotionally and said,
"I'm fine."

Bolding looked at him for a moment. "I'm sorry, Mike, but
I don't agree. Jim and I are worried about you. You're taking
too many chances." He picked up a teletype. His tone became
more official. "There's a special being run out of Bureau
headquarters. I'm sending you back for a breather. Have you
heard about the wacko down at Disney World with the deadly
viruses?"

"That sounds a lot less dangerous."

Bolding gave a short laugh. "Unlike the Super Bowl MVP,
you're not going to Disney World. You'll be in Washington
reviewing files."

"Reviewing files? In Washington? Thank God, for a second
there I thought I was being punished."

"I've given this a lot of thought, and I really do feel it's for
your own good. Try and relax while you're there. It's only
for two weeks. Think of it as a paid vacation." When Devlin
didn't answer, Bolding said, "Mike, this is something we're
trying to do for you. Don't turn it into a problem." Then, after
another moment of silence, he said, "I hate ultimatums, but
either accept this or I'll have to find another squad for you, one
with a lot more indoor responsibilities."

Devlin considered his options; there really were none. He
thought about having to leave his family again. Knox would
understand; she always did. He had not told her about the
arrests the day before because she would have seen it as another
burning building. But if he wasn't taking chances, why was
he keeping it from her? Maybe there was some validity to the
ASAC's concerns. Maybe he was being, as Knox liked to put

it, a little too immortal. Washington might help him find out. "Just two weeks?"

The tension narrowing Bolding's eyes eased. "Just two weeks, I promise."

Devlin stood up and shook both men's hands. As he reached the door, Bolding asked, "Mike, just out of curiosity, where did you get the electronic equipment you used to track the van?"

Within the Bureau, there existed an underground of agents who trusted each other when something unauthorized was needed, agents who still remembered why they had joined the FBI. Devlin had gotten the beeper from the office's head technical agent. But there was an unwritten rule these individuals refused to break: They never gave each other up. Devlin said, "I'll ask you again: Are you sure you want to know?"

The ASAC smiled softly, and Devlin was reminded that a long time ago Eric Bolding had been one of these agents. "Enjoy Washington, Mike."

III CHAPTER 4 III

"Washington? Why are they sending you?"

Her tone was supportive, but he could tell that it held the beginnings of suspicion. She had discovered that each time her husband received an abrupt change in assignment, she could depend on an elusive explanation that was usually traceable, through determined investigation, to some breach of FBI protocol or procedure. He would not lie to her, but she knew he was not above rerouting the truth, especially when it was for "her own good." Her dark blue eyes waited. Their objective: to find the unraveling point of his defense.

From past interrogations, Devlin recognized the warning signs. Her jaw was set for conflict, and he was about to become the enemy. He knew his chances of keeping the truth from her were remote, but maybe vagueness would delay its discovery. "We pulled a stunt on some arrests yesterday that the ASAC didn't like."

"We? So the others will be going to Washington with you?"

He could see that his clumsy sleight of hand was not going to work, so he opted for a quick retreat. "You do understand that compassion is the real reason I tell little white lies?"

With the same inflection she'd used the first time the question was asked, she said, "Why you?"

"You're not going to like the answer."

"There's a surprise."

"Okay. Bolding thinks I took some chances during the arrests." She continued to stare at him, waiting for the details he was obviously avoiding. Her eyes had always been a sanctuary for him during life's little storms, but now they were unrelenting, inquisitional. He told her what his role had been in the capture of the bank-robbery gang.

"And he thought that was dangerous?" she asked facetiously.

He laughed. "I thought he was overreacting too."

"I guess this just isn't registering."

"What isn't?"

"That everyone else sees you're developing a problem."

"A problem?"

"Can you honestly sit here now and tell me that getting in a car with three armed bank robbers and driving like a maniac is just another day at the office?"

"Somebody had to do it."

"Did they? Did anybody *have* to do it? Or was this another chance for Mike Devlin to guzzle testosterone? Wouldn't they have been caught anyhow?" When Devlin didn't answer, she asked again, "Wouldn't they?"

"Possibly."

"Possibly? You really don't see what you do as dangerous. I used to think you did it for the adrenaline rush, but that's not it, because there has to be fear before those glands will pump. Something else is driving you, and it's scaring the hell out of me."

"I know this isn't what you want to hear, but I think you're taking this a little too seriously."

She turned away for a moment and then looked back at him carefully. "God, I hope you're right."

"You should know better than anyone, I'm not that easy to get rid of." She shook her head slowly trying to prevent the smile that was pulling at the corners of her mouth. "And for the next two weeks I'll be sitting at a desk in Washington reviewing files, so you can stop thinking about it for at least that long. Who knows, maybe I'll learn to like it."

"You do, and I'll really start to worry," she said. "But while you're there, take a look at all this and make sure you're right and I'm wrong."

"I will, I promise. Anything else?"

"Take me to bed."

"Is that an order?"

"It is."

"That's one good thing about being a file reviewer—we are a submissive bunch."

||| CHAPTER 5 |||

Devlin walked up Pennsylvania Avenue and past the FBI police who guarded the J. Edgar Hoover Building. A surprisingly long line of tourists stood in the crisp January weather, waiting for the 8:00 A.M. tour. When he entered through the Tenth Street door, one of the security people wearing the unofficial uniform of a blue blazer and gray slacks asked if she could help him. Devlin flipped open his credentials and said, "I'm in from Detroit to work a special." The guard studied his photograph and then his face. Her eyes searched his, looking, he thought, more for motive than identification. "Expecting trouble?" he asked half jokingly.

Satisfied, she smiled and in a conspiratorial whisper said, "We have to be careful. We're only supposed to let in a couple of the lunatic fringe a day."

"I guess it's a good thing I got here early, then." The guard gave him a pleasant smile and copied his name from the identification. She asked him to wait while a security pass was prepared.

A few minutes later, he was handed the badge and told to report to room 621. He had expected to be shuffled off to one of the building's small, windowless cubicles that were normally reserved for management underlings. The penal-colony nature of the rooms was, according to the lore of the rank-and-file agents, exactly what these future Special Agents in Charge deserved for leaving the real FBI.

Room 621 was marked SECTION CHIEF: VIOLENT CRIMES AND MAJOR OFFENDERS SECTION.

When Devlin entered, he was greeted by the secretary.

"Good morning," she said brightly.

For Devlin, Bureau secretaries had always been one of the uncelebrated sources of the FBI's success. Usually they were hired as stenos or typists, and if they could demonstrate a flawless ability to get the job done in spite of inconsiderate agents, endless drudgery, and insulting wages, they could eventually become an FBI Secretary, a title they were curiously possessive of. And while "their" agents were looking for anything from bad guys to badly sliced golf balls, these women jealously guarded the reputation of the agency. Whether their lunch hour was spent typing a late report or talking a fugitive into surrendering, they did whatever was necessary to maintain the Myth. In the "real world," they could have doubled their salary and halved their workload. But they stayed, and although it was not part of their job description, they reminded everyone what real dedication was all about.

"Hi, I'm Mike Devlin. I'm in from Detroit. I was told to report here."

"Oh, yes. I'm Sharon. Welcome, Mr. Devlin."

Devlin lowered his voice. "Sharon, out in the field, where everyone knows that the secretaries are really in charge, they call the agents by their first names."

She feigned surprise. "No kidding. Next time I'm in Detroit, I'll call you Mike." Devlin laughed and shook his head in appreciation of secretarial tenacity. She picked up her phone. "Mike Devlin is here."

Almost immediately, the section chief's door opened and Devlin was surprised to see Tom O'Hare. "Mike, how the hell are you?"

A few years earlier, O'Hare had been Devlin's ASAC in Detroit. He looked the same—tall and trim, with dark, thoughtful eyes. His hair, richly curled just above the collar, was also unchanged but now seemed noticeably longer than the standard length of his Hoover Building peers. It reminded Devlin that the man who would be giving him orders for the next couple of weeks had never been one to surrender to the comfort of conformity and was never guided by the criteria or precedents of others. Devlin had witnessed these things first-hand, during the only arrest they had ever made together. The story was one Devlin had sworn never to tell. It violated law enforcement's most irrevocable rule: Never give up your gun.

The case involved a Top Ten fugitive who had escaped from an Alabama prison while serving two consecutive life sentences for a double murder. Bureau policy dictated that an SAC or ASAC was to be present at all such high-profile apprehensions. Normally, agents were less than enthusiastic about dragging managerial baggage through an already difficult situation, but before becoming an administrator, O'Hare had spent ten years in the trenches of Philadelphia, and he knew his way around the street. While he served as an ASAC in Detroit, the agents found that O'Hare's decisions were unselfish and always made with their best interests in mind. He was, they decided, one of them.

As the Top Ten arrest assignments were being given out, the case agent hesitated when he had to choose someone to cover the rear of the house. Seasoned fugitive agents loved action and did not consider the back door the place to be during a time when the possibility of physical confrontation was so high. O'Hare understood the problem and eliminated it by asking to be sent to the back. As soon as he got there, the front door was kicked in. After ten minutes of fruitless searching, panic that they had somehow let this rare trophy slip through their fingers started to set in.

Then came a knock at the rear door, its rhythm and volume unexcited. Once it was opened, the ASAC pushed the hand-cuffed fugitive inside. They were both out of breath, and their clothes were torn and dirty. O'Hare explained, "I heard the front door go down, and the next thing I know, he comes bolting out the back." The agents searching the house assembled around O'Hare and, while glaring at the prisoner for not having the courtesy to be caught within the area of their search, they stole admiring glances at their ASAC's ripped clothing.

As everyone started to leave, O'Hare discreetly asked Devlin, "Can you stick around a minute?" When he was certain everyone was gone, he led the way to the backyard. "I need you to help me find my gun."

"Did you lose it during the scuffle?"

Half grinning, O'Hare said, "This stays between us." Devlin nodded. "When he ran out, I drew down on him and yelled, 'Freeze.' He looked me dead in the eyes and said, 'Go ahead and kill me, motherfucker, because I ain't going back to prison.' So I had to either shoot him, which in Michigan would probably have sent *me* to prison, or wrestle him into handcuffs. But I was afraid if he got lucky, he'd wind up with my gun, and that seemed even less attractive. So what do you do?"

"Tough call. I don't know."

"Well, I didn't know either, but the only thing I could think of at the time was to throw my gun as far as I could and then jump him. I know it was stupid, but—"

Devlin laughed. "I'd call it creative." O'Hare laughed, a little relieved by Devlin's approval. "Just out of curiosity, Tom, what would you have done if he had gotten away?"

"The same thing we're going to do now—keep it quiet."

"And what would you have done if after you threw your gun away, he pulled out some sort of weapon?"

Just then O'Hare found his gun behind a bush, reholstered it, and said, "Then I'd have shown that fugitive some real running."

As Devlin followed O'Hare into his office, he glanced again at his hair and could not help but think that the next two weeks might not be so bad after all.

After they sat down, Devlin said, "Section chief. I'm impressed. I guess this means that you have officially become one of them."

"You know what they say, 'Washington is a city of great architectural *and* personal facades.' And don't be throwing any stones. You're a big part of the reason I got this job."

"I've been in this building less than fifteen minutes, and I'm already being blamed for something."

"Well, you did solve the Puget Sound murders. And after I told the Bureau how it was the result of my inspiring leadership, they promoted me."

"You have no one to blame but yourself; you're the one who allowed us to commit all those felonies."

"I hear you're still committing them."

"Sounds like you've been talking to Detroit."

"I have, but I'm not referring to your new career as a getaway driver—I'm talking about the Gentkiller," he said, referring to a serial murderer whose targets had been FBI agents. Devlin's surprise was obvious. "Come on, Mike, did you think no one was going to figure out you were responsible for solving the murders of four agents? As soon as I heard about it, I could see your fingerprints all over it." O'Hare leaned back, looking for Devlin's reaction. "Funny how the killer died so mysteriously."

Devlin stared back solemnly. "Detroit can be a funny place."

"If you mean funny in the eye-for-an-eye sense, I agree. Especially the cases you work. I have always been amazed at how justice seems to follow you around."

"Don't get too close or you'll find out what really follows me around."

O'Hare smiled. "Eric Bolding did call to let me know you were coming. He thinks your toes are hanging a little too far over the edge."

"Well, for the next two weeks, I'll be reviewing files, so he can breathe easy. Of course, there is the death of a thousand paper cuts to consider."

"Don't worry. I reminded him that we're very proud of our cowardice back here."

Devlin laughed. "Was he hoping some of it would rub off on me?"

"He knows you better than that, but I think there is such a thing as too much bravery," O'Hare said. "I remember once in Vietnam, I was assigned this platoon sergeant who was half black. He was twenty, maybe twenty-one, and he had made the rank of staff sergeant, which was unbelievable at that age. I'd been in-country about a month when one night we're up on a hill and started taking mortar fire. Ever mortared over there?" Devlin nodded. "Then you know how terrifying it is. I was down in my foxhole, scared to death. I looked up and here's this magnificent bastard standing up with a compass and a radio, taking an azimuth on the tube flashes and calling in counter-mortar fire as casually as if he were checking the wind direction. I can close my eyes right now and see him standing there, oblivious to the exploding rounds. It was the bravest thing I have ever seen. It's the bravest thing I ever *will* see. A couple of months later, I had to force him to go on R and R, literally threaten him with a court-martial. Two days later, I get word from the rear that he tried to kill himself. The psychiatrists said it was some sort of deep-seated guilt about his parents being interracial. He was evidently trying to commit suicide through bravery."

"Well, if they ever start mortaring Washington, don't expect me to stand up and take an azimuth."

"See, the cowardice around here is contagious. Have you seen the morning paper?" O'Hare handed him a newspaper. "Just read 'The Message.' " The front-page headline read: FREEDOM'S LAST DANCE. Off to the side was a boxed article entitled "The Message":

The life span of a democracy is 300 years; 100 years to build, 100 years to enjoy, and 100 years to destroy. America is well into its third hundred years and disastrously ahead of schedule. This has happened because you have become so immune to freedom that you are unable to enjoy its pleasures or mourn its loss. There can be no democracy without freedom for every man. You are no longer capable of maintaining or deserving such independence, so someone must assume leadership. It has become my duty to reverse history's course. I will deploy any tactics necessary to accomplish this mission. Take a moment to look around and witness freedom's last dance. You have two weeks to comply.

Devlin looked up from the article. "Comply with what?"

"No one's sure, but a second vial of virus is still missing. Everyone around here is worried that if we don't 'comply,' he'll find an even deadlier spot for it."

"Couldn't he thaw it out and use it to make more virus?"

"Christ, Mike, no one's supposed to figure that out. But you're right, he could go on regenerating that stuff indefinitely. Flood the whole country with it. That's why we've got to solve this and recover the other vial as soon as possible."

"Any leads?"

"A Disney employee who dresses up as one of the Seven Dwarfs got a good look at him when he was pushing the research tech around in the wheelchair. We've got our best artist down there working with him on a composite. But he was wearing a hat and sunglasses, so it won't be much."

"That's it?"

"Atlanta's running background and neighborhoods on the tech to see if we can identify the subject through past associations."

"Any contamination at the park?"

"Fortunately, the subject was not familiar with Disney's procedures. Ever been down there?"

"No."

"Security is unbelievable. They are constantly looking for potential problems. After the subject killed the victim, he dumped the vial down his shirt. Then he left him in the middle of the street. But one of the security people spotted the victim immediately and could see he was dead. Since Disney frowns on stiffs littering the grand concourse, he wheeled him to one of the first-aid stations and called EMS. They showed up and, after opening his shirt to check his vitals, spotted the vial. The name of the virus was marked on it, so they knew exactly what they had. It hadn't thawed out, so they don't think there will be any problem. But they do have the security man and the two paramedics quarantined."

"Lucky."

"Damn right. Let's hope we get him before he learns from his mistakes."

"What about the wheelchair?" Devlin asked.

"It's up at the lab, but it's been sanitized."

"So, you want me to—"

"Do you know who Dr. Murray Craven is?"

"The psycholinguistics consultant?"

"I want you to go see him at Syracuse University. He knows you're coming."

"What do you expect to get from him?"

"He's helped us in the past with some tough cases. I think you'll be surprised at what he can come up with. But let him know we're not looking for something that will stand up in court; we're just looking for leads. Anything at all."

"Is he going to want to examine the original document?"

"That's another problem. The subject E-mailed the message to *The Real Deal*, that tabloid TV show, so there is no original document. And another problem is that their studio is located in New York. When we approached them about putting a trap-and-trace on the line, they told us they wanted a court order."

"A court order?"

"They're milking it. As long as this guy is giving them every exclusive, do you think they want us catching him?"

"How many lines do they have going into the studio?"

"I don't know, but I gave the SAC in New York until five o'clock today to have traces on all of them. The U.S. Attorney is also working on court orders for taps."

"That'll work fine if he's calling locally."

"I know, I know. If he's out of state, he'll never be on long enough to pinpoint. But that's all we've got."

"I guess I had better get to Syracuse."

"How's Knox?"

"I think she's glad to have me out of her hair for a couple of weeks."

There was a soft knock on the door, and Sharon walked in with a teletype, which she handed to O'Hare. As he read it, she watched him more closely than was necessary, stirring Devlin's curiosity. He hadn't taken the time to realize how attractive she was when they first met. Flawless skin accented her high, round cheekbones and well-defined jaw. Thick, fleshly lips, though slightly parted, clung together sensually at their lip-sticked corners. Dark, luxurious eyelashes guarded her wide, attentive eyes. She stood in front of O'Hare's desk with the erectness and poise of a professional dancer. Her legs were slender but muscular, and the rest of her figure was sleek and amply feminine. O'Hare finished reading the communication and gave her some instructions. Her eyes never left his. Whatever he was selling, she was buying. It was not unusual for a Bureau secretary to admire her boss, even to have an occasional impure thought about him, but there was something more in the way she was looking at him, something more committed, more impulsive. O'Hare finished his instructions, and her eyes remained on him a second too long, looking for some special level of understanding between them, and then she left.

After the door closed, Devlin said, "You're a lucky guy, Tom. An office with a window and a good-looking secretary."

"Sharon's quite a woman."

"*Woman?* Sounds like someone's pen has been in Bureau ink."

"It's a long story."

"With a familiar headline. You are still married, aren't you?"

"Susan and I are not good."

"In what way?"

"How many ways are there?"

"Does Susan know it's not good?" O'Hare looked at Devlin briefly and then turned away without answering. "So right now you're just taking Sharon out for a little test drive?"

"God, you're a pain in the ass."

"I'll take that as a yes?"

"It's not that simple," O'Hare said. "The truth is the fire between Susan and me has gone out. She's a great person, but it just doesn't work for us anymore."

"Did you realize that before or after Sharon?"

"Like the chicken and the egg, some things are impossible to separate into cause and effect."

"I've found that cause and effect are usually ambiguous only when it serves someone's purpose."

"Oh, really?" O'Hare folded his arms across his chest comfortably. "Then tell me, which *did* come first, the chicken or the egg?"

Devlin leaned back in his chair and put his hands in his pockets. He stared off in silence for a moment and then said, "My guess would be the chicken. If the egg had come first, there would have been no one to sit on it and hatch it."

"That's very cute, Mike," O'Hare said. "So maybe I don't want to know whose fault this is, but the last line on the last page is still the same—whatever there was between Susan and me is gone now."

"Two women. You're much more ambitious than I am."

"We all have our vices, Mike. At least mine will kill me slowly."

Devlin laughed. "I don't know. I think Sharon could stop my heart."

"Are we all through with the counseling session?"

"You're the boss."

"Boy, I wish I had a dollar for each person you've sucker-punched with those words. But that is exactly why I've arranged it so you'll report only to me. I know most of your *techniques*. I want you to lie back for these two weeks. Just handle a couple of grounders for me, have some laughs, and maybe get a fresh angle on things."

"Like R and R?"

"Yeah, like R and R."

||| CHAPTER 6 |||

He heard the key turn in the front door; it was a sound he had grown to hate. Again his life was being invaded. Although objections had been frequently voiced, his father's justification was always the same: As long as he was paying the bills, he had the right to "check up" on his son. Besides, he always called first. But the calls always seemed more a scheduling confirmation than a courtesy. There was a certain dignity in privacy, the subtle power of earned solitude. Unfortunately, it was a luxury his father would never allow him. But that was not the worst part of the "visits"; what he hated even more was the conversation that was about to take place. It was driven by three generations of misdeeds and guilt.

"Hello, son."

Son. His father never called him by his name and had a way of saying *son* that made it sound accusatory. Invariably, it was the precursor to a lecture, the guidon of a perceived failure. The burning laser point of patrimonial disappointment. It reminded him of *Mister*, the always condescending identifier of upperclassmen. They would spit it in his face several times a paragraph to prove their worthiness and, more important, his insignificance. "Father," was his emotionless reply.

"How are you?"

With equal insincerity, he answered, "Just fine, Father." He knew this would be a short visit because his father had not taken the time to sit down; somewhere in the Washington area a business meeting grew near. That was good. Dialogue would take the short course tonight. The only variable was how long his father, who saw himself as a great motivator of men, would take to offer the word *failure* as the only incentive necessary to right the distracted course of his son's life. His father undoubtedly perceived his pronunciation of the word as a subliminal whisper, but for his heir it arrived with the impact of a recoilless rifle.

"How goes the job search?"

"I've got an interview next week at a Baltimore engineering firm." It was a lie, but he knew his father, normally a suspicious man, would trade logic for avoiding the truth when it came to his own son. Denial had become part of the family's genetic code.

Actually, he had a job. It was very blue-collar, but that was not the reason he didn't want his father to know about it. He fought the urge to laugh out loud. He was tempted to take his father into the bedroom and pull out the uniform that was carefully hidden among some other clothing in the closet. He'd see if his father could put aside his disappointment and notice that the identification badge hanging from the pocket, while bearing his face, was in another name. But of course he wouldn't do that; there was too much at stake. His father took out a check and handed it to him. "That's good, son, but it wouldn't hurt to have more than one iron in the fire, you know, have more than one interview lined up at a time. The only real tragedy in life is the failure of hope."

There it was! Well disguised, but definitely the f-word. Fortunately, it meant that within seconds the closing ceremonies would begin, and that would be it for another week. Despite his father's jackhammer use of the concept, he felt as though he was becoming better at overcoming failure's usually paralyzing wake. Even though the Disney World venture had accomplished most of what he had hoped for, it had been a failure of sorts: there had been no massive outbreak of disease and, more important, no widespread dying. He would not be taken seriously until there was. But he had learned from his mistake. He could now look his father in the eye; he was no longer a failure. He wanted to tell him that America would not be able to ignore him anymore. This time, his success was guaranteed—a lot of people were about to die.

"Good-bye, Father."

III CHAPTER 7 III

Dr. Murray Craven's office was neatly cluttered with things that, to Devlin's limited knowledge of psycholinguistics, seemed unrelated. On a single shelf, under rows of books that covered subjects from Egyptology to gourmet mushrooms, sat a microscope. Next to it were a clarinet and a half dozen jazz CDs. By the window, dozing in half-shaded light, was a healthy bonsai tree. A set of delicate pruning shears lay next to it. On another shelf was a stack of awards that sat unframed and apparently forgotten. Sitting on top of a long, narrow credenza next to his desk were two projects in progress: an ancient gold pocket watch, partially disassembled, and the lower jaw of a human skull with an accompanying set of dental X rays. The only object that hung on the room's walls, which were covered almost entirely with crammed bookshelves, was a poster-size photograph of Frank Lloyd Wright's Falling Water, with all its mysterious angles and shadowed recesses, hovering over a busy, unviolated stream.

Without warning, a computer printer in the corner started up as if it were an alarm objecting to Devlin's presence. He went over to it, turned his head sideways and, watching the paper emerge, tried briefly to decipher the secret scientific garble of the psycholinguist.

On the desk were two framed photographs, one of a woman and three children and one of a man, presumably the Ph.D. himself, in a Mediterranean-blue kayak, wearing a yellow helmet and matching life vest. The craft was momentarily suspended on a foamy white peak of some angry river, the professor's paddle useless as it clawed the air. Devlin studied the paddle in the photo and then recognized it as the same fractured device that stood somewhat misplaced in the corner of the room, the dusty trophy of a distant day.

The office's door swung open and a man Devlin recognized as the kayaker smiled. "Agent Devlin?"

Although Craven was sixty, he moved toward Devlin with an athletic efficiency. He was bald on top, but the hair around the sides and back was full and textured, balancing his head elegantly. If Devlin hadn't known who he was and had to guess his history, he would have decided that Craven was turn-of-the-century royalty—at least half a dozen deaths from being able to ascend the throne and thereby forced to survive by his grace and charm. "Please, call me Mike." They shook hands.

"Sorry I'm late. Weekly basketball game."

"Did you win?"

"We don't keep score. It makes lying afterward much more conscionable." Devlin smiled. "But you're here to talk about— what is the media calling him—the Freedom Killer? An interesting oxymoron, don't you think?"

"Nothing sells papers better than an intriguing murder with an accommodating oxymoron."

As though the final winning lottery ball had fallen into place, Craven proclaimed, "Chicago!"

Devlin was confused for a second and then smiled his congratulations. "Very good, especially since, between the Marine Corps and the Bureau, I haven't lived there for almost twenty years."

"You've been in Detroit for—?"

"You can hear Detroit, too? Fifteen years."

"That's what threw me for a minute. Your time in Michigan has softened those tough Chicago t's."

"I'm impressed. Now, if you'll tell me who the killer is, I'll be on my way."

"If I could do that, I'm afraid your job wouldn't be nearly as interesting. But maybe I can tell you a few things about the person you're looking for." Craven opened a drawer and took out several pages of notes. After he looked them over for a few seconds, he picked up a book with an oddly colored dust jacket and started leafing through it. Across the Day-Glo orange and optic-lime cover was printed the title, *Psycholinguistics and Threat Analysis*. Its author was Dr. Murray L. Craven. "First, he is a white male."

"I've read that communiqué a dozen times. How do you determine something like that?"

"You have to remember, our conclusions are nothing more than educated guesses; but that's really what social sciences are. You're an experienced investigator; you can look at a case and, more times than not, tell where the guilt lies. It is the same with psycholinguistics. We have studied language patterns for so long we can make good guesses about the psychology of their users. Take this individual—he is a man who is psychotically outraged about whatever he perceives society's ills to be. Never once does he mention race; therefore, race is not an issue with him. A black man, similarly disoriented, would most certainly bring up race, and, if not directly, then in time-tested expressions that vent his race's historical frustration—phrases such as 'power to the people,' 'oppressors,' or 'exploitation.' For generations, blacks have used these to communicate their feelings among themselves, so it is doubtful that they would not use them during a tirade such as this one. Similarly, the aggression level and grandiose scope of the threat is definitely male in nature. His syntax and use of language, coupled with his complex interpretation of the concept of freedom, qualify him as an educated American. And based on the lack of proletariat rhetoric, he probably is, or at least was raised, middle-class. As far as his age, the use of 'reverse history's course' is a youthful ideal, and the three-hundred-year concept plus the lack of clichés used by people a generation older—I would put him in his late twenties or early thirties. Although it's difficult to say without hearing the actual voice, certain phrase selections make me think he might be from the eastern United States."

"I understand you don't like to get too far out on the guessing limb, but we're looking for avenues of investigation. Can you give us any starting point?"

"Let's look at his message and see if we can figure out what he's trying to say. The message is probably interpretable on more than one level. It is actually divided into three distinct parts: the historical, the accusatory, and then his role as military enforcer. In the historical, he talks about the life span of a democracy and how we have corrupted even that pessimistic timetable. Which takes us right into the accusatory 'this has happened because *you* . . . !' It is not only meant to be accusatory, but also to humiliate. Humiliation is very important to him because, if you humiliate someone, it means one thing: You have control over them. You do understand that this is all about control?" Devlin nodded. "It's always about control.

"Now, that brings us to the sentence containing 'no democracy without freedom for every man' in it. For me this sentence is the most interesting. If you read the entire message a number of times, you will see that that sentence does not exactly flow with the rest of the text. His use of words is so economical and his transitions are so refined that to the trained ear, this one sentence has a few ragged edges. That usually indicates one thing: Whatever stressor caused this individual to go over the edge is contained in this sentence. For me, the word *every* is the key. The Constitution says 'all men,' and that is what nine hundred ninety-nine out of a thousand would say, but by saying 'every man,' I think he is referring to a specific individual. He is railing at one person's freedom being taken away, possibly his own."

"What about—what did you call it—the military-enforcer segment?"

"Something you have to understand about this type of person is that he invariably sees the establishment as not only the enemy of his life, but also the aggressor in that war. He is using a military identity or fantasy to present himself in a comparable framework to challenge the establishment. What he is trying to do by setting himself up as a military figure is to insult the government and maybe, more specifically, the military. So his adopting this military persona is another act of humiliation. He's saying: Since you can't stop me, my military skills are better than yours, which makes me better than you."

"Do you think he was thrown out of the military?" Devlin asked.

"I think that's a strong possibility. Or he may also have done some military prison time."

"Is he going to be satisfied with just threats in the future, or is he going to do something again?"

"That's where he's a little vague. Most of the time these individuals find the power they seek in the threat alone, but he's already tasted real power, the power over life and death, when he killed that research technician. He says, 'You have two weeks to comply.' That sounds like he's not going to do anything until that time; but because he doesn't tell us what we are supposed to do to comply, as cunning and vicious as his first act was, I think he will give us further input before the deadline."

"Further input?"

Craven hesitated and seemed reluctant to answer, as if his prediction would come true once pronounced. "During the next two weeks, he is going to kill a lot more people."

||| CHAPTER 8 |||

Devlin hung up the phone and looked at his watch. He had just enough time to get to his plane. As he walked through the Syracuse airport, he watched the people as they hurried off, concerned with little else than their own schedules. How had the communiqué described it?—"immune to" their own freedom? Predictably, the country was observing the killer's vague threats "to comply," as well as its own independence, with equal boredom. Devlin thought about Craven's forecast of more deaths in the name of freedom and wondered if the killer wasn't counting on that indifference.

When Devlin had called O'Hare and given him Dr. Craven's analysis, the section chief said, "That doesn't give us much to go on. Maybe it'll match up with something later. When you get into Dulles, rent a car."

"Am I going somewhere?"

"I set up a meeting for you with the Behavioral Science Unit tonight. Do you know Bill Hagstrom?"

"I met him once in Detroit."

"Good, he's expecting you around seven. I want you to give him what you got from Craven. Then put your heads together and see what you can come up with. BSU is no longer at Quantico. If you've got a pen, I'll tell you how to get there."

Devlin wrote down the directions. "Anything happening?"

"We got the composite from the Disney employee. It'll be on the networks tonight and in all the papers tomorrow. But I'm not getting my hopes up—it's pretty nondescript. I've got to go; the Director is waiting for an update. I'll see you in the morning."

Dusk was surrendering the last of its somber light when Devlin turned his car off the highway and into the parking lot of a small, unnoticed office building near Quantico. It was the new home of the FBI's Critical Incident Response Group.

When Devlin knocked on the door, Bill Hagstrom answered it himself. "Mike Devlin, you old bank robber, how are you?"

"Is there anyone in the Bureau who doesn't know about that?"

"I don't know, I've called everybody I know."

"I'll have to find a way to thank you."

As the two men walked through the empty office, Devlin could see it was a place simply for work. There was no reception area, no piped-in music or magazines, no employees' lounge or dime-store art hanging on the walls—just worn gray desks covered with open files and pads of paper partially filled. Pens were left uncapped, drawers open, and trash cans filled with crumpled, abandoned theories. Nothing had been put away because the agents had worked until the last possible moment, until their minds, no matter how sharply prodded, refused to go on. They had left abruptly, searching for distraction— something frivolous, something healing.

All of it reminded Devlin of the painful realities of the group's work. For the men and women of the Child Abduction and Serial Killer Unit, the luxury of pretense and ceremony did not exist, because their workdays were guided by two whipsawing facts: the excellence of their product could save a life, and their rate of production would never match that of those they hunted.

The first thing Devlin noticed in Hagstrom's office was a large board with photographs of dozens of children pinned to it. The majority of them were the kind seen on MISSING flyers—posed, formal, and slightly blurred from excessive copying. But some were bright and crisp originals, the camera catching the spontaneity and joy of the moment. It was apparent that these were children who had been recovered due to the efforts of Hagstrom's unit.

"Bill, how come you have all those mixed together?"

Hagstrom turned around and looked at the photographs. "That's my reality board. If I just had the kids who were missing on it, I think I would eventually lose all hope. But by mixing in some of our victories, it keeps me focused on why we do this."

Devlin also noticed that there were no pictures of Hagstrom's own children in the office. Given the parental nightmares the profiler faced every day, Devlin imagined it would not have been difficult for him to visualize his kids' photos making the leap from his desk to the board every time they were late coming home.

Devlin had not seen him in almost two years. Since that time, Hagstrom had been put in charge of the unit. His face had become hollow and gray with exhaustion, but his eyes were bright and, as always, demanding of the truth. At the moment they were locked on Devlin. "The last time I saw you, you were looking for the Gentkiller. I heard he died," Hagstrom said, his tone inviting a confidence.

"Sooner or later justice does prevail."

"And now you're going to ask me about the Freedom Killer. Do you think the same thing will happen to him?"

"All you can do is hope," Devlin said. "But you're the expert—you're supposed to tell me how we go about catching him." Devlin's tone was flat and uninviting.

Hagstrom recognized the resistance in Devlin's voice, so he picked up his annotated copy of the killer's message and reread it. "Obviously, he needs to be in control. But you have to understand why these people need to demonstrate their authority. It all stems from a sense of powerlessness. At one time or another, we all experience that kind of frustration. I know I do every April fifteenth, because no matter what I do, there is no way to prevent the IRS's control over me. But after a while, the normal person simply denies that powerlessness. I would say to myself, 'Everyone else has to pay taxes and *they* survive, and I will too. So they really don't have that much authority over me.'

"But individuals like this are different. Because of their psychological history, they have no self-worth and, consequently, no ability whatsoever to affect their world through normal means. They perceive everything as an assault on their self-importance, which in turn increases their feelings of powerlessness. Invariably, they have no social network to fall back on, no social identity, no support from family or friends, no one to tell them: 'Yes, we also have to pay the IRS.' Our killer is convinced that society is conspiring to destroy him, so he becomes enraged enough to assert himself through these destructive acts and prove that he is not powerless, which is really what power is all about. And as far as his methods are concerned, the greater the death and destruction he can create, the greater his feeling of self-worth."

"Let me tell you what Dr. Craven said." Devlin took out his notes and began reading them.

When he finished, Hagstrom said, "I agree, especially that the 'every man' phrase is hiding whatever triggered him. And in the previous sentence, he says we are 'unable to mourn its loss.' That indicates that someone did lose their freedom, possibly him. I think that is what he wants us to do, to lose ours—partially to instruct us on how it feels, but mostly to punish us for whoever lost theirs. He starts by telling us what's wrong with America and ends by claiming he has no choice but to fix it. In other words, he would have us believe it is not a power trip but rather his 'duty.' "

"So he's rationalizing what he's doing."

"That's right. And whatever the event was that set him off, it left a void that can only be filled by violence. That's normal with this type of offender, but he is different. Whatever happened to him, as far as he is concerned, cannot be rectified, so his acts are not only a demonstration of his significance, but are also meant to be a punishment for the enemies of his life."

"How does the military fit into all of this?"

"He's definitely got some sort of grudge with it. A bad discharge, or maybe they wouldn't accept him. Remember, his reason does not have to be real or rational, just perceived. His entire perceptual system is out of focus. Let's assume his problem was that, in some way, he was not allowed to serve his country in the military. So now he wants to demonstrate to everyone the mistake that has been made. There is no better way to illustrate that than by taking away the one thing he would have protected if he were in the military—America's freedom. In other words, without him, our independence is gone—when in reality, he's the one trying to take it away."

"Does he really think he can destroy our freedom?"

"Not only destroy it, but destroy it in the next"—Hagstrom looked at his calendar—"twelve days. Which brings us to the *most* unique thing about his message: the two-week limit. Because these individuals are driven by compulsion, they can never stop. But he's saying in two weeks he will. So this is as much about revenge as it is about power."

"We have twelve days *to comply*. What do you think he means by that?" Devlin asked.

"My guess is he wants us to comply with his authority to take our freedom away. Give him our freedom."

"How are we supposed to do that?"

"To answer that, I think we have to consider the one act he has already committed. Where is there a greater demonstration of freedom in this country than Disney World? Why attempt to infect innocent people, many of whom are children, with a deadly virus? What is he ultimately trying to accomplish?"

Devlin thought for a second. "I guess by his utter disregard for the children, he's trying to convince everyone that there is nothing he won't do to achieve his 'mission.' "

"That's right. And he had the research tech steal two vials of the virus so everyone would be worrying about him doing it a second time."

"So he wants to keep everyone from going back into the park," Devlin said.

"Exactly, and because the virus was stolen in Atlanta and exposed in Florida, he's also telling us he's mobile, willing, and capable of planting more viruses in ball parks, zoos, museums, or anywhere else people go in mass to enjoy themselves. He's ordering America to stop having a good time."

"How far will he go?"

"Like all serial offenders, as far as his wits will take him. And don't underestimate him. He's a helluva lot smarter than most anyone we've been up against before."

"Do you think he's set this deadline because he plans his own destruction as part of his final act?"

"It's clear he's a narcissist, so I doubt if he has thought about the possibility. But if his grand design for revenge fails—which would prove in the end that he is indeed powerless—he could become suicidal."

"Why is he so extreme?"

"I was afraid you'd ask that. Because I've never seen anything like this before, I'm going to have to enter crystal-ball territory. Based on the planning and execution of the murder, the precise approach to his demand, and his obey-or-be-punished intolerance, I think he is an unusually regimented person. This would indicate he was in an institutionalized setting during his formative years, mid- to late teens—maybe a prison or, more than likely, the military. And during those years of discipline, all this self-hatred was seething, trying to boil over. Because these two completely opposite forces were tearing at him, his mind had to adapt or explode. So he mutated, and like all mutations, his new psyche is now better adapted to its new purpose—mass murder. But the real goal of mutation is survival, and the strongest evidence of that adaptation is the deadline he has set. Normally, the more death and destruction these people are involved in, the heavier the psychological toll is on them. But he has offset these feelings by establishing a cut-off date. The reason he can be so violent is because he knows it is going to last for only two weeks."

Devlin said, "So he is moving the guilt that is inherent in these things up front by putting a time limit on it."

"That would be my evaluation."

"Is he crazy?"

"You can't measure him in those terms. He's beyond anything modern psychology has encountered. Malignant narcissism, a severe personality disorder that leaves the individual grandiose, paranoid, and ruthless—someone like Saddam Hussein probably comes the closest. Human beings mean nothing to him. Either they're objects that he can get something from, or they're obstacles. He is interested only in satisfying what he perceives as his needs. And what he needs is control. A serial killer murders to take the ultimate control over his victims, but this man is unique in that he is trying to control not just individuals but our entire society."

"You know what's odd? Every message I've ever seen before has been signed with some sort of symbolic alias, like the Symbionese Liberation Army or the Zodiac Killer. But not this guy."

"You're right. These people want credit for what they're doing. It becomes their identity, a persona worthy of notice and respect. I think because he did not sign his message, he's saying that in two weeks, he and his destruction never existed. He has, in fact, developed a new defense mechanism. It's the safety-net part of his mutation."

"What do you think he'll do next—the virus again?"

"He's going to be almost impossible to anticipate. The virus would certainly be the easiest, but he didn't mention it in his communication, so he may have something else in mind. If he doesn't use it, he knows we're still threatened by it, and that may be its greatest value to him."

"So the only thing we can do is sit and wait?"

"Remember one thing, Mike," Hagstrom said, smiling. "When I have to theorize too much, I can lose track of what is real and what isn't. I may be seeing black where there's only white. Hopefully, we'll never hear from the Freedom Killer again."

Devlin watched closely as Hagstrom smiled to punctuate his last sentence with optimism. But an army of liars had taught Devlin that for a smile to be genuine, the face had to have more than the customary lip and eye formation. The eyebrows had to be lowered. Hagstrom's were not. It was a subtle cue, but an undeniable one. Devlin leaned back and tilted his head slightly, letting the unit chief know his words were suspect.

Hagstrom immediately realized his mistake. "It was the eyebrows, wasn't it?" Devlin gave a short laugh of confirmation. "It's just that sometimes I try to be optimistic even though it's not my gut feeling." Hagstrom took a deep breath and released it cautiously. "My best guess? It won't be long before we hear from him again. And this time he'll attempt something even more cataclysmic." Hagstrom stared off for a moment, then he let a smug smile lower his brow. "Since this is a new type of antisocial behavior, we'll need a new psychological category. What do you think of *cataclysmist*?"

"Cataclysmist? Couldn't you come up with something a little more difficult to pronounce? You know, I think you actually have to be able to spell the word before you can accept the Nobel Prize."

"You don't like it? Then that's it—cataclysmist!"

"How about delusions-of-grandeurist?"

"That's not nearly encompassing enough to describe him."

"I didn't mean him."

Hagstrom laughed. "You know, Mike, you'd probably make a helluva profiler yourself."

"I'll take that as an insult. However, my crystal ball does tell me that you're about to meet up with a couple of beers."

"A couple? That hardly seems adequate for a delusions-of-grandeurist."

When Devlin walked into his hotel room three hours later, he noticed the flashing red message light on his phone. He dialed the voice mail service and listened to the recording. "Mike, this is O'Hare. Be in my office at six A.M. He's hit again."

III CHAPTER 9 III

The sixth-floor corridor, lined with the tarnish of predawn light, led Devlin toward room 621. His footsteps echoed, disturbing the building's overnight calm. Sharon was not at her desk, so he walked into O'Hare's office. He was already on the phone. "I don't give a good goddamn who you have to wake up. And I care even less what time it is where you're at. I hope this won't ruin your day, but people are dying all over this country; and unless we find out where all those shipments went, there'll be more. Call me in an hour. And I better not have to call you." O'Hare slammed the phone down. "You heard about it on the news?"

"Yes. They said eight dead."

"It's up to thirteen now, and God knows how many haven't been found yet."

"All heart-medication poisonings?"

"Every one. The best we can figure at this point is that he broke into the manufacturer's warehouse in Kansas City and poisoned shipments going all over the country. Now there's a million people out there afraid to take their heart medication and having anxiety attacks because they can't. The hospitals are overrun, and I imagine every doctor in the country has been up all night answering calls."

"How long before the drug companies can ship replacements?"

"Day and a half, minimum. But the problem is paranoia. Everyone who takes *any* kind of medication is worried. I can't say I blame them. The thing that scares me is how creative this guy is. He's done two things, so different we will never be able to anticipate his next move."

"Do we have *anything*?"

"Just this." O'Hare handed Devlin a sheet of paper. "It was E-mailed to *The Real Deal* two hours ago." Devlin looked at the message.

Freedom can never be won, nor sustained, without the loss of life. It seems, without war, America is all too willing to forget this truth. So I am declaring war to remind you of the importance of liberty. I hope you will respect your freedom while you still have a chance. I am not optimistic. Comply or suffer the consequences. You have eleven days.

"What does this guy want?" O'Hare asked.

"After talking to Craven and Hagstrom, I think he wants to shut the country down. Take away everyone's freedom."

"The most powerful and freest society in the history of the world? Now, there's a power trip."

"You've got to admit, he's had a hell of an opening week."

Knowing it was true, O'Hare scowled at Devlin's comment. "What else did they have to say?"

"White male, mid-to late twenties, at least some college, but may not have graduated. High IQ and meticulous in his work and personal habits. He will more than likely be an obsessive record keeper. When we find him, there will be extensive documentation of everything from his life to his philosophy to his crimes. Probably spent time in the military. And if so, had a less-than-honorable discharge. From the eastern United States, and middle-class."

The phone rang. "Tom O'Hare ... just fine, Mr. Jackson . . ." O'Hare looked at Devlin and rolled his eyes. ". . . and how are things at the White House? . . . Yes, we're identifying and seizing all shipments right now . . . as soon as possible . . . no kidding, the President has taken a personal interest in the case. Well, that's good to know because normally we like the death toll to reach two or three dozen before we get up off our asses, but if the President's interested, we'll pull out all the stops right now . . . Am I being facetious? Does the President know how poor your people skills are . . . You're going to call the Director? Hold on, I'll transfer you myself." O'Hare switched the call to the Director's office and hung up.

Devlin smiled. "I guess there'll be no holding back that promotion now."

"The moron did say the President was holding a press conference today. 'To reassure the nation.' I hope he's not going to say something to set this guy off again."

"I don't think anyone is setting him off. It's my guess he has this all carefully scheduled. Take this heart medication tampering—he had to do that days ago, maybe even before Disney World. So far, he's way ahead of us."

"I hope you're wrong."

"I assume Kansas City is investigating the drug company break-in, trying to identify the—" Devlin remembered Hagstrom's tongue-in-cheek use of *cataclysmist* and wondered how long it would take to work its way from O'Hare's office to the White House news conference. Washington loved those buzzwords, especially the ones that took everybody's mind off the questions they should be asking or answering. Besides, he owed Hagstrom for that crack about the bank robbery.

"The what?" O'Hare prodded.

"Hagstrom said this guy is in a whole new category. He called him a cataclysmist."

"Cataclysmist. I like that. It'll take the heat off of us while everyone tries to put their own spin on it." Devlin was careful not to smile; it was already working. O'Hare continued, "Yes, Kansas City is investigating the break-in."

"And they'll be getting an employees list: disgruntled, fired, et cetera?" Devlin asked.

"I'll make sure they do. What did you have in mind?"

"You could send someone over to the Pentagon and check the cataclysmist's profile against their computer." Devlin found that he was starting to like the word; the syllables had a nice rolling rhythm. "And then interface it with the list from Kansas City. It's a long shot, but when we're done, if nothing else, we would have a couple of databases for future reference."

"Good idea. I know an Army major in personnel over there. He'll get you cleared."

"Me?"

"It's your idea."

"I don't know anything about computers."

"I'll get you someone who does."

"Oh, I get it. You've changed your mind. Now you *want* me to commit suicide."

O'Hare was not amused. "You're assigned to me, and this is what I need you to do. Stop down at Records Management and see if there's anyone around you can use. Call me with their name, and I'll get it okayed."

Devlin started to say something but decided that whoever was keeping score of such things was simply paying him back for the *cataclysmist* stunt.

III CHAPTER 10 III

By the time Devlin found the Records Management Office, it was almost 7:00 A.M. A huge room was partitioned off into single-employee workstations, each housing its own computer terminal. Although he could not see anyone, he heard the plastic clicking of a keyboard. He followed the sound to one of the most isolated pods. A man in his mid-twenties with dark hair and a taut, clenched jaw was typing at an incredible, almost angry, rate. His eager eyes were focused on the monitor, and he didn't notice Devlin. "Excuse me." The man looked up. "I'm Mike Devlin."

His eyes searched Devlin's face and then returned to the screen. "Tony Bonelli," he said, and then his long, powerful fingers resumed their work.

"I'm in from Detroit on a special."

"The Freedom Killer?" Bonelli asked without looking up.

"Yes. Have you heard about the poisonings?" Bonelli nodded while he continued to type. "I'm working directly for Tom O'Hare, and he's sending me over to the Pentagon to generate a list of suspects from their computers. And since I don't know a thing about computers, I've been authorized to shanghai one able-bodied computer operator."

Bonelli stopped typing and looked up at Devlin. There was something unfriendly in his gaze. "And you think that might be me."

"The way you handle that keyboard, I was hoping it would be. And I like the fact that you're in here early. I'd be surprised if you're getting any overtime for it."

Bonelli shut off his computer. "No, I don't get paid for it. I feel I should come in an hour early every day just to show people that I wasn't hired"—he reached under his desk and pulled out a pair of metal canes, slipped his overdeveloped forearms through the metal loops, and stood up stiff-legged—"because I have muscular dystrophy. Fortunately for me, you need someone who is *able-bodied,* so I won't have to go."

Devlin's smile surprised Bonelli. It was not the reaction he thought his little drama would bring. "No, no. This is great. I've been looking for someone to be the brains of the operation. You have no idea what a full-time job being the brawn is."

Unamused, Bonelli said, "I'll pass," and turned away. As he started walking, Devlin watched. Each step seemed excruciating, punctuated by a teetering repositioning of his canes. Twenty-five feet away, Bonelli filled a coffee cup and sat down.

"I'm going to need someone who likes to work," Devlin said.

"Do you know how hard it is for me just to get here every morning? The Pentagon is a hundred times the size of this building."

"I'll bet this place seemed a hundred times bigger the first time you walked in."

"Hey, I've earned the right to be left alone. I'm comfortable here. I like my work."

"I hope you're lying to me, Tony. Because anybody who works in Records Management and thinks he likes it needs extensive therapy."

"Well then, I guess I need therapy, because I'm satisfied with it."

But Devlin could see he wasn't. He'd regret his flash of anger as soon as he realized he was losing an opportunity to escape the suffocating tedium of a clerk's workday. "I'm going to get the car. When someone able-bodied gets here, send them down."

Fifteen minutes later, Devlin sat in his rented car in front of FBI headquarters and watched Tony Bonelli drag his disobedient legs toward him. Devlin let him open the door and waited while he tossed his backpack containing his laptop computer into the backseat. When Bonelli was finally seated, he looked at Devlin, who was smiling patiently.

Sullenly, the clerk turned and looked straight ahead. With genuine anger in his voice, he said, "Anyone ever tell you what a pain in the ass you are?"

Devlin pulled out into traffic. "You're the second one today."

Bonelli was still glaring at the windshield. "And it isn't even seven-thirty yet."

||| CHAPTER 11 |||

The Pentagon housed the Departments of Defense, Army, Navy, and Air Force and was considered the world's largest office building. Taking up over 3.5 million square feet, it used 45,000 telephones. The corresponding bureaucracy was equally labyrinthine. Devlin needed over an hour to locate O'Hare's Army contact. He, in turn, assigned one of his sergeants to assist the two men from the FBI.

Somewhat familiar with the military's computers, the sergeant informed them that the discharge information was available, but each branch of the service maintained its own system and would have to be queried separately. Devlin and Bonelli went to work.

By the end of the first day, a routine had developed. Based on the killer's estimated age, Bonelli, working year by year, generated a list of less-than-honorably-discharged soldiers, with their dates of birth and Social Security numbers along with a brief narrative of the facts upon which the discharge was based. Devlin reviewed the list. When an individual looked particularly suited to the profile, his name was given to the sergeant, who called St. Louis, where the repository of permanent Army records was located, and had the file faxed to the Pentagon. Devlin then analyzed the information in it. If the individual met the more extensive dimensions of the profile, he was slated for interview by agents in the field. At the same time, Bonelli created his own database of suspects by taking the names Devlin had chosen and entering them into his personal computer.

But the more names they processed, the more Devlin realized the futility of what they were doing. There were thousands of discharges that would meet the profile, and he soon became aware that their investigation was unlikely to identify the killer.

At five o'clock Devlin went over to Bonelli, who didn't seem to notice that everyone was leaving the building. "Tony, it's five. We can knock off if you want."

"I'm fine. But if we stay, you're going to have to give me a ride home."

"You don't drive?"

"It's easier to pay someone." Bonelli's words were rapid and toneless, almost rude, intended to avoid any further discussion.

Devlin wondered how he would have reacted to the question if he himself had the disease. Not only did Bonelli have to literally fight against every degenerating effect of the affliction—

he had to overcome an even more devastating attack on his pride. "Do you think we're making any headway here?"

Bonelli stopped typing and looked at Devlin, apparently surprised to be asked for an opinion. "I really haven't thought about it. My job is hacking on this computer."

"Well, I've done things like this a few times before, and I think I had a bad idea. There are far too many discharges for us to narrow it down this way. So if you want to pull back on the stick a little, it's okay."

Bonelli nodded his agreement with the logic of Devlin's assessment and then continued to type at his normal, urgent speed. Devlin watched him and understood that not unlike the Freedom Killer, who defined himself through destructive acts, Bonelli let his work explain who he was.

"You want some coffee?" Devlin asked.

Without looking up, Bonelli answered, "No thanks."

In the employee lounge, a television hung from the wall, and the evening news was on. The station was reporting the President's address earlier in the day. The newswoman said he had called the killer "a maniac" and "a coward." He assured the people of the United States that all the poisoned medicine had been seized and that it was safe for everyone to resume not only their normal dosages but their daily lives. "Lastly," she said, "the President described the killer as a demented individual who would be caught quickly and punished to the fullest extent of the law."

The President's threats, outrage, and assurances seemed somehow predictable, and Devlin knew if he felt that way, the killer, as carefully as he had orchestrated everything to this point, had probably anticipated these things also.

Then the President was shown turning the microphone over to the attorney general to field questions. Devlin sat drinking his coffee, half listening until one of the reporters asked if the

FBI had a profile for the killer. The attorney general read directly from his notes. " 'The individual responsible for these acts is believed to be a white male in his mid- to late twenties of above-average intelligence, raised in the eastern part of the United States, and from a middle-class family. Has had at least some college and has probably spent time in the military. He is a meticulous person, a prolific record keeper, and if he was in the military, he would have, in all likelihood, been given a less-than-honorable discharge. The FBI's Behavioral Science Unit believes that the so-called Freedom Killer is a new category of murderer-terrorist. He is being classified as a cataclysmist.' " The attorney general paused for dramatic effect, and the reporters murmured appreciatively at the term. Something new—something theatrical—had been fired broadside into their lexicon.

A woman reporter asked, "What's the difference between a—" she hesitated, as if she expected to have trouble with the pronunciation, and then easily said, "—cataclysmist, and a serial killer?"

The attorney general replied, "It's my understanding that a serial killer murders to take ultimate control of his victim. But this person kills on a larger scale, using cataclysmic destruction to ultimately take control of society."

The anchorman came back on. "In a story related to the cataclysmist . . ." Devlin wished he could see Bill Hagstrom's face. "The Disney corporation has announced that attendance at Disney World, in Orlando, Florida, is down almost sixty percent since the murder of research technician Nathan Walker. They feel that the cataclysmist's previous attempt to contaminate tourists with the Lassa virus at the park and his subsequent warnings are responsible. Most people currently attending the facility are thought to be foreign tourists." The station then showed some tape taken at the park. It seemed almost empty as the camera found some Japanese tourists, who were boarding the "Nautilus" submarine attraction without waiting in line.

America was starting to comply.

III CHAPTER 12 III

William Blake turned off his television and sat down at his worktable. On the wall directly over it was a framed photograph of a man in an Army officer's uniform. The vague, brown photography, as well as the uniform's details and less-than-tailored fit, were World War II vintage. The man smiled smugly, almost condescendingly; he was apparently in possession of a great secret. Blake loved that smile, because he knew its secret. And now he had his own. "Cataclysmist. I think Grandfather would have been pleased that *my* crime has become a new psychological disorder. Very flattering."

Off to his left, he lit a small white candle. From a bag on the floor, he took out sixteen small, identical plastic bottles and lined them in a neat row. Something occurred to him: L-U-P-I-N-E: *a six-letter word for a clustering flower*. He picked up the crossword puzzle he had been working on and wrote in the letters. There were still three words that eluded him, preventing its completion.

He turned his attention back to the bottles. They had screw tops that doubled as medicine droppers, the rubber bulb portion of which were protected by tamper-proof plastic caps. The tops of the bottles were entirely sealed with clear plastic shrink-wrap. Carefully, he opened a dark brown bottle that was filled with carbon tetrachloride, an industrial solvent— five milligrams of which would kill a 150-pound human being in under a minute. He inserted the needle of a syringe into the clear liquid and filled it.

S-P-A-L-L. He set the syringe down and wrote in the five-letter word for a stone chip. The P was common to LUPINE.

He picked up the first eyedropper bottle, turned it upside down, and then heated the needle over the candle. Gently, he punctured the center of the plastic bottle's bottom through its seam. He injected fifty milligrams of the poison into the container and withdrew the syringe. Still holding it upside down, he dabbed a small drop of clear epoxy on the pinhole. After thirty seconds it was dry and undetectable. He turned it right side up and wiped it with a brown paper towel, looking for any spots darkened by leaking moisture. There were none.

Blake finished seven more bottles before he remembered: *A five-letter word for mother of pearl:* N-A-C-R-E. One word left: five letters, beginning with N, for Indian governor. He injected the last eight bottles and tested them; only one leaked. He did not attempt to repair it, because another drop of epoxy might have been noticeable.

After he blew out the candle, he leaned back and looked at the photograph of his grandfather. Then he put each of the altered bottles back in their cardboard boxes and carefully glued shut the lids he had razor-bladed open. When the last box was sealed, he packed all of them into a suitcase on the floor. N-A-B-O-B, of course. He filled in the last puzzle spaces.

Blake closed his suitcase and put on his overcoat. "Well," he said out loud, "it *is* the cold and flu season, so I'd better get these bottles of children's aspirin delivered. Cataclysmist—I like it."

||| CHAPTER 13 |||

Bonelli's apartment was in Hyattsville, Maryland, just north of Washington. It was in an older eight-unit building, the kind with high ceilings and drafty windows. Devlin pulled to the curb. Without looking at him, Bonelli pronounced an unconvincing "Thanks." It wasn't that he didn't appreciate the ride; he did. But more than anything else in his life—even the disease, which he pretty much accepted as his position in the pecking order—he hated that people had to do things for him. Not having the independence to do anything and everything for yourself was what disability really meant. He shunned even the simplest of courtesies offered to him. He felt that when people did things for him—even the driver he paid—he was inconveniencing them, as though his handicap were wasting their time, too. The worst part of his disease was that as it crept through him slowly, its ever-tightening circle of dependence was strangling his spirit. As he started to get out of the car, Devlin said, "I ate a lot of computer dust today. I don't suppose you got a beer in there."

Bonelli felt awkward, defensive. He had never had a visitor other than his parents. He wanted to say no. "Sure, come on in." After seeing hundreds of smiles that failed to hide their owner's pity, he sensed a genuine kindness in the patience Devlin had showed him the entire day.

On the third floor, Devlin followed Bonelli into his apartment. "Not bad."

"It's probably bigger than I need. But my folks come down every other weekend. My mom brings me food and cleans. I don't know if I'd want this much room to take care of otherwise." Bonelli unslung his backpack and pointed to a chair. Devlin sat down while his host labored over to the refrigerator and took out two cans of beer. He walked back, handed one to Devlin, and sat down.

"Where are you from originally?" Devlin asked.

"Baltimore. That's where my folks live."

"This all works out pretty well, then."

Bonelli smiled crookedly. "Everything but being in Records Management."

"Why work there, then?"

"They hired me, and loyalty is important to me."

"How long have you been there?"

"Seven years."

"Seven years! I think you've crossed that fine line between loyalty and sadomasochism. There must be some other place you'd like to go in the Bureau."

"Sure." Bonelli smiled. "New Agent Training." Devlin said nothing and took a sip of beer. "Funny, a month ago my mom was clearing out a bunch of old boxes of my stuff from as far back as grammar school. In fourth grade, during a career day, we had to write essays about what we were going to be. I chose FBI agent; it's all I could ever remember wanting to be. But when I was a junior in high school, I was diagnosed with MD. Once the initial shock wore off, I realized life was going to go on with or without my permission. So after finishing college, I applied to the Bureau. They have some pretty good-paying clerical positions. Because my degree was in computer science, they offered me a job as a specialist contingent upon moving to Washington. All in all, it's been worth it."

"I can't imagine being a support employee at headquarters. The *agents* in that building think they're little more than clerks. It must be *really* tough on you."

"Sometimes it does seem like I get paid not to think. The thing I miss the most is the chance to be creative, to pursue an idea, to find an answer that no one else has. It must be great being an agent and having that kind of latitude."

"Most of what we do is sausage—throw everything in one end, turn the crank long enough, and out comes a predictable shape. But there are some days when all that work and all those chances finally line up and unlock the impossible case. It's a hell of a feeling. From then on you can say, 'Yeah, I made a difference.' " Bonelli sat transfixed, lost in Devlin's words. "Sorry, sometimes I get a little carried away."

"No, not at all. My job's fine—I have nothing to complain about. It's just when I hear something like that, I guess I feel a little shortchanged."

Devlin felt awkward and looked around the apartment for something to change the conversation. "An electronic keyboard—is that a decoration?"

"Since I was big enough to climb up on the bench, my mother had me take piano lessons. When I couldn't work the pedals any longer, my parents bought me that."

"Do you do requests?"

Bonelli got up on his canes and made his way over to the keyboard. "The most common request is for me to stop. How about some Motown?" He started playing Marvin Gaye's "I Heard It Through the Grapevine."

Devlin watched him, and although his playing was average, he seemed to be dependent on the instrument. Respectfully, he touched the keys and released the soft notes as if they were so many characters on a computer screen, each representing a little more impact on a world that might have never noticed his withering life otherwise.

Devlin downed the rest of his beer and got two more. After putting one on a table next to Bonelli, he walked to the window. He stared at the street below and thought about the madman who was out there trying to take away the nation's freedom—freedom that everyone, including Devlin, took for granted until they met someone like Tony Bonelli.

‖‖ CHAPTER 14 ‖‖

The next afternoon, FBI Kansas City faxed Devlin a list of the drug company's ex-employees. It took Bonelli less than three hours to run the names through the military computers. There were no matches. When Devlin called O'Hare to report the results, the section chief said, "I guess that would have been too easy."

"Are you getting any good tips off the hotline?"

"*Good* tips? Yeah, since the release of the composite and profile, we're getting hundreds of *good* tips. I'd trade them all for one *great* tip. How are you doing there?"

"I think we're wasting our time."

O'Hare said, "Good, keep at it," and hung up.

Evidently, O'Hare had enough problems and felt he had one less with Devlin stuck at the Pentagon.

By the third day, Devlin and Bonelli had lapsed into a half-hearted pattern of work. While their file and computer searches occasionally produced someone who needed to be interviewed by one of the Bureau field offices, that one "great" suspect never materialized. Early in the afternoon, the sergeant assigned to them walked up and told Devlin, "Sir, you're supposed to call Agent O'Hare ASAP."

"Tom, it's Mike. Tell me you've got somebody in custody so I can get the hell out of here."

"You'd better get over here. He killed some kids this time."

When Devlin walked into O'Hare's office, Sharon said the section chief would be right back and handed him a teletype to read. It was from the Director to all field offices and was entitled "Freemurs," the Bureau code name for Freedom Murders. The communication stated an unknown subject had injected poison into bottles of children's liquid aspirin in Dallas, Detroit, San Francisco, and Washington, D.C. Four children were known dead. Devlin dropped the teletype. "Sharon, let me use your phone!" Before she could answer, he was dialing his home number. The first ring went unanswered. *That damn Pentagon. The world could come to an end and you'd never know about it in there.* Second ring. Devlin was trying to remember his next-door neighbor's number when his wife answered. "Knox, have you heard about the aspirin?"

"It's been on the news all morning. What's the matter?"

Devlin sat down. "Sorry, I *just* found out about it, and—the kids are all right?"

"Other than Patrick inheriting his father's eagerness to question authority, they're fine."

O'Hare walked in, his face grim. Devlin said, "Tell them I miss them, and I'll call tonight."

"It's going to be longer than two weeks, isn't it, Mike?"

"Not if I have anything to do with it." He hung up and followed O'Hare into his office.

"Read the teletype?" O'Hare asked.

"He was in *Detroit!*"

"Mike, I've got enough emotional people to deal with. This

maniac is depending on everyone getting upset. He set up the President for that tirade, knowing he was going to make him look like a fool with the second wave of poisonings. He cannot succeed without mass hysteria. That's his greatest weapon right now."

"When I saw Detroit, the only thing I could think of was my kids."

"That's how he wants it to work. Your kids are okay, aren't they?" Devlin nodded. "Can you do this?" O'Hare could still see the anger in Devlin. "Can you detach yourself emotionally?"

Devlin thought about the four dead children and knew he couldn't. "Yes."

O'Hare looked at him closely. "You're lying, aren't you?"

"Have you ever solved a tough case—I mean really tough, the kind that takes everything from you before it's done— without getting emotionally involved?"

O'Hare was silent for a moment. "Even though you're the best investigator I know, I swore that I wasn't going to let you get involved in this, no matter what happened. But these poor kids."

"Tom, this is headquarters. How dangerous can it be?"

"It's also Washington. If someone wants to paralyze this country, this is a good place to start."

Devlin shrugged his agreement. "Do we know how he got the poison into the bottles?"

"The lab's working on it right now, but it looks like a liquid industrial poison was syringed in through the bottom of the plastic bottles and then they were resealed. It's January. Kids are sick a lot, so he probably figured it wouldn't take long to get the stuff out into the general population."

"Pretty small window of opportunity after the President's speech. I would guess he didn't break into the manufacturer's warehouse this time. Since the aspirin is available over the counter, he probably planted it himself."

"You're right. One of the stores where it was found had just opened. Their stock had been stored at the location for a month. So he had to have put it there himself in the last couple of days."

"Any security cameras?"

"No, all the stores were in low-crime areas. I'm sure that was another consideration in his selection process."

Devlin said, "Why Detroit, Dallas, San Francisco, and Washington? There are bigger cities where this would make more of an impact. And why only four cities?"

"I don't know. Do you think he's connected to those cities?"

"Possibly."

"We've collected thousands of bottles to inspect for contamination. So far we've found eleven that were poisoned and still on the shelves. They're being processed for prints. Retailers are panicking in every city in the country. They're calling their local FBI offices, demanding that agents be sent out to inspect every nicked or dented container."

"So he has the entire Bureau tied up on things other than looking for him," Devlin said.

"There's no question he knows what he's doing. Some of the press is already claiming the President is responsible."

"A house divided."

O'Hare nodded. "That seems to be his goal."

"Did he E-mail a message this time?"

"No. You'd think he would want to gloat after outsmarting everybody in the government, especially the White House. And now that we finally got the trap-and-traces on those lines, there's no message. He's probably figured that out, too. Have you got any ideas?"

Involuntarily, Devlin's thoughts raced away from him. No longer was his mind working logically, trying to follow the killer's trail one plodding step at a time. The long, tedious pathway that reason was normally forced to follow, methodically looping around logic's mile markers, was being bypassed, overridden by some authority outside Devlin's control, causing an almost telepathic insight. For a brief moment he was being shown the full design of the Freedom Killer's plan. What Devlin was experiencing had happened only a couple of times before, and as tenuous as its origins were, he had learned to trust the message. Everything the killer had done so far had a dual purpose. Each destructive act, designed to strip away freedom, was also intended to provide a psychological predisposition from which the next outrage could be launched.

"I'm going to need Bonelli for the duration."

"That's no problem."

"A room to work out of. Phones, fax, and a computer terminal. And copies of all the teletypes."

O'Hare distrusted the look in Devlin's eyes. "You're going to have to promise not to take any chances."

"We've been through all this."

"Then you shouldn't have any trouble promising me."

"Do you want me to lie to you?"

"If you have to."

"I promise."

O'Hare released an almost imperceptible sigh. "I'll take care of Bonelli. Sharon will handle everything else you need."

After Devlin left, O'Hare felt an unexpected twinge of optimism. But as he reread the teletype describing the ruthless efficiency with which the Freedom Killer had ended the lives of four unsuspecting children, it quickly disappeared.

III CHAPTER 15 III

Two hours later, Devlin and Bonelli sat in a room on the seventh floor of the Hoover Building. It was equipped with everything Devlin had requested, plus three separate phone lines.

"Any ideas, Tony?"

"I wouldn't know where to start."

"Ever seen an FBI agent get the Nobel Prize for investigation?"

Bonelli chuckled. "No."

"That's because what we do is not that difficult. It just takes a little logic and a little luck. Now, what do we know about this?"

"Uh, we think he is a white male, in his mid- to—"

"Forget the profile for a minute. Concrete things. Like, where has he been?"

"Oh, ah—Atlanta, Disney World, then Kansas City, Detroit, Dallas, San Francisco, and Washington."

"Okay, when was he there?"

"Well, he killed the research technician on—let's see— January fourteenth. And we think the kidnapping was the night before, on the thirteenth, in Atlanta."

"Now, let's figure out when he was in Kansas City. The information from there indicates that the contaminated heart medication was shipped on January tenth. And the only possible point it could have been tampered with was at the manufacturer's warehouse. It had been moved there two days before, on the eighth."

Bonelli interrupted. "So he had to be in Kansas City on January eighth or ninth."

"Right. Now, let's see if we can figure out his timetable on the aspirin poisonings. One of the stores in Dallas was new and didn't open until the sixteenth, which was one day before the President's speech, so he couldn't have done it any earlier than that. I'm going to guess he wanted to wait until after the speech, to make sure what was said fit into his plan; but just to be sure, let's include the sixteenth."

"So he had to plant them on the sixteenth or seventeenth of January."

"And he knew that once the source of the poisonings was discovered, it would be just a matter of hours before all the bottles were pulled off the shelves. So when he went in the stores, I'm sure he put his bottles up front so they'd be taken first. That would ensure maximum casualties in as little time as possible. But it probably took him more than one day to get to and from four cities, so let's add a day on the back end and figure the eighteenth also. What does all that tell us?"

Bonelli looked at him for the answer, but Devlin just stared back patiently. Bonelli leaned back and closed his eyes. After a minute he sat up. "If he was in all those cities in such a short period of time, he had to fly."

"I told you this wasn't that hard."

"But there were probably tens of thousands of people flying on those days."

"How many do you think flew to Detroit, Dallas, San Francisco, and Washington?"

"Probably very few."

"*Very* few."

"It still seems like a needle in a haystack to me."

"It is. But at least we now have a haystack. And no one does haystacks better than the FBI. The good news is that because this is headquarters, someone will have liaison with all the airlines. You just have to find out who that is and start making calls."

"Me?"

"If not you, who?"

"You're the agent."

"That's what being an agent is all about: I create a stupid idea, and the clerks run out the leads. *How* long have you been working for the Bureau?"

"Okay, but what if someone asks me if I'm an agent?"

"As long as I've been doing this, no one has ever asked me."

"Yeah, but you *are* an agent."

"Then lie."

"I've never been a great liar."

"Then whatever gave you the idea you could be an agent?"

Bonelli smiled tentatively. "I really don't know if I can pull it off."

"Do you know what attitude is?" Devlin asked.

"I think so."

"If you *think* so, you don't. Attitude means that Tony Bonelli's stuff is at least as important as anyone else's. And probably *more* so. All you have to say is, 'Good afternoon, this is Tony Bonelli, I'm with the FBI, and I'm working on the Freedom Murders. I was wondering if you could help us.' You'll be talking to some airline employee, who is going to be thrilled to help with such an important case. After they hear 'FBI,' you could tell them you molest cattle for the Bureau and it wouldn't matter. Put a little strut in your voice. You're Anthony Bonelli; you've overcome problems these people couldn't even imagine."

"I'll give it a try."

Sensing Bonelli's reluctance to pose as an agent in his presence, Devlin picked up a file and said, "I've got a few things to do." Bonelli looked at him, his uncertainty obvious. Devlin took out his credentials and placed them on the desk in front of the clerk. "Place your left hand on my creds." Bonelli obeyed, and Devlin raised his right hand. "Do you promise to defend this mutha against all enemies until death do us part?"

Bonelli laughed. With comedic enthusiasm, he raised his right hand and said, "I do."

"You are now the recipient of a Mike Devlin battlefield commission. God help you." He picked up his file and headed for the door. "Call O'Hare's secretary. She can tell you who has liaison with the airlines."

"I'll take care of it."

"Hey, I think I hear attitude." Bonelli reached for the telephone, and Devlin said, "Tony, this guy is a long way from being done. Just remember why we're doing this and you'll be fine." He was about to further lecture his new apprentice about the correlation between success and determination when he noticed Bonelli's canes propped up against the wall and remembered it was unnecessary.

||| CHAPTER 16 |||

It took Devlin almost three hours to read and reread all the Freemurs teletypes. As always, they were written in the dispassionate language that agents called "bureauese," a bland, chronological, fact-reporting style that the agency had used since Dillinger robbed his first bank. Theories, suppositions, and guesses were never set forth but were left to the creativity of the recipient. Although these official communications were without literary merit, they were rich with accuracy.

Devlin sat in a small, isolated room and tried to determine in which city the killer's latest death trek had started and finished. Presumably, it would be in the general area of where he permanently resided. Kansas City was a possibility. Maybe he lived there or had worked for the drug manufacturer. That would explain how he got the idea to contaminate the shipments. But not necessarily. Once a particular product was chosen, it would not have been difficult to determine where it was manufactured.

Investigation by the Kansas City office had determined that entry into the warehouse had been gained through the adjoining corporate offices. The warehouse was protected by an alarm system, but its offices were not. Two small holes were found in the glass that framed a side entrance into its headquarters, indicating that a BB gun was used to test for the presence of an alarm. It was an old burglar's trick. A shot through the glass would set the system off—if there was one. Then he would hide at a safe distance and wait. If the police did not respond, he would know there were no alarms and could go to work on the door with whatever method he chose. And later, if the police happened to cruise by while he was inside, they would not be able to spot the two tiny holes in the glass. This evidence told Devlin that the killer was not an ex-employee, who would have known which parts of the building were electronically protected.

Of the four cities where the poisoned aspirin had been planted, Devlin could not see any pattern that indicated a starting or finishing point. Hopefully, Bonelli would have more luck with the airlines.

The only two times and places that were pinned down were those involving Atlanta and Disney World. The killer had obviously driven from Atlanta to Florida, because he had to transport the drugged research technician. Maybe Atlanta was his home base. FBI Atlanta had interviewed all the technician's friends, neighbors, and co-workers. They had not developed one decent lead that might help reveal the identity of the killer.

Devlin closed the file. Teletypes, though full of information, were merely summaries of the investigation. The file in Atlanta would have much more detail in it than had been forwarded to Bureau headquarters. He wondered if O'Hare would let him go there and take a look around.

Bonelli, engrossed in his telephone conversation, did not hear Devlin come back into the room. "Yes, sir, you're the third person I've been switched to . . . I'm Anthony Bonelli, with the FBI in Washington. We're working on the Freedom Killer case and need some help. I'm looking for passenger lists for any flights . . ."

As Bonelli continued, Devlin noticed that the authority in his voice seemed more natural. After giving the person his fax number and asking if the list could be transmitted ASAP, Bonelli hung up.

Devlin asked, "So, how are we doing?"

"We?" the clerk asked defensively.

Devlin laughed. "Talk about attitude. Now I know how Dr. Frankenstein felt."

"Sorry," Bonelli said good-naturedly, "I was on kind of a roll there. We're doing fine. I've talked to most of the majors, and they're sending us passenger lists. But because we don't know where he started or in what order he went to those cities, their computers can't search for one person traveling to those cities. Besides, he could have used a different airline for each flight."

"Then what use are these lists they're sending us?"

"I'll load them into the computer and then interface them. Anyone who was on more than one of those flights should pop."

Devlin nodded his appreciation for Bonelli taking the investigation a step further than had been outlined. "Pretty clever."

"Thanks."

"While you're doing that, I'm going to run down to Atlanta tomorrow. Will that cause you any problems?"

"Not at all; I'll be here holding down the fort."

Devlin noted Bonelli's use of the word *fort*. Building fortresses around himself seemed to be a constant undertaking. When they had first met, the clerk had squirreled himself away in a corner pod, surrounded physically by hardware and emotionally by work. Although he had always dreamed of doing an agent's work, he had been reluctant to leave the sanctuary of his routine when the opportunity was offered. And his apartment—Devlin almost had to go to the 9-millimeter to get invited inside. Even his initial reaction to people was safely unsociable. Devlin understood it was the disease and all its emotional cargo that caused Bonelli to seek the comfort of walls. But fortresses, while full of security, were reciprocally devoid of freedom.

||| CHAPTER 17 |||

Devlin got off the plane in Atlanta and scanned the crowd of people who were meeting passengers. O'Hare had said that someone from the field office would pick him up. Surprisingly, the section chief had thought it was a good idea that Devlin make the trip. "There has to be a connection between the killer and that research technician; see if you can find it."

"I should be back tomorrow night."

"What about Kansas City and Disney World—think there's anything there?"

"I thought about it, but Atlanta's the only place he made more than chance contact with someone. Let me see if I can find anything there first."

"Mike, we need a break on this. That's why I'm letting you go. The answers have a way of finding you."

Devlin spotted a black man in his early thirties, dressed in a suit. He was patiently searching the stream of passengers coming through the gate. When his eyes found Devlin's, he nodded and walked toward him. "You Devlin?"

Sensing an intentional lack of camaraderie in the agent's tone, Devlin understood the message: *We don't need some headquarters puke down here second-guessing us.* It was a good sign. Whenever agents became territorial, it usually meant that they were proud of what they were accomplishing and resented someone else's ego elbowing its way in, looking for a cheap massage.

Devlin held out his hand. "*Mike* Devlin."

The agent shook his hand. "Nelson Roberts."

Roberts's grip was deliberately unresponsive, hinting that unless this turf problem was addressed, a long, unproductive day lay ahead. "Nelson, let me explain something. Like you, I'm a street hump. I'm from Detroit and was hijacked to Washington for this special. I'm not here to look up your skirt to see if you're missing anything. My purpose is to get inside this guy's head and see if we can guess what's next. Now, I'm going to need some help. Will that be you?"

Roberts considered what Devlin had said and then allowed one corner of his mouth to smirk. "That'll be me."

Devlin smiled back. "Good. I'd like to see three things: Nate Walker's apartment, the Centers for Disease Control, and the case file."

Once they were in the car heading to Walker's apartment, Devlin asked, "How long have you been working this case?"

"From minute one."

"What's the best guess why Walker stole the vials?"

"According to everyone we talked to, he was a compulsive spender. It didn't matter if he had money or not—he would charge, beg, borrow, and, maybe in this case, steal it."

"So you think it might have been a bribe?"

"As theories go, it does fill in the blanks."

"Did you get his bank records?"

"I gave the clerk a subpoena this morning before I came to get you. By the time we get back to the office, they should be there."

"Well then, let's go see how Mr. Walker spent his money."

Walker's apartment building had a desolate, no-frills quality. A large tan concrete cube, it appeared to be of modular construction and therefore defied an accurate assessment of its age. It could have been five years or twenty-five years old. The lawn in front of it was two weeks too long, and a couple dozen tiny shrubs, terminal brown in color, surrounded the structure.

As they got out of the car, Devlin asked Roberts, "Have you been here before?"

"No. When this thing broke, the SAC sent me to CDC because at that time our main concern was the missing virus. Another squad was sent here. They said the manager was a pain in the ass. Insisted on a search warrant before he would let them in."

"Did they find anything?"

"Nothing that helped. Think we should get a search warrant?"

"I don't think there's enough time. I want to be on that late flight back to Washington. Besides, I would think that a couple of charming guys like us could persuade the manager to come to the aid of his country."

Roberts adjusted his tie with mock vanity. "Absolutely."

Roberts scanned the names of the residents that were pasted over the individual mailboxes and below the doorbells until he found E. WARD—MANAGER. He rang the bell. When there was no answer, he tried it again. "I guess he's not in."

Devlin said, "Let me check something." He walked around to the rear of the building. Bulging black and green plastic garbage bags overflowed from the Dumpster, and another dozen were carelessly stacked next to it. Devlin counted eighteen parking slots, five of which had cars in them. The space nearest the back door had MANAGER stenciled across the front of it and was occupied by an old two-door sedan. Its color, Devlin thought, was dark green or blue; it was difficult to tell under the grime that covered everything from the tires to the vinyl top. The interior was blanketed with fast-food wrappers and an occasional soft-drink container. The ashtray was open and full of cigarette butts. Devlin walked back to the front door.

Roberts asked, "Any luck?"

"He's in there." Devlin pushed the bell and held it in.

After almost a minute, an angry voice answered. "Hansen, if that's you again, I'm gonna kick your ass."

Devlin continued to press the button. From somewhere inside, the two agents heard a door slam. Devlin released the buzzer and said, "Stand by for a little bull-riding."

Roberts's grin was short-lived as the front door was ripped open. "Who the fuck are you?" the manager thundered. He was well over six feet tall and weighed close to 350 pounds. He was dressed in shower shoes, khaki slacks, and an orange tank top. Stenciled white letters across the front of it read: EYE WATCH BAYWATCH. Devlin held up his credentials. As the manager studied them, Devlin slowly turned them sideways and watched the mammoth head in front of him rotate accordingly. Then he slowly righted them. The head followed. Finally, Ward said, "Yeah, so?"

"So, we want to see Nate Walker's apartment."

The manager snorted disdainfully. "You got me up for that? You don't look like you got a search warrant."

Roberts stepped in front of him. "That's just what this country needs—another self-appointed constitutional scholar. You want a search warrant?" Roberts took out one of his business cards and a pen. On the back side he wrote something, then wedged it into the nameplate above the manager's mailbox.

Devlin liked Roberts's aggressiveness, but the manager didn't. He realized his usual tactics were not going to work with these two agents. The confidence they showed was dissolving the intimidation he relied on. Devlin could see he did not want to acknowledge their authority by looking at the card, and was apparently afraid that reading what the black agent had written would somehow make him answerable to its intent. As he peered at it out of the corner of his eye, Devlin and Roberts watched him patiently, knowing that someone so well acquainted with self-loathing would find its obviously negative message irresistible.

Finally, he turned and read the neat black letters that had been printed on the card: SEND MY MAIL TO THE FULTON COUNTY JAIL. Ward's breathing could now be heard in his speech; his voice climbed a half an octave: "Because I won't let you conduct an illegal search, you think you can put me in jail? That's a laugh."

Roberts stepped up in front of him and lowered his voice as if he did not want to be overheard. "Don't you read the papers? We're the FBI. We killed JFK and Martin Luther King. Do you think we'd think twice about locking up a pimple like you?"

While uncertainty caused Ward's falsely confident smile to fail, Roberts's face remained stony with conviction. The manager looked at Devlin for some proof that the black agent was bluffing. Devlin shook his head defenselessly. "I could be way off base here, but you don't look like the type who could survive on bologna sandwiches and cold coffee."

As Ward looked back and forth at the agents, Devlin could see that he realized just how expensive his bravado was becoming. He had passed the break-even point and was now sliding quickly down the scale of diminishing returns. "Wait here," he ordered in a final face-saving maneuver.

A minute later he was back with the key to Walker's apartment. "Put it in my mailbox when you leave."

The one-bedroom apartment was on the fourth floor. Roberts unlocked the door and led the way in. The walk-through kitchen had a few dishes in the sink but was otherwise clean. The refrigerator was virtually empty. It contained ketchup, mustard, soy sauce, and three beers. Devlin said, "I guess he liked to eat out."

A small couch, console TV, and recliner filled the living

room. The bed was unmade and a used towel lay on the floor, apparently where Walker had left it a week before.

Searching through a tall white antiqued secretarial desk in the dining area, Roberts found Walker's personal papers. As he started going through them, Devlin checked the bedroom, which was equally neat and uncluttered.

After finding nothing significant, Devlin joined Roberts and started examining the research assistant's personal documents. "Whatever squad searched this place was certainly neat." An hour later, they were done and had found nothing to indicate Walker's connection to the killer. When they left, Devlin dropped the apartment key in the manager's mailbox. The two agents smiled when they saw that Roberts's card had been removed from the nameplate.

The Centers for Disease Control was a half-hour drive away. Roberts had been there a number of times previously to interview Walker's co-workers. He introduced Devlin to one of the security people, who escorted them through the facility, discussing how Walker had evidently gained access to the two vials of virus kept in the superfreezers, which maintained such samples at a temperature of −160 degrees Fahrenheit. Finally, they were briefed on the new security precautions that had been implemented to prevent any recurrence of employee theft. The entire tour took less than an hour.

Four and a half hours after picking Devlin up at the airport, Roberts pulled his Bureau car into the federal building's basement garage. They took the elevator to the FBI office. As Roberts led the way to his squad's area, he asked, "Well, *did* we miss anything?"

Devlin studied the relaxed expression on the Atlanta agent's face and was satisfied the question was devoid of any combativeness. "From what I saw—nothing."

"Good," Roberts said, and nodded at a desk. Three volumes of the Freemurs case, along with scores of loose pages, were stacked on top. "There's the file. The rotor clerk hasn't had time to put all the serials in it, so I had her pile them up here until she could get caught up. Do you need anything else?"

"Just a few hours to read."

It was almost five o'clock when Devlin finished. He stood up and stretched. Roberts came over. "Any luck?"

"I couldn't find anything to light my fire. How about the 1-A's?"

"I've been working on them at my desk, trying to get them numbered." The 1-A section of an FBI file was the repository for less important evidence that was not likely to become the object of testimony during trial. Things such as photos, phone books, and identification cards were numbered into small envelopes and then grouped together in a larger envelope at the back of the file. Roberts carried back about thirty of the small envelopes and placed them on Devlin's desk. "Looking for anything in particular?"

"Walker's bank records."

Roberts scattered the envelopes until he found the one Devlin wanted. "Here. I was just looking at them. About five weeks ago, he deposited four thousand dollars in his account."

Devlin scanned the pages. "And he had withdrawn almost all of it by the time he disappeared."

"Do you think it could have been the down payment on a bribe?"

"If it wasn't, where did he get four thousand dollars? It doesn't look like he ever had that much money in his account before."

Roberts said, "I guess we should reinterview everyone to see if he ever mentioned anything about a windfall."

Devlin flipped through the 1-A envelopes, reading the description of the contents listed on the outside of each one. "Do you have any idea what he was doing around the time he made the deposit?"

"No, but that's something else we can ask."

"Good idea." Devlin shuffled back through the envelopes until he found what he was looking for. "Did you look at his credit cards?"

"He only had the one, and it was maxed."

Devlin leafed through several photocopied pages. "According to this, the weekend before he made that deposit, there was an inquiry but no charge from the Raintree Hotel on Duke Street in Alexandria, Virginia."

Roberts leaned over Devlin's shoulder. "Let me get the address. I'll send a lead up there."

Devlin did not answer. He was thinking about the aspirin poisonings. One of the four cities targeted had been Washington, and now Alexandria, Virginia, just across the Potomac River, had come up. Was it a coincidence? Probably. But the solutions to most cases started with coincidences. Devlin flipped back through the envelopes until he found the photos of Nate Walker. He took one out and put it in his coat pocket.

"Don't bother, Nelson. I'll run it out myself tomorrow."

||| CHAPTER 18 |||

At 8:00 A.M. the next morning, Devlin went to O'Hare's office to brief him on the trip to Atlanta, but according to his secretary, the section chief was already in conference with the Director. She said she would call as soon as he returned.

Devlin found Bonelli as he had left him, typing information into the computer. "How was Atlanta?" Bonelli asked after realizing Devlin was there.

"If you're asking me if we identified the killer, the answer is: keep typing."

It was almost 11:00 A.M. when Sharon called and told Devlin that O'Hare would like to see him.

"Did I miss anything while I was gone?" Devlin asked the section chief.

"I don't know. Did you have any pains in *your* ass while you were down there?"

"That bad?"

"And a whole lot more. The Director is taking a ton of crap from those boy wonders at the White House. And he's such a stand-up guy, he won't let any of it roll downhill, which makes me feel that much worse. It was bad enough when they were calling every half hour. Now there's a different one of them here every day to sit in on our meetings. If you were ever curious about what happened to all those twerps in high school, the ones who didn't find serial killing to be enough of a power trip, just check the White House staff."

"I suppose they have some suggestions about what we should be doing."

"Of course. Today's mastermind wanted us to offer a two-million-dollar reward—as if someone knows who this guy is."

"Are the field offices coming up with anything?"

"Between running out tips and having to check out every suspicious container, they are completely overwhelmed. They don't have time to do anything but put out brushfires. There is no in-depth investigation going on at all."

"I've got to tell you, this guy has my attention," Devlin said. "Not only has he found new ways to commit mass murder, but he has figured out how to keep us from investigating it at the same time."

"Well, I think the Director has found a solution to that. There's an immediate teletype going out right now to all SACs instructing them to form Freedom Murder task forces with other federal, state, and local agencies. It's the first time the Bureau has had to ask for help like this."

"The killer has got to like that—he's become a national priority."

"And that means we've got to do whatever is necessary to stop him. Did you find anything in Atlanta?"

"Not really. They've pretty much covered all the bases."

"What does 'not really' mean?" O'Hare asked. When Devlin hesitated, he said, "Come on, Mike. I need some joy on this."

"It's probably nothing, but Nate Walker had heavyweight money problems. About a month before he was killed, he deposited a mysterious four thousand dollars into his checking account. According to his credit card, the weekend before this unexplained windfall he was in Washington."

"Why hasn't Atlanta notified us?"

"They just got the credit card report yesterday."

"Any idea what he was doing here?"

"Atlanta's going to do some reinterviewing and see if they can find out."

"What were the charges?"

"Just a hotel."

O'Hare looked at him closely. "Mike, it worries me when you say 'just.' "

"I was going to check it out myself before I bothered you with it."

"Bother me now."

"It really isn't much. It's not even a charge, just an inquiry. I called the credit card company this morning, and after a two-hour runaround, they told me he was evidently staying at the Raintree Hotel in Alexandria and charging everything to his room. When he checked out, he tried to use the card. That's when the hotel made the query and found out he was overloaded."

"How'd he pay the bill, then?"

"That's what I was going to try and find out."

"Give me the information; I'll have someone run it out."

"I'd like to do it."

"You were told no heavy lifting on this," O'Hare said.

"This is not heavy lifting. I'll go over there and stroke some hotel employee until I get a computer printout. At most, I'll interview a bellboy. I'll be back before you could find someone to handle it."

"The hotel and nothing else."

"Whatever you say."

"Save that crap for someone who doesn't know you."

"Whatever you say."

When Devlin pulled up in front of the Raintree Hotel, he flashed his credentials at the valet parking attendant. "I'm sorry, sir, but I have to charge you."

"I'm just going in to see the manager."

"I could lose my job. Sorry, it's three dollars."

"Nothing to be sorry about." Devlin handed him four dollars and waited while the valet walked around the back of the car and wrote the license number on the claim ticket. He handed it to Devlin and thanked him for the tip.

Devlin found the manager's office, knocked, and was buzzed in. After he showed the secretary his identification, she took him to a small inner office and introduced him to the manager. He was a dark-skinned black man who wore an expensive single-breasted suit and spoke with a South African accent. "How may I help the FBI?"

"On or around December thirteenth, you had a guest here by the name of Nate Walker. I'd like to see any records you might have for him."

The manager lowered his voice. "The hotel will not be receiving any complaints from Mr. Walker about giving out this information, I trust."

"Not unless the hotel can find a way to reattach Mr. Walker's brain to his spine. I'm looking for the individual who performed the surgery."

Devlin's less-than-picturesque description of Walker's death had a purpose to it. Too many everyday, hardworking people held the misconception that the FBI, for a lack of something better to do, spent a good portion of its time peeking into ordinary people's private lives. From his reaction, Devlin could see the manager now understood the seriousness of his inquiry. "In that case, right this way." He led Devlin into another small office, this one with a computer. He typed in a query, waited briefly, and hit the PRINT button. They waited, listening to the electronic rhythm of the machine. When it finished, the manager handed Devlin a copy of Nate Walker's hotel bill.

Devlin took a quick look at it. "How did he pay this?"

The manager scanned the computer screen. "From the transaction codes, he apparently tried to use a credit card and that was rejected, so he paid cash."

Evidently, Walker liked to spend money. Although he had stayed only three days, the bill was almost doubled because of charges for hotel services: parking, mini-bar, valet, room service, in-room movies, hotel bars and restaurants, even the gift shop. Surprisingly, there was not one long-distance phone call. Devlin did some quick math and determined that Walker had charged over a hundred dollars at the hotel bar. "Is there any way to tell what he was doing in the Washington area while he was staying here?"

"We host a lot of conventions. Do you know what he did for a living?"

"He was a research technician at the Centers for Disease Control in Atlanta."

The manager typed the dates into the computer. "Yes, there was a three-day seminar on communicable diseases while he was staying here."

The killer, after he came up with the idea of spreading the deadly disease, had to first get his hands on the necessary biological material. Devlin wondered if he had gone to Atlanta with the idea of breaking into the CDC as he had in Kansas City but, because it was a federal facility, found the security too difficult to circumvent. Maybe bribing an employee seemed like the next best approach. But which employee would be vulnerable? Somehow, the killer had found out about the seminar. Maybe, because he used his own computer to send messages to *The Real Deal*, he had found out about it by searching the Internet. Conventions were well known as places where people unwound and let their weaknesses be exposed. With strangers mixing, there was always an abundance of alcohol and loose talk. It would not take long to find out about

Walker's legendary money problems. "I see he ran up a large bar tab."

The manager looked at the bill. "Pretty good size. Hardly a record, though."

"Would it be possible for you to tell me who was working the bar on those dates?"

"Afternoons or evenings?"

"I know some people come to these things and never attend a lecture, but let's assume he was at the seminar during the day. Who was working nights?"

From the printer table, the manager took a clipboard and leafed through work schedules. "The waitresses were Sandy Morton and Barbara Dalton. The bartender, Rodney Harris."

"Would they be working tonight?"

"The waitresses start in about an hour."

"And Harris?"

"Ah, no. We had to let him go."

"For . . . ?"

"Shortchanging customers."

"Do you have an address for him?"

The manager hit a couple more keys on the computer and then wrote down Harris's address. "He may not be that easy to find. I think the police have a warrant out for him. There was also a couple thousand dollars' worth of liquor missing when he left."

Devlin thanked him, went to the gift shop to buy a newspaper, and headed to the bar.

An hour later, the two waitresses showed up. Devlin showed both of them Nate Walker's photo and asked about the dates he was a hotel guest. Neither of them could recall having seen him before.

The parking attendant saw Devlin coming and brought his car around without being given the claim check. Devlin got in and showed the attendant the address the manager had written down. "Man, I know you're the police, but I wouldn't go in that neighborhood alone."

Devlin felt a surge of adrenaline. "How do I get there?"

III CHAPTER 19 III

The postcard perfection of Washington, D.C., quickly dissolved as Devlin neared the address he had been given for Rodney Harris. The architecture was different than Detroit's, but the decline and despair were not. Graffiti was everywhere, warning the stranger who could recognize such urban markings that civility and diplomacy were now as useless as the Dow Jones averages. Devlin drove past boarded-up storefronts, decaying apartment buildings, exhausted cars, and lethargic people, who seemed oblivious to the surrounding chaos.

Two men argued outside of a liquor store, reminding Devlin that confrontation was a primary communication skill here and that those who stepped aside first usually lost. He started feeling comfortable. It was a place, unlike FBI headquarters, where he understood the rules. Harris's address was one half of a red-brick two-flat. Devlin rang the bell and a black man in his sixties, wearing freshly pressed gray work clothes, came to the door. Devlin showed him his identification. "If you're looking for Rodney, he ain't here."

"Do you mind if I come in?"

"You can come in, you can search my house, but my son ain't here."

Devlin followed him into the living room. They both sat down. "First of all, Mr. Harris, I'm not going to search your house. I just want to ask Rodney about something he may have seen when he was working at the Raintree. I know he's had some problems with the law, but I don't care about liquor being stolen, unless it happens to be my own."

The old man smiled politely. "You know, I done my best to bring the boy up right. I settled down with his mother and got a regular job. But when she passed eight years ago, Rodney got wild. I done my best, but sometimes I guess it just ain't enough." Harris's lips tightened and he slowly shook his head in disappointment.

"How old is Rodney?"

"Thirty."

"I wouldn't give up on him yet. He may not be doing exactly what you want him to, but kids figure that's their job."

The old man sensed that Devlin's words were sincere and nodded his appreciation. "What's this about?"

"Have you heard of the Freedom Killer?"

"Sure, I listen to the news. That little black girl that died, the one from here who was poisoned, her people live over by where I used to work."

"That's what I need to talk to Rodney about. The man who is responsible for these deaths may have been drinking at the Raintree bar." Devlin could see the reluctance in the old man's face. It was the same every time he asked parents where he could find their son or daughter. "If you don't want to tell me where he's at, that's fine, but it's not about him. We only want to find this killer."

"The Purple Camel."

"What's that?"

"Bar he hangs out at all day and night. It's probably where

he sold the liquor he stole. I'm sure he's there right now, gamblin' and hoodlumizin' with those bums he calls friends."

"How do I get there?"

"You going by yourself?" Harris asked. "I don't think a white man should go there by hisself, whether he's FBI or not."

"Don't worry about me. I've found I can overcome most obstacles with stupidity."

III CHAPTER 20 III

Devlin pulled his car to the curb and got out. He had been going into bars like the Purple Camel alone since he was nine years old. Weekly, on payday, his mother would send him in search of his father and the elusive bricklayer's paycheck. When Devlin was lucky enough to find him, he would be sitting on whatever stool was closest to the bartender, his work cap cocked jauntily on his head. To preclude any question of his solvency, he would have all his cash stacked on the bar in front of him. Often, there would be a woman sitting next to him. Devlin knew that his father plus money plus a woman equaled zero for the family. So even if he couldn't convince his father to come home, he knew that the money was a more than acceptable alternative. Much to the dissatisfaction of his father's companion, Devlin was usually able to cajole the majority of the remaining money from him. Dutifully, he would walk home with his hand squeezed tightly around the wad of bills in his pocket and turn it over to his mother, never mentioning who his father had been with.

And for the last fifteen years, warrants for men like Rodney Harris had taken Devlin into dozens of Detroit bars, giving him a working knowledge of the protocol necessary when entering such places. Invariably, the only laws enforced there were those legislated from within. But he did have one advantage: The customers would be wary of him, because a white man, especially a cop, would not be crazy enough to invade their sanctuary alone unless it was a trap.

The door closed behind him. The only light came from a series of electric beer signs behind the bar. Devlin stood motionless until his eyes adjusted to the darkness.

The lone person there was the bartender, and he stood behind the bar reading a newspaper, intentionally ignoring the man who was obviously the law. Devlin stood in front of him and waited. A full minute passed, and neither of the men moved. Finally, the bartender looked up from the paper and glared.

Devlin stared back. "Rodney Harris."

"Don't know him."

"Maybe you know him by a different name."

The bartender sucked his teeth defiantly. "Don't know him by that name, either."

Devlin sensed a tenseness in the bartender's face that he had seen before. Something was going on. "Let me describe him to you. He's black, thirty years old, and sold you the liquor he stole from the Raintree Hotel."

The bartender's eyes flickered dangerously. A ruthlessness settled comfortably on his face. "You mean Tombo. He's in the backroom." His words were slow, seething, and impudent. Their message was: I hope you're foolish enough to go in there.

Devlin decided he was. As he put his hand on the doorknob,

he heard the muffled cheer of a dozen voices. He looked back at the bartender, who still wore the same sadistic smile. "Yeah, go ahead."

Devlin waited a moment until fear knotted his stomach, then pulled open the door.

The backroom was large, and rap music throbbed indecipherably. A makeshift bar sat shadowed along the rear wall. Languid blue smoke rose and disappeared into the beams of half a dozen recessed ceiling lights, which illuminated only the center of the room. The walls and corners remained hidden in darkness. A few dozen men formed an oval around two individuals who stood twenty feet apart, facing one another. Balanced on each of their heads was an unopened can of beer. In the waistband of the man facing him, Devlin could see an oddly shaped gun butt that he recognized as a CO_2-powered BB pistol. Several in the crowd argued loudly, making bets. A stout man in his fifties wearing a gray silk suit put his hand on the shoulder of the contestant facing Devlin and said, "I got two hundred on Tombo that needs to be covered." He held up the other hand, which had several folded bills threaded between his fingers.

Someone said, "C'mon, T-Bone, give us some weight. How about two to one?"

Everyone waited for his answer. The man grinned slowly, exposing an electric-white smile filled with well-maintained teeth except for one of the upper canines, which was solid gold with a half-carat-diamond inlay. "What do you think this is, a motherfuckin' soup kitchen lookin' to give your raggedy ass a handout? And before you ask, no, I ain't takin' no food stamps, neither."

Everyone laughed, including the person T-Bone had berated. It was a good sign for Devlin. The men were not easily insulted; they were concerned only with the action. They were true gamblers, and gamblers, because they witnessed their own shortcomings daily, were usually a tolerant bunch. Apparently, T-Bone made not only the odds in the backroom but also the rules. Devlin decided he was the key.

Finally, another man said, "I'll take ten dollars of that, T-Bone."

The diamond disappeared as T-Bone's face became comically confused. "Bitch, you better take that ten home to your old lady so she can buy herself some new underwear, because you obviously wearing hers."

Again everybody laughed. But then fear of becoming T-Bone's next target set in, and the men grew quiet, reluctant to attempt their own modest bets. Sensing their reservation, he said, "Put all your sorry Salvation Army asses together probably ain't two hundred dollars in the whole room."

Devlin closed the door with a thud and stepped out of the shadows. With the exception of the music, the room became silent while militant eyes measured him cautiously. "I'll take the whole load, T-Bone."

Everyone waited for the man in the gray silk suit to respond. He considered Devlin's motives for being there. This man was alone and obviously a fed. Feds would have no interest in these minor-league activities, so T-Bone figured that whatever Devlin's game was, it was about to cost the government two hundred dollars. His diamond winked at Devlin. "Now, that's what I mean—some big, white money."

Devlin walked up to him and took out two hundred dollars. "Who holds this?"

T-Bone pulled four fifties from between his fingers and handed them to a thin old man in his seventies, wearing a black suit, white shirt, and tie. "Digger's the referee here." Devlin handed his wager to the old man. The gambling chatter started again.

Finally Digger looked at Harris. "Tombo, you ready?" Harris nodded. The old man looked at his opponent. "R.J., you ready?"

R.J. nodded, and Digger took a couple of steps back. The rest of the crowd followed his lead, enlarging the oval.

Although Devlin had not asked for the fine print, he had a pretty good idea what the match was about. But the subtleties of the contest were not important to him, because he knew that any close calls would go to the house anyway. It didn't matter; he wasn't there to collect money.

As the crowd sensed the beginning of combat, their excitement rose. Small side bets were finalized as the bettors urged their favorites on. Digger held his hand high in the air. He looked from one contestant to the other. They both nodded. He slowly lowered his hand, and the gunfighters tensed. "Draw!"

R.J. got his shot off first, but it was fired too quickly, hitting low and ripping a one-inch gash in his opponent's forehead. The can on Harris's forehead remained balanced, so he took his time. He raised his weapon slowly, aiming, for a moment, at the middle of R.J.'s face. Then he lifted it slightly, squeezed off a shot, and the surprisingly powerful shot caused the beer can to explode. Half the men cheered while the other half swore.

R.J. shook hands with Harris and apologized for having shot him. Harris laughed good-naturedly. T-Bone flashed his diamond at Devlin as Digger handed him the four hundred dollars and asked, "Want to go again?"

Devlin smiled back. "Not just yet."

Another man walked inside the oval with two cans of beer and handed one to Harris. The challenge was met with another rush of betting. Devlin went to the bar and ordered a beer. R.J. came up behind him and said sarcastically, "I thought the FBI was supposed to be smart."

"Well, I guess this has been very instructional for you, then."

"That was a sucker bet."

Devlin ordered him a beer and said, "Why's that?"

R.J. was surprised that someone he was trying to goad

would buy him a drink. His words softened. "If Tombo knows someone is faster than him, he'll let him take the first shot even if it means he's going to get hit in the head."

Digger was stepping back and raising his hand.

Devlin said, "If you knew he was going to wait, why didn't you take an extra second to find your target before shooting?"

R.J. laughed. "It's a helluva lot easier standing here talking about it than getting in there and doing it."

Digger slowly lowered his hand.

R.J. said, "Watch Tombo this time. He's faster than this guy and will win on speed."

The old man yelled, "Draw!" And as R.J. had predicted, Harris fired so quickly his opponent never got the shot off.

The crowd rang with cheers and good-natured boos. Harris lifted the beer off his head and held it up in a toast to his fellow gamblers. R.J. said to Devlin. "I told you, man."

T-Bone asked if anyone else wanted to try. There were no takers, so he sat down at a table with Harris and started paying him his share of the winnings. Devlin ordered another beer, picked it up, and said, "Excuse me, I got to go to work."

He walked over to the table T-Bone and Harris were sitting at and pulled up a chair. Harris glared at him for a moment and then said, "I hope you're not here about me."

"I am."

"And you think you can take me out of here?"

"That's not why I'm here."

"Then why me?"

"I'm here to talk."

"About . . . ?"

"The Freedom Killer."

"That sounds like a white problem to me."

"Why is the death of a three-year-old black girl a white problem?"

"She's the only one of the four who was black. It doesn't matter what color any of them were, because *you're* white."

"This guy wants to destroy this country and that doesn't bother you?"

"Take a look around. Does this look like the land of mother-fuckin' opportunity? How many white people you know who would take a shot in the forehead for nickels and dimes?"

"So it's always going to be us against you?"

"That's right, because you white boys ain't got the heart to deal with any of this." Harris sneered. "Or you thinking about trying me, Suburbs?"

Devlin understood Harris's reference: White people lived in the suburbs and couldn't imagine what it was like in the inner city. And no amount of talking was going to change his mind. But Devlin had an idea and it started the adrenaline buzz again. "Why not? But since you have the home field advantage, I'll need a couple of concessions."

Harris was already on his feet. "You can have whatever you want."

"I want double or nothing on the two hundred. And if you lose, you cooperate on the murders."

"Man, this is a dream come true. You betting against your own money. I can't lose. I hope I don't shoot you in the eye by accident." Devlin knew Harris wouldn't allow himself to lose intentionally for any reason; it was all part of the pre-contest intimidation ritual. The two men walked to their positions. Digger handed Harris one of the BB guns. As he offered one to Devlin, Harris said, "What's the other condition?"

Devlin refused the pistol and drew his 9-millimeter. "That we do this like the big boys." Again, the only sound in the room was the music. Devlin reholstered his weapon.

"You're bullshittin'," Harris said.

Devlin stood with his hands hanging comfortably at his

sides. "I know there's got to be another gun in here. You *do* want it, don't you?"

Two opposing fears twisted the brown-and-tan planes of Harris's face. As frightening as Devlin's challenge was, losing the respect of friends had always been his greatest fear. "Digger, give me your shit."

"You sure?" the old man asked.

"Just give it to me!"

From his back pocket, Digger reluctantly drew a chrome-plated revolver and handed it to him. Harris searched Devlin's eyes and saw sparks of something he had witnessed countless times growing up—insanity. "I want a drink first."

Devlin knew this was, at least in part, another attempt to intimidate him, implying that if he drank, his aim could be off the mark. "I'll have one, too."

The bartender poured them each a shot of cognac. Harris threw his back. Devlin hated cognac but downed the flinty liquid in one gulp. He smirked at Harris. "Time to lock and load, Rodney."

Reluctantly, Harris walked back to his position. Someone in the crowd sensed his apprehension and yelled, "Come on, Tombo! Don't let him scare you." Other voices chimed in, urging him on.

The room was becoming more barbaric, more dangerous. Never had the thrill of betting been so horrifyingly seductive. Everyone wanted to run from this trouble, but no one could move. Devlin felt invulnerable. All his body's emergency chemicals were spilling over, igniting his senses. His vision accelerated, measuring everything quicker, more often. Images slowed; he could see several things at once: Digger argues with T-Bone; R.J. orders another drink; two men are making a bet. He could now see into the darkness along the walls and in the corners. His hearing intensified. He could hear low, over-lapping conversations: Digger wants T-Bone to stop the match;

R.J. is ordering cognac instead of beer; one of the men wants odds if he takes Devlin. He could read every microscopic nuance in their faces: T-Bone wants to see this no matter the cost. R.J. is fascinated but glad it isn't him; Harris is scared. Devlin was euphoric, but calm. He felt a power over everything that his senses touched. He could not be beaten.

Devlin took his suit coat off, exposing his gun. He reached down and thumbed back the 9-millimeter's hammer to the full-cock position.

Harris, seemingly in a need to answer Devlin's aggressiveness, broke open the revolver's cylinder to ensure it was loaded. He closed it and stuck it in his waistband. Both men placed the beer cans on their heads. Everyone moved back against the wall and out from behind the combatants.

Devlin put his hands into his pockets casually and said to Digger, "Whenever you're ready." A scraping of feet could be heard as everyone tried to get even closer to the walls.

Harris took a moment to review his life and decided it hadn't been all that great. And without the respect of his friends, it would be nothing. "Fuck it, I'm ready."

Devlin shifted his weight onto one hip comfortably while keeping his hands in his pockets. From the wall, Digger lowered his hand slowly.

Anticipating the command, Harris's hand edged toward the revolver. Devlin remained motionless.

"Draw!"

Harris clawed at the unfamiliar gun. When it cleared his waistband, he shifted into a gunfighter's stance. Fearing Devlin's sureness, he fired too soon. The bullet struck the floor four feet to the left of where Devlin stood. Harris's movement had started the beer sliding off his head. It hit the floor.

Devlin stood relaxed, his hands in his pockets, the can on his head unmoved.

Suddenly, the men in the room realized it had all been a

bluff. They howled appreciatively. Several of them crowded around Harris, clapping him on the shoulder and congratulating him on his courage.

Devlin took the beer off his head and offered Harris his hand. "Can I buy you a drink?"

All at once Harris was relieved. No one had gotten hurt, and his reputation had been enhanced by not backing down from the deadly challenge. "Yeah, I think I could use one." He ordered a double cognac and Devlin cracked open the beer in his hand.

They took their drinks to a table and sat down. T-Bone came over and gave Devlin his money back. "Never seen nothing like that, man." He shook Devlin's hand and moved to the bar, where everyone was drinking and talking excitedly.

Devlin said, "About five weeks ago, there was a man who stayed at the Raintree. According to his bill, he spent a lot of time in the bar. He was a research technician at the Centers for Disease Control in Atlanta. He was there for a conference on diseases. Ring any bells?"

"Man, they had so many conventions, I never paid much attention what they were about."

"His name was Nate Walker. Ran a tab in your bar one night of over a hundred dollars."

"Lot of people do that."

Devlin took out Walker's photo. Immediately, Harris said, "Oh yeah, big tipper. One of them people trying to prove something by throwing money around. He was in there a couple of nights, early. Double vodkas. And he wasn't half steppin'. Told me he'd double my tip if he never had to ask for the next one, so I kept pouring and he kept drinking."

"Ever see him with anyone?"

"People like him are there to drink, not to make friends, but the last night I saw him, another guy came in and started buying. Bought the rest of the night and never tipped me a dime. Before long, these two start this serious whispering. For a while I figured maybe they're sissies. Just before they left, the one you got the picture of, he writes down something like a phone number and the other guy hands him an envelope. I can't see what's in it, but the tipper looks into it like you do if it's money."

"What did the other one look like?"

"White dude. Average size, maybe late twenties. Suit and tie. I think brown hair. Glasses and a beard. His hair a little too long to be as neat as the rest of him."

"Think you'd know him if you saw him again?"

"I don't know. With those glasses and all that hair, it'd be tough. If he shaved and cut his hair, it could be you. I don't think I'd know him."

"Anything else about him you remember?"

"Nothing special."

"How did he pay?"

"Cash. All fifties. And not a penny for me."

"Could he have been staying at the hotel?"

Harris thought for a second. "No, that's right. When they were leaving the bar, he said he had to get back to his hotel. So I guess not."

Devlin felt a familiar disappointment. If the killer had stayed at the Raintree and charged the night's drinking to his room, he would not have been difficult to identify.

Harris agreed to come to the Washington field office the next day and work with a composite artist to define the face of the man he had seen in the bar with Nate Walker. Devlin asked, "Can I buy you one last drink before I go?"

Harris threw back the rest of his drink. "Sure." Devlin took out his money to pay. On top of the bills was the parking claim check from the hotel. He asked Harris, "Since he wasn't staying there, what do you think the chances are that he used the Raintree's parking lot?"

"The closest hotel is too far to walk, so he either took a cab or used the valet-parking. There's no place around there to park without getting towed."

Devlin offered Harris his hand. "If you can help us with this, we'll try and get you some air on that liquor thing."

"I would appreciate it," Harris said, "but let me ask you a question. What do you figure the odds were of me shooting that can off your head?"

"About a million to one."

"Then what were my odds of hitting you?"

Devlin stared off ponderously. "Considerably better."

||| CHAPTER 21 |||

Devlin sat in his car outside the Purple Camel. He closed his eyes and tried to make sense of what he had just done. He was back inside. This time he stood in the oval behind Harris as Digger yelled, "Draw!" He watched himself as Harris drew and fired. There was something different about him—something he had seen too many times before in the men he had hunted, a darkness that was contemptuous of life. Harris's bullet was on its way toward Devlin so slowly that he could see the rotation of its flight. At the last moment, he flinched and opened his eyes.

He laughed at himself for being so dramatic. Involuntarily, the laugh replayed itself and Devlin was surprised at its uncertainty.

Maybe he did need some time off. As soon as this case was solved, he promised himself, and drove off.

If Devlin's suspicions were correct and the Freedom Killer was from the Washington, D.C., area, he would probably have driven to the hotel for his meeting with Nate Walker. Devlin headed back to the Raintree.

The manager was gone for the day, but his nighttime counterpart proved to be equally cooperative. She was a middle-aged Hispanic woman with a no-nonsense set to her jaw. In the vaguest terms possible, he explained why he needed the parking stubs, if they were still available.

"We keep them for six months. Then an auditor comes in to make sure no one is pocketing the fees. The only way we can do that is by accounting for all the tickets. Of course they're numbered, so we'll know how many have been used. Which night did you want?"

"We know he was in the hotel bar December twentieth, but I have a feeling that he may have been here one or two nights previous to that, collecting information. So the eighteenth through the twentieth."

"It'll take me a few minutes to get them," she said.

"Can I use your phone to make a collect call?"

"Sure. Punch line three to get out."

Devlin dialed his house, and Knox answered. "Were you sleeping?"

"Just drifting off." Her voice was like warm brandy. "How are you?"

"I'm good. A little lonely, but good."

"I know, but a week from now you'll be home." He didn't say anything. "Is that your way of telling me they're keeping you longer?"

Devlin hesitated while he focused on her question. "Ah, not that I know of."

"Is something wrong, Mike?"

"No, no, I'm sorry. It's been kind of a long day."

"What have you been doing?"

Although he thought he had programmed his mind not to return to the Purple Camel, the stage lights went up, and he and Rodney Harris were again at center of the oval. But he would not burden Knox with the vapors of his imagination. "Right now I'm an overworked clerk. They have me at a hotel checking records."

"At this time of night?"

"This thing's keeping us all pretty busy. How are the kids?"

"They're good. I'm not supposed to tell you because he wanted to himself, but Pat got a hat trick tonight."

"That's great," he said. "And I had to miss it."

"He understands."

"No, you ask him if he understands, and because he's a good kid, he says he does, but the only thing he knows for sure is that he scored three goals and his father wasn't there."

Knox laughed disarmingly. "What's the matter, Mike, no one there to beat you up, so you're doing it yourself?" She waited a moment for him to respond. When he didn't, she said, "How about I fly out for a couple of days? There were some cheap air fares to Washington in the paper today."

"I don't know, what about Katie and Pat?"

"I could call Mom and Dad. Maybe they won't remember how exhausting the kids were the last time they watched them."

"I'm working pretty long hours."

"Hey, Devlin, I'm throwing myself at you here! How about faking a little enthusiasm?"

"Sorry. It's just that I don't want you to come out here and I'd be too busy for us to enjoy it."

"That's okay. At least we'd get to spend some time together. And you remember Cindy; she lives in Washington. I could give her a call."

Devlin laughed lightly. "Okay, but you've been warned."

"It'll be a couple of days. I'll let you know as soon as I get everything arranged."

The manager walked back in. Devlin said, "I've got to go. I love you."

Knox said she loved him, too.

The manager set down a cardboard box containing the stubs. "I'm sorry, but they're out of order. I'll have to go through all of them."

"That's okay." Devlin opened his briefcase and pulled out a pair of evidence gloves. "You've got plenty to do. I can take care of this."

"I should get back to work, but if you need anything, just call the concierge desk and they'll track me down."

During the next hour and a half, Devlin went through four months of tickets. Checking the date-time stamp on each, he separated those that had been issued on the dates of the seminar on communicable diseases. There were 263 of them, each with a license plate number written on the back.

Driving back to his hotel, Devlin turned on the news. According to the radio announcer, a poll had been taken that day and it revealed that people across the country, in spite of governmental assurances to the contrary, were hesitant when purchasing not only medicines but also food. Sixty-four percent did not feel completely safe in the purchase of food and over-the-counter medications. Thirty-eight percent felt the same way about prescription drugs. After the President's failed guarantee for safe consumption, 52 percent felt their government could not be trusted to protect what they purchased. Nationally, drug stores reported their sales were off by almost 40 percent. Supermarkets reported sharp declines in the purchase of perishable items, while the sale of canned products was soaring. And government offices across the country were receiving in excess of six thousand calls a day, demanding that something be done.

Devlin shut off the radio. The killer had taken away a little more freedom and replaced it with a healthy dose of anarchy. Disorder was something he was starting to master. But one thing gave Devlin hope: Of the quarter-billion people in America, he might have the Freedom Killer's license plate in his briefcase.

It was midnight by the time he got back to his hotel. He went to his room and started making a list of the license plate numbers. He divided them by states. Predictably, the majority of them were from the Washington area. When he finished, he rough-drafted a teletype to all the FBI offices and outlined leads for those covering states that had license plate numbers listed in the teletype. At 2:00 A.M., he went to bed.

By 6:30, he was back at the Hoover Building. Bonelli was already there, loading long airline passenger lists into the computer. Devlin said, "You did go home last night, didn't you?"

"One of the—and I'm lacking a better word here— *advantages* to muscular dystrophy is I can't sleep more than four hours." Devlin could see something new in Bonelli's demeanor—a change of direction for his energy, and excitement. He asked, "How'd you do at the Raintree?"

Devlin explained what he had learned at the hotel and from Rodney Harris.

"Christ, Mike, that's got to be it!"

Devlin smiled. "You're going to have to become a little more cynical if you want to do this for a living. Whoever Walker was talking to in the bar could be anyone from a colleague to a one-night stand. If it was the killer, we don't even know if he had a car. In a major case like this, if you let yourself be distracted by quick-kill leads, you'll lose control of the broad thrusts of the investigation, which, more times than not, lead to a solution. You want to be investigating as many logical avenues of approach as you can reasonably handle. If you abandon them all every time one promising lead presents itself, you're probably not going to find the answer. We're going to check these license plates, but we'll also keep on with the airlines and anything else we can think of." Devlin handed him a sheet of paper. "Here's the list. How about loading it? If one of the names match someone in the airlines' database, then we can both get excited. Right now I've got to update O'Hare."

A vinyl couch sat against the wall opposite Tom O'Hare's desk. The cushions together were barely five feet long, which was causing the tall section chief to sleep in an uncomfortable ball. Devlin entered the office and closed the door with enough force to wake him. Squinting at the intruder with only one eye, O'Hare asked in a hoarse whisper, "Time?"

"Six forty-five."

O'Hare's confusion did not dissipate. "A.M. or P.M.?"

"A.M."

He sat up and took ten seconds to let his head clear. When he noticed the papers in Devlin's hand, he asked, "He hasn't hit again?"

"Not that I know of."

"Then tell me you are the messenger of *good* news."

"The possibility of good news."

O'Hare was pulling on his pants and stopped, one leg in. "What, you want me to beg?"

"It's just that I'd feel better if your pants were all the way on. You know, in case this information arouses you."

O'Hare finished with his trousers, then found his shoes and put them on. He walked over to a small coffee maker and poured the remaining three quarters of a cup that had apparently been thickening through most of the night. He swallowed a mouthful without grimacing. "Okay, my brain is as fully engaged as it gets."

Devlin handed him the rough draft of the teletype that outlined the previous day's investigation. There was no mention of the Purple Camel's backroom.

O'Hare read it quickly. "I let you loose for only one day, and you come back with all of this." He glanced at the "Leads" section of the teletype. "I see you want all offices to obtain driver's-license photos of the vehicle owners who were parked at the hotel. Are you going to show them to this Rodney Harris?"

"Yes, but he's already told me he doesn't think he can make him. I thought it would be good to have them in case we get a better witness later on."

"Okay, I'll have Sharon send this out as soon as she gets in."

"Did they get anything off the bottles of aspirin they seized?" Devlin asked.

O'Hare scanned the top of his desk until he found what he was looking for. He picked up a green sheet of paper. "They found two additional bottles containing poison—carbon tetrachloride. It's used in manufacturing fluorocarbons, also utilized as a dry-cleaning agent, and even found in fire extinguishers, so it's not that hard to get. Very quick and very lights-out. Ident didn't find any latents of value." He gave the lab report a disgusted toss.

"I'm going to take the parking stubs up to Latent Prints," Devlin said.

"I noticed there were no leads set out for the Washington Metro Field Office."

"I thought I'd get together with the case agent there and maybe give him a hand with the interviews."

O'Hare's brow darkened with suspicion. "And are there any particular leads you'll be picking out for yourself?"

Devlin smiled. "You know, any white males in their twenties."

"Let me see the list." Devlin handed it to him. "You've already gotten the registrations?"

"I called them over to the WMFO last night and had them run. I picked up the printouts on the way in this morning."

"I know we wouldn't have these leads without you, but I've got ten thousand agents at my disposal; I'll make sure these leads get covered—without you."

"Do you think that's fair?"

"Fair? Evidently you're confusing the Bureau with the Boy Scouts. Next you'll be demanding justice. Your real value to this case is devising these avenues of investigation. And I need you to continue doing exactly that."

"Whatever you need."

Devlin's words set off an alarm in O'Hare. It was not natural for him to agree so easily. "Mike, I don't want to hear that some mysterious agent with a Detroit attitude has been out contacting these owners before the WMFO agents can get to them."

"You won't, I promise."

O'Hare sat silently, analyzing the end of their conversation, looking for loopholes he might have left for Devlin to sneak through. When he couldn't find any, he said, "Good, I'll have the white males in their twenties checked out first." But when Devlin left without further protest, the section chief felt certain he had missed something.

After taking the valet tickets to the lab, Devlin waited for the elevator to take him back down to his floor. From his inside suit pocket, he pulled out a smaller list of owners that he had selected and failed to record on the document he gave O'Hare. Based on race, age, and residence, he felt they were the most promising of the bunch. Devlin decided he was not the type of person, as O'Hare had suggested, to demand justice. However, he wasn't above stealing it.

By the time he got back to the room, Bonelli had finished

entering all the registrations into the computer. Devlin asked, "Anything match?"

"Nothing so far. And all the airline manifests are now loaded. So much for a quick kill."

"Just remember, a quick kill is like quick sex—it has very little afterglow."

"Shakespeare?" Bonelli asked.

"Wile E. Coyote."

"So what do you want me to do now?"

Devlin showed him the list he had gleaned. "How long will it take you to add these to the registered owners?"

"About two minutes."

"Good. Then call the names over to the clerk at WMFO who's running down the DMV photos and ask him to get those, too."

"Why am I getting the feeling that the front office doesn't know about these?"

"You're getting good at this, Tony."

Bonelli smiled. "None of this will take long. Anything else?"

"I'm going to start interviewing the people on that list. Want to come along?"

"Are you serious?"

"Yep."

"Couldn't you get in trouble for taking me along?"

"I could get in trouble for taking *me* along. What's the difference?"

Devlin could see that Bonelli was struggling with leaving, but finally he said, "Yeah. Sure."

"You'll have to wait in the car. You know, in case I don't come out. It's a rental. Someone will have to return it."

Bonelli laughed. "I can do that."

"While you're calling the field office about those DMV photos, I'm going to talk to Behavioral Science and see what we're looking for." Devlin dialed Bill Hagstrom's private number.

"Hagstrom."

"Yeah, this is the Cataclysmist. I understand you've been looking for me."

"Go ahead and laugh it up, Devlin. But don't forget—I've been taught by experts how to hide the bodies." Devlin laughed. "Is there some official purpose for this call?"

"I need to know if you have adjusted your profile because of the poisonings."

"No. In fact, he's acting pretty much the way I thought he would. Unfortunately."

Devlin related what he had learned about the communicable diseases seminar in Washington and his theory about how the research technician had been compromised. He also told Hagstrom about the bartender and the parking stubs.

"How did the bartender say he looked?" Devlin told him about the beard, glasses, and the hair that seemed a little too long. "Good. If he hadn't disguised himself in some way, I'd have to change my analysis."

"How so?"

"If he had presented himself so that he could be identified, I would have had to categorize him as less organized than I thought. This individual is the most regimented subject I've ever seen. He seems to anticipate everything, and because of that, he is going to be difficult to identify. He takes very few chances, and really enjoys orchestrating all this at a distance. He gets close if he has to, but only if he can minimize exposure. He's going to hit again—something different, but something he can further intimidate the public with. Each act has to be more dramatic and more intimidating because of his self-perceived aura of increasing invincibility. People are starting to see him as being in charge."

"I'm going to interview some of the people who parked in the Raintree garage. Anything I should look for?"

"Number one thing: If you find the right person, he'll be working *you* for information. This is his chance to find out not only what the law knows about him, but how smart an opponent the FBI is. I'd give him a little taste to start the interview, something like: 'I'm looking for the Freedom Killer, and we think he was in Washington on these dates.' That gives him the opening to ask you for more. If he bites on it, he'll be pushing you pretty hard for answers. Then you can turn it around a little bit and find out how much he knows about the killer. Maybe discuss the cities where the poisonings took place, only throw in one that's incorrect, like Houston instead of Dallas. See if he corrects you. Take that as far as you can, and then start insulting him. Tell him this individual is a coward and a perverted killer of children. There's only one person in this country who should find that offensive."

"Just out of curiosity, if we do get this guy in, what are the chances of a confession?"

"You have to understand the way he's been thinking. He committed the first act, the murder of the technician, because he was filled with all this rage. Once that pressure is relieved, he becomes paranoid with worry, just waiting for the police to come and get him. When that doesn't happen, he becomes more contemptuous, more narcissistic with every act. Right now, he's probably feeling that if the police do come to his door, they are not smart enough to prove it's him. So, no, I don't think you'll get a confession, especially if he gets a few more murders under his belt before we can find him."

"One-on-one, is he dangerous?"

"If he thinks you have found him out and you're going to stop his plan, he'll kill you before you can take your next breath."

"Maybe I should do these interviews on the telephone."

"Seriously, Mike, if you use some of those techniques I described, you'd better be very subtle. As smart as this guy is, he'll sense what you're doing."

"So by giving me those interviewing tips, you're trying to get me killed."

"I've got to pay you back for that cataclysmist stunt somehow."

||| CHAPTER 22 |||

For the next eight hours, Devlin and Bonelli tracked down the owners of the vehicles that had been parked at the Raintree during Nate Walker's stay. By day's end, they had located and interviewed six of them—three in Virginia, two in Maryland, and one in Washington. Only one of them had been there for the communicable diseases seminar. The others seemed to have legitimate reasons for being at the hotel. Devlin did detect deception in the response of the man from Washington. After being pressed, he admitted he had gotten a room with a woman who was not his wife. Devlin dropped Bonelli off in front of FBI headquarters and went to park the car. It was six o'clock and the last of winter's shadowy light had faded into the western horizon.

In Los Angeles, it was three hours earlier, seventy degrees, and sunny. A 747 from Chicago was touching down at LAX. The Freedom Killer watched as the other passengers made their final preparations so they could hurry off the plane. Amused, his lips drew back tightly into the same hostile expression his grandfather permanently wore in the photograph. Both were fueled by the power that came from possessing the secret of impending slaughter. Enjoy your freedom, people, he thought. Things are about to change.

Forty-five minutes later, with his luggage in the trunk, he drove a rental car along the freeway, looking for a tall parking structure that would meet his needs.

This was his fifth city in two days. He had spent the morning in Chicago, as he had in the other cities, planting bombs. There were two more to set, and the last one was going to be the most challenging. He checked the clock on the dashboard. In seven more hours, he would be landing at Washington's National Airport, his last bomb safely hidden on the plane. He blinked his eyes in pleasure, feeling the warm exhaustion of work fulfilled.

He spotted the type of parking garage he had been to in the other cities. At the entrance gate, he pushed the button and took the ticket. He drove up the coiling ramp until the parked cars started to thin out. Then he found what he was looking for: a new four-wheel-drive vehicle parked by itself. The owner probably had chosen its location, away from other cars, to prevent door dings.

He pulled in on the far side of it so anyone driving up would not immediately notice him. From his suitcase he took a brown paper bag. He lay down between the cars and crawled easily under the extra distance of the four-wheeler. The bag contained a small but efficient bomb, consisting of C-4, an electrical blasting cap, a battery, and a wristwatch. He rechecked the setting. It was programmed to detonate at 8:00 A.M. the next morning. Like the other cars he had set bombs in, chances were this was a commuter's car, and if so, the driver would be on the way to work when the bomb exploded. Using thick gray duct tape, he secured the device tightly to the car's frame next to the gas tank. Five minutes later, he was paying the parking attendant and asking for directions back to LAX.

After returning his car to the rental lot, he took the shuttle bus back to the airport. Once inside, he found a telephone close to the security check point. While he pretended to be making a call, he watched the individual guards. There were four of them processing carry-on luggage through their X-ray machines. He was looking for the one who was least attentive. He knew that statistically, white males were the most likely to own and understand laptop computers—not that anyone but a design engineer would be able to detect what was hidden in his. But he had gotten this far by minimizing risks. Because he felt she was the least likely to question the inner workings of anything electronic, he considered the one black female guard. He watched her process four passengers, and not only did she check their bags, she studied their faces. She would not do. Working at the machine next to her was a white female who was overweight and seemed to be a compulsive talker. She addressed each passenger, and they politely but briefly returned her small talk. During the lulls, she would fire quick comments to the other guards, who didn't seem interested in answering. Blake headed for her station.

He carried his two bags up to her machine and laid them flat on the conveyor belt. She looked up at him. "How are you today?"

The laptop passed in front of her. Dozens of pieces of metal components stared back, daring her to detect the one that didn't belong. She let it pass. He answered, "Just fine, how about yourself?"

His second carry-on, a shopping bag, passed under her screen. She studied its contents and did not answer. She frowned. "You have two items piled on top of each other. I'm going to have to put them through one at a time."

He could feel his face trying to give him away and was glad he had decided not to go through the black woman's station. "Oh, I'm sorry. Those are some toys I'm bringing back for my son. He's two."

She pulled the first box out of the bag. "Play Clay," she said. "My nephew likes this gunk, too."

"I hope my wife doesn't think it's too messy." He chuckled.

She passed the box under the screen and saw that nothing was hidden in the blocks of colored dough. She examined the second box. "A remote-control car. Hmmm, the box says for five years old and up."

"You caught me," he said. "Guess I'm just a pushy parent." He laughed, a little more convincingly this time.

She inserted the box and watched it. "This one already has a battery in it. I didn't think the toy makers did that anymore."

"I had the sales clerk put it in so Tommy could play with it as soon as he opens the box."

She looked at him inquisitively for a moment. "Looks like your son has a good father. Have a nice day, sir."

"I will."

As he walked through the metal detector, the tone sounded. "Please empty your pockets, sir," a male guard requested. Blake emptied his keys and change into the plastic tray and walked back through. Again the tone halted him. "It's probably your wristwatch." The guard held out the tray. Blake took off his watch and placed it in the tray carefully. He did not want anyone to see that the back was missing. This time there was no alarm.

Once William Blake's flight was in the air and the attendant announced it was okay for electronic devices to be used, he took out his laptop and pretended to be having trouble with it. Removing a panel from the back, he palmed the thin, innocuous-looking three-and-a-half-inch silver tube with the two wires coming out of the bottom. There was probably not a person on the plane who could tell the difference between a computer component and an electrical blasting cap, but he still wanted to be cautious. He tried his computer again and then shook his head, demonstrating that it still wasn't working. He put it away and took out the remote-control car. After he stripped the battery out of it, he stowed it under the seat.

When the plane landed in Detroit for a one-hour layover, most of the passengers got off to stretch their legs. William Blake picked up his bag containing the Play Clay and headed to the aircraft's rear restroom.

||| CHAPTER 23 |||

The next morning, Devlin arrived at the Hoover Building at 7:00 A.M. Bonelli was already there and told him that O'Hare had called twice and needed to see him ASAP.

As soon as Devlin walked in his office, O'Hare said, "Where were you yesterday?"

Devlin couldn't tell him he had been interviewing people who, according to the section chief's list, didn't exist, but he didn't like lying to him either. "Mostly spinning my wheels."

O'Hare stared at him for a moment, weighing the purpose of the ambiguous answer, and then decided he had enough problems. He handed Devlin a fax. "The Title Three we have on *The Real Deal* intercepted this an hour ago." Devlin started to read it as O'Hare looked at his watch. "Never mind, you won't have to." He picked up a remote control and switched on the television in the corner of his office.

The announcer's voice and the accompanying music seemed obtrusive, much too dramatic for the early morning. "This is another *Real Deal* exclusive. One hour ago, this program received the third communiqué from the individual known to the government as the Cataclysmist." The screen went blank. Then a message typed its way slowly across it, in an attempt to give the listeners the impression that the declaration was being aimed at each of them:

AIR THIS MESSAGE BEFORE THE MORNING RUSH HOUR

You continue to abuse your freedom in the name of license. License is but the brief reward that can come only from participating in the life-and-death struggle for freedom. You must be taught the difference.

In a continuing effort to evoke your compliance, I have discovered a gasoline additive the government developed some time ago. When processed through an internal combustion engine, it will cause some of those engines to explode violently.

I have contaminated gasoline supplies in New York, Miami, Chicago, Los Angeles, and Washington, D.C., and they are just the beginning.

If you wish to live, do not drive your cars.

The government will tell you that no such additive exists and the explosions were caused by something other than what I have said, but remember the hollowness of their assurances in the past.

If you as a country choose not to comply, I will be forced to proceed with another implementation. This additive works equally well on jet engines. Five days.

* * *

The announcer came back on the screen, and O'Hare turned the set off. There was a brief knock at the door, and a tall thin man with a permanently distracted look on his face came in. "Mike, this is Dean Hatton, one of our Ph.Ds. He's in charge of the Explosives Unit." They shook hands. "Well, Doc," O'Hare said, "is there any such additive?"

"I've discussed it with some of the others in the unit. There are some adjuvant reagents that when introduced into high performance racing cars, especially drag racers, can cause the thousands of little explosions to intensify during that quarter of a mile, something like nitroglycerin. But those are in a relatively concentrated state and are carefully measured and added directly to the tank. To contaminate huge fuel reservoirs with something similar would take enormous amounts of the product. We're confident this is all smoke."

"What about the military? It sounds like something they'd like to have."

"I thought of that. I sent one of my people over to the Pentagon to check with them, but the chemistry and physics of what he has claimed is not plausible. And it is unlikely that any such additive could be developed. It would be tantamount to trying to contaminate the Atlantic Ocean with a spoonful of poison."

O'Hare said, "Thanks, Dean. Let me know what the Pentagon has to say."

"I'm going to make some calls myself to some other research people. You'll be the first to know, but I'm telling you, it's all smoke."

After Hatton left, O'Hare asked, "What's this guy up to—is he bluffing?"

Devlin stood up and went to the window. He stared out for a long time. Without turning around, he said, "Today, in those five cities, cars will blow up."

"But Hatton said that was impossible."

"What the subject wants, at least today, is that no one should drive their cars. He knows that such an outrageous request would never be taken seriously unless cars do blow up."

"But how?"

"Just like he did when he poisoned the aspirins: He's gone to those five cities and planted bombs in cars."

"Jesus Christ, what can we do?"

Devlin glanced at his watch and faced O'Hare. "Absolutely nothing."

||| CHAPTER 24 |||

After Devlin left O'Hare's office, he had Bonelli call all the airlines again to get new passenger lists for the cities that were named in the latest message. Because Washington, D.C., had come up in all three incidents now, he told him to concentrate on it as a start-finish point for the killer's travels. The trip, Devlin estimated, had taken place within the last seventy-two hours. Although compiling and comparing the passenger lists would again be a lot of work, if they could match any of the names with those already stored in the computer, it might provide the break they needed.

The first bomb exploded at 7:15 A.M. EST just outside New York City, killing the driver, a thirty-two-year-old father of three.

* * *

While Bonelli worked on the airline lists, Devlin called Dr. Murray Craven. "Did you receive my fax, Doctor?"

"Yes, I've just been studying it."

"Anything jump out at you?"

"A couple of things, the most interesting of which is that it now appears he was hiding himself a little bit in the first two communiqués. In this one, his use of language is more sophisticated. If anything, I underestimated his intelligence."

"Why was he hiding?"

"Why does anyone hide? He was afraid of being caught. However, the more he gets away with, the bolder he'll become. It's a normal progression with this type of individual. Other than that, I really can't add much."

"Do you think he's going to blow up a plane?"

"That's an interesting question, because he only teases us with the implication. He may try, if he can figure a way to do it risk-free."

"We'll continue to send you any messages we get."

"I'm sorry I can't be more help. Even though his language is a little more elaborate, he is still being very careful."

"Knowing that he's still being careful might be helpful. Thanks, Doctor."

The second bomb detonated at 8:05 A.M. EST in Miami, killing a man and his wife on their way to work. The third went off at 8:20 A.M. EDT in Washington, killing a twenty-five-year-old female law clerk.

Devlin was called back to O'Hare's office. "You've heard?"

"We had the news on downstairs," Devlin said.

"I just got a call from Chicago. Number four. A woman and her two-year-old daughter, both dead."

Both men sat in silence. Finally, O'Hare said, "We can't let ourselves get overwhelmed—he's depending on that."

"I've got Bonelli working on some things with the airlines. He said everyone he's talked to is getting overwhelmed. They're being buried with cancellations."

"It's hard to believe people are buying this."

"Hey, we know all the facts. Would you fly right now if you didn't have to?"

"This whole gasoline ruse seems so unbelievable."

"I saw a statistic on CNN the other night that twenty-seven percent of the people in this country think aliens have already landed. That's over sixty million people. How much evidence do you think they'll need to take a couple of days off from work? And when someone from the government goes on television and sounds the all-clear, who's going to believe them? He's already shown that the President didn't know what he was talking about. In this morning's message, he warned everyone that we were going to try and deceive them again. Not everyone is going to buy it, but if he can take out twenty-five percent, he'll cripple this country."

"I just hope he's not going to blow up an airplane tomorrow to make his point."

"He hasn't let us down yet."

"I can't imagine him trying it. With his message today, airports are going to spend millions tightening security. Flights are going to be delayed, and Americans inconvenienced. He's getting everything he wants without any risk."

"You don't think he sees it as a challenge? Don't forget that his ego is getting harder to feed. If he could blow up a plane after warning us and in spite of the increased security, he would reach a new level of credibility and humiliate us that much more."

The phone rang. O'Hare answered it and listened for a few seconds. "Great, thanks." He hung up. "The fifth bomb just went off in L.A., the driver was out of her car—maybe our luck is changing."

"Do we know anything yet about what kind of timing devices were used?"

O'Hare shuffled through his messages until he found the one he was looking for. "The NYPD bomb squad is doing the crime scene on the first bombing. They're still there. They've found fragments from a day-date wristwatch."

"That's bad news. The Weather Underground used them in the seventies. They'd put them in bank safety-deposit boxes to explode months later, at some politically important date. If I remember right, they were pretty accurate, and because the combination of day and date was needed to complete the circuit, they could be programmed to detonate more than a year later."

"You mean we could put this guy in prison and still have bombs going off a year later?"

"I don't think so. He couldn't afford to have them under the cars for too long. People have their oil changed, or repairs are needed. He knows they would be found. And don't forget—he has said that he's quitting in five more days."

"If there aren't more set for later, why use such an elaborate timing device?" O'Hare asked.

"Because he knows the history of that type of timer and the FBI's experience with it. So when we find out he has used them, we'll think there are more of them out there. Why do you think he had Walker bring him a second vial of the virus?"

"To keep us worried about it being used."

"Exactly. His primary objective is not to kill, but to control through fear."

"But why is he warning us ahead of time?"

"Based on the message's language, Dr. Craven thinks he's getting bolder, but let's call Hagstrom."

Devlin hit the speaker phone button and dialed the Behavioral Science Unit.

"Hagstrom."

"Bill, it's Mike Devlin and Tom O'Hare on the speaker phone."

"How are you guys doing up there?"

"Have you seen the latest message?" Devlin asked.

"I was just going over it."

O'Hare asked, "We were wondering. Why is he warning us? Until now, he's only communicated after the fact."

"Tactically, I'm sure you can see the advantage. If a bully beats you up every day, he doesn't have to actually hit you to provoke your fear; he just has to draw his fist back. He's already proven he's a mass murderer. And psychologically, not unlike the bully, he gets off on intimidation. It demonstrates that he is better than us. And because he is so much better than everyone else, he can tell us ahead of time and we still can't stop him. He's growing in confidence."

Devlin said, "I talked to Dr. Craven this morning, and he reads him pretty much the same way. He also said this message was more sophisticated."

"Well, this one was certainly more complex. It starts out with a capitalized header with instructions, as if it were a corporate memo. And then he's not only using paragraphs, but one-sentence paragraphs. Very dramatic. I think we will find his terroristic technique is also growing in complexity and drama."

O'Hare asked, "Do you mean blowing-up-a-plane dramatic?"

"This latest communiqué has two warnings in it: the cars, which has already happened, and then the planes. Because planes are harder to get at, he may just be the bully pulling his fist back. But I wouldn't bet my paycheck either way."

"Then there's still no way to anticipate what he will do next?" asked O'Hare.

"Like I said before, if he was doing the same thing each time, I think we'd have a shot at him, but he uses a completely different method every time. And all of his techniques have been ingenious. The one thing I would bet my check on is that next time he will warn us. Humiliation is a progressive need. For it to be nurturing, he has to increase its dosage, which means he'll have to give us a bigger advantage each time so we'll look increasingly inept."

O'Hare asked, "What are the odds he is going to blow up a plane?"

"Better than even."

||| CHAPTER 25 |||

Bonelli was not in the room when Devlin returned, but neatly stacked on his desk were dozens of faxed airline manifests. The pages that had already been logged into the computer had a red line drawn diagonally across the front. Devlin leafed through them and was amazed by how much had been completed.

Fifteen minutes later, Bonelli returned. "How'd it go upstairs?"

"BSU thinks there's better than a fifty-fifty chance he's going to try to blow up a plane. And soon."

"What do *you* think?"

"I think we had better put everything we've been doing on hold. I've got an idea."

"I hope it's a good one, because there'll be hundreds of planes flying in the next few days."

"I know," Devlin said. "See if you agree with this: You're

the bomber, and you have two or three days to get to five cities to plant the devices. How do you do it?"

"You fly."

"Right. But then what?"

Bonelli thought for a second. "You have to find the cars to put bombs under."

"But how do you get to those cars?"

"Best guess for the poisonings was taxis."

"Right, but you can't tell a cabbie, 'Wait here, I got to go plant this bomb.' "

"Rented cars?" Bonelli ventured.

"That's the way I'd go. Let's make a list of the rental agencies that have booths at the airports in the cities he was in. We'll call them. What we're looking for are males renting cars in one or more of those five cities within the last seventy-two hours. He probably would have had the car less than twelve hours from check-out to check-in time. I think there's a good chance we're going to find one person who has rented cars in four of the five cities."

"And the fifth city is his home, so he wouldn't need to rent a car. Still think it's Washington?"

"If I'm right about this, we'll know for sure," Devlin said.

"But wouldn't he use a different alias every time he rented a car? That's what he probably did on the planes."

"If you go to the airport to fly and hand them cash, you can give them whatever name you want. And if you should have to show a driver's license, they're a dime a dozen. But when you rent a car, you have to show a license *and* a valid credit card. Phony credit cards are much more difficult to come up with these days than licenses, and he'd need four of them. The only thing he could do to disguise his movements is use a different rental agency in each city."

Bonelli opened the phone book. "I'll start with Alamo."

Devlin looked at the same page. "I got Avis."

For the next four and a half hours, the two men worked furiously. Initially, they were both making calls and much of their time was spent on hold, waiting while the different agencies ran the computer inquiries they requested. Once the lists started arriving on the fax machine, Bonelli stopped making calls and began loading the names. As Devlin was finishing a call to one of the two remaining companies on his list, Bonelli said, "Got one!"

Devlin looked over at him anxiously and asked the person on the phone. "Can you fax it right away? . . . I appreciate it." He hung up.

Bonelli continued. "William Blake. One Hertz, one National."

Devlin picked up one of the unprocessed faxes from Bonelli's desk. The clerk took another. Devlin ran his finger along the pages and then stopped. "Blake, Budget."

Bonelli scanned his completely. "Avis, negative."

"While you check the rest of them, I'm going to call the last agency. When you're done with that, check all the poisoning and bombing flights for William Blake."

Devlin called the last car rental agency. He had them check only for William Blake. After a few minutes they reported that an individual using that name had rented a Ford Taurus at LAX the day before the bombings, for less than two hours.

Bonelli looked up from his computer screen and smiled slowly. "Last night, at one forty-five A.M., William Blake arrived at Washington National from Los Angeles."

Devlin took a marker from his desk and, in large letters, started mapping out William Blake's movements directly on one of the room's white walls. Using Bureau abbreviations, he wrote the five cities across the top:

NY   MM   CG   LA   WDC

"That's the order he traveled to those cities, based on the times he rented the cars."

Then he listed the rental companies by name under the appropriate cities and the dates and times they were rented and returned:

NY	MM	CG	LA	WDC
Hertz:	Budget:	National:	Alamo:	
Jan 7	Jan 7	Jan 8	Jan 8	
9:03 a.m.	3:20 p.m.	9:37 a.m.	3:30 p.m.	
12:08 p.m.	6:01 a.m.	12:47 p.m.	5:03 p.m.	

Devlin studied the chart for a few minutes. "I think it's safe to say that he started and finished in Washington. There was no rental, and he arrived here on a late flight last night. He probably had his own car at the airport."

"That sounds logical," Bonelli said.

"From the rentals, we know the approximate time he got to each city. You've already compiled all the flight information for those days, so let's figure out which flights he was most likely on."

"What good will it do to know the flights if he used aliases?"

"I'm not sure, but there's something rolling around in the back of my head. Maybe this will pin it down."

Bonelli grabbed a stack of faxes from the floor next to his desk and started going through them. "The trouble is there were so many flights going in and out of New York around that time, he could have been on any one of eight or ten different flights."

"There has to be a way to narrow it down."

Both men lapsed into silent thought. For what seemed like a long time, they sat motionless, letting their minds race to find an answer.

Bonelli slammed his fist on the desk. "Luggage!"

"Luggage?"

Bonelli started typing frantically. "How much did each of those bombs weigh?"

Devlin didn't know but tried to guess. "I suppose anywhere from three to five pounds."

Bonelli stared at the monitor. "Okay, there were five of them, so that means his luggage was ten to fifteen pounds heavier when he left Washington."

"I don't see how that helps us."

Bonelli pointed at a line on the screen. "William Blake, when he flew from Los Angeles to Washington, checked two suitcases, which together weighed a total of twenty-one pounds. Adding ten to fifteen pounds means we're looking for someone on the Washington-to-New York flights who had two suitcases weighing thirty-one to thirty-six pounds. Since those flights are mostly one-day business flights, there shouldn't be many passengers carrying two suitcases weighing that much. I just have to scan the passenger lists for anyone with luggage in that weight range. Hopefully, there won't be too many."

Devlin was fascinated as he watched Bonelli's hands move rhythmically across the keyboard, just as they had the night he played music in his apartment. At an incredible rate, he scrolled through the endless lists he had loaded into his database. Twice he stopped to make notes. When he finished, he read from the sheet of paper in his hand. "There are two possibles: United flight 1401, arrived at Kennedy at eight thirty-five A.M., and USAir flight 518 got in at eight forty-five. The passenger on the United flight is from Chicago." Bonelli looked up at Devlin confidently. "But the passenger on USAir, a Martin Rich, listed a Maryland area code. That's got to be him."

"It probably is, but let's include the United flight to be on the safe side," Devlin said. "That's amazing. How did you come up with that?"

Bonelli laughed. "I guess I've been waiting since fourth grade to do something like this. It just never occurred to me to try it before."

"Well, I'm impressed." Devlin wrote the two flight numbers on the wall under the New York entry.

Bonelli noticed he wasn't listing the arrival times. "Isn't *when* he got there important?"

"I don't think so. We needed the rental times only to help us identify the flights. I don't want to clutter this up any more than it already is. Now, how about Miami?"

When they were finished, there were seven possible flights the killer could have taken, including the American Airlines flight on which he had flown back to Washington.

Devlin moved his chair back so he could look at the strange mural he and Bonelli had created. The thick blue-black letters seemed irrefutable, as if they were a new message from the Freedom Killer. There was something there warning Devlin. He settled back in concentration and waited for the answer to reveal itself.

For twenty minutes, he studied the wall. Bonelli sat as quietly as he could, occasionally realizing that he was holding his breath.

"Christ!" Devlin grabbed the phone and called O'Hare. "Tom, it's Mike. We're down in room five-eleven. I think you better get down here."

Bonelli asked, "What is it?"

Devlin held his hand up as he reanalyzed his thoughts in silence.

O'Hare came through the door. "Tell me you've got something!"

Devlin continued to concentrate on the wall for a few seconds longer. "Let's say he did set up a second wave of bombings. What would he expect us to be doing right now with that hanging over our heads?"

O'Hare thought for a second. "Exactly what we are doing—warning people to have their cars checked."

"That's right. But he has to make it look like two separate acts. Just like the poisonings, the second set of bombings would be a punishment for ignoring the initial ones. And to make sure they were separated in time, the soonest he would have set any of the timers for is drive time tomorrow morning."

"That sounds like the way he thinks," O'Hare said.

"Okay. Now what happens if, because of our warnings, one of the bombs is discovered before it detonates?" O'Hare didn't answer. "It would tell everyone that he really didn't cause those explosions with a gasoline additive. But more important, it would prove that the *government* was telling the truth, destroying everything he has worked so hard to orchestrate. Now, look at the other side. If we tell everyone that bombs were the cause of the explosions and because of that they check their cars and don't find anything, it would lend further credence to the existence of his mysterious additive."

O'Hare's face lightened. "So there are no bombs?"

"Everyone is in a panic, wanting to believe *bomb* instead of *gasoline*. But if they find no devices, even though the government insists they were the cause of the explosions, and then there's another deadly explosion, he will win again. This time even bigger."

O'Hare stared at Devlin, hoping he would contradict what the section chief was thinking. Finally he said, "A plane?"

"I think so," Devlin said, and nodded toward the wall. "We figured out what times the killer was in those cities planting bombs. From that, we've come up with seven flights he could have been on."

Bewildered by the rush of conclusions, O'Hare stared at the notations on the wall as if they were the illegible language of ancient cave dwellers.

"How?"

"Let me explain that later. The key here is the time period he was in Los Angeles. A city that high-profile would be a most desirable target for him if he was going to set more bombs. The second largest city in the country, and with probably the biggest dependency on personal transportation. But he was there only an hour and a half. He would be lucky to get one device planted in that amount of time. So if he didn't plant more than one bomb in L.A., he probably didn't do it anywhere. But he *was* on five flights in two days. It makes sense that he's targeting an airplane. If he was successful, it would shut down air travel. And that's exactly what he wants."

"So you think he put a bomb aboard one of those planes?"

"Why not? He was already on it legitimately. But the real genius is that he would have planted it before he tells us he's going to blow up a plane. People cancel flights, security increases tenfold, and the plane explodes in spite of our efforts. Now he's perceived as someone who can't be stopped."

"How does he get a bomb aboard?"

"Airport security is set up to detect metal, nothing else. What goes into a bomb? Plastic explosive, which doesn't show up on an X ray and can be shaped into anything. A watch and a battery, both no problem. The only metallic object that might be suspicious, if the guard has ever seen one before, is the electrical blasting cap. And that's small enough to be concealed in another metal object like a pen or a calculator. We've got to locate those seven planes and get the bomb dogs aboard."

O'Hare said, "I've got to clear this with the Director. You'd better come with me." He pointed at the wall. "And bring a copy of your notes."

As Devlin started duplicating the killer's schedule, he told Bonelli, "Start calling the airlines. Have them identify and locate those seven planes. Don't tell them what it's about. Then call the car rentals. Have them isolate the four cars Blake rented so we can process them for prints. Tell them there'll be agents on the way with search warrants. Get every bit of information about the credit card and any driver's licenses he used. Make sure we have the names and locations of the employees who actually waited on him so they can be interviewed. Also, run a check on Martin Rich and the phone number he used."

Bonelli was writing furiously. "Anything else?"

"Yeah. Keep your fingers crossed that this bomb isn't scheduled to go off before tomorrow."

||| CHAPTER 26 |||

When O'Hare informed the secretary that it was urgent that he and Devlin see the Director, she, having been seasoned by such requests, nodded reassuringly and said it would be just a moment—he was on the phone with the White House.

The reception room surprised Devlin. It was not large, and he immediately realized it didn't contain the trappings of self-importance that were so standard in Washington. The furnishings were minimal. Aside from the secretary's desk, there was a large wine-colored leather couch and two gray upholstered armchairs grouped around a simple wooden coffee table. The only thing that hung from the walls was a wooden plaque with dozens of small brass plates covering it, each inscribed with the name of an FBI agent who had died in the line of duty. The carpeting, thick and dark green, gave the only clue that a visitor was about to meet someone of importance. Devlin wondered why there was no security protecting the Director and then decided that hidden somewhere in the walls was a pinhole surveillance camera behind which armed agents waited.

The two men sat down on the couch. Devlin had expected the Director's office to be teeming with frantic activity, but instead he felt a strange, relaxing calm. Semiclassical music barely whispered. The lighting, grainy and off-white, was provided indirectly by hidden fixtures. The only exception was the green glow from the shade of the banker's lamp on the secretary's desk. The walls were covered with thickly ribbed platinum-gray cloth designed to deaden secondary sound. Even when the secretary answered the phone, her voice was barely audible. Devlin leaned back, closed his eyes, and accepted the offered tranquility.

The Director opened his door and waved both men inside. O'Hare introduced Devlin, and they sat down.

Robert August looked more like a young enlisted Marine than the head of the FBI. He was extremely fit, with dark hair, and moved with a relaxed economy of effort.

In an attempt to expedite the situation, O'Hare reduced the purpose of their visit to one dramatic sentence: "We think the Freedom Killer is going to blow up a commercial airliner."

Robert August, or "Bob" as he insisted on being called, had become an FBI agent immediately after finishing law school. When his promised three years of service was completed, he resigned to take a job with the United States Attorney's Office as a federal prosecutor. Later, after a short but impressive career as a federal judge, he was made the Director of the FBI. The Bureau's rank-and-file agents liked his let's-get-the-job-done style, and felt if he could somehow learn to ignore the politicians, he would likely become the best Director the agency ever had. And if he didn't, at least he was one of them.

Devlin watched the Director's reaction to what O'Hare had said. Although the statement was designed to bring about an urgent response, August received it with monastic calm, unwilling to have his judgment distorted by emotion. Devlin could see there was a patience in him, a confidence that injustice would, in time, give way to virtue. "How do we know this?" August asked.

"Mike figured it out, so I'll let him explain it."

For the next fifteen minutes, Devlin explained the investigation that he and Bonelli had conducted and the reasons for their conclusion.

August switched on the speaker phone and dialed. A slightly impatient male voice answered. "White House."

"This is Bob August. I need to talk to the President."

"I'm sorry, he's just gone into a staff meeting."

"How long?"

"It's hard to say, but it'll be a while."

"This is urgent."

"I can let you talk to Ralph Larsen."

"Okay, I guess he'll have to do."

As the call was being switched, Devlin looked at O'Hare questioningly. "He's one of those power-tie hemorrhoids who has been brightening my life since this all started."

Larsen came on the line. "Bob, how are you?"

"It looks like we might have a bomb aboard a commercial airplane."

Larsen's voice went from mildly condescending to fully self-protective. "What are you doing about it?"

"We've got it narrowed down to seven specific planes. We're going to ground them and conduct searches."

"Wait a minute. How sure are you that one of them has a bomb aboard?"

In an abbreviated version, August brought him up-to-date.

Larsen said, "Sounds like a long shot to me."

"Whether it's long or not, it won't hurt anything to search them."

"On the contrary. The public's confidence in what we're doing is low enough right now. If you go out and start searching passenger planes based of some *psychic premonition*, it's going to cause more panic in this country."

"I understand. But what do we tell the public if we don't conduct a search and a bomb goes off?"

Larsen hesitated. "Are you at your office?"

"Yes."

"I'll get back to you."

"When?"

"As soon as I can."

August disconnected the call. O'Hare asked, "How long will that take?"

"Until the crisis is over." The two small, well-developed muscles at the hinge of the Director's jaw knotted almost imperceptively. "Do what you have to do."

O'Hare and Devlin stood up to leave. August asked, "Can you spare Mike for a couple of minutes?"

"Uh, sure," O'Hare answered, and left quickly. Devlin sat back down.

"I've been hearing some interesting stories about you," the Director said.

Devlin smiled. "*Interesting* is an interesting choice of words."

August smiled and held up a personnel file so Devlin could see his name printed along the side. "I've been doing some reading, too. Your career certainly hasn't been boring."

"I can't complain."

August started riffling through the pages of the file. "The Puget Sound Murders. The bank robbery case that got you sent here. Numerous high-profile fugitive arrests. Kidnappings. Extortions. You've done some nice work."

"Thank you."

August closed the file and put it down. "Let me mention one other case that doesn't seem to be in your file—Gentkill."

"The reason it's not mentioned is because the SAC wouldn't allow me to work on it."

"Something else I noticed during my reading were numerous memos implying you were never a slave to any SAC's wishes. Would an order from a superior really have kept you out of the investigation?"

"I've always found *superior* to be a subjective term."

August laughed. "I'll bet you have. And since that response is meant to either ignore my question or challenge my authority to ask it, I'll just say that I took the murders of those four agents very personally. I think of myself as a Christian person, but I was not sorry to hear that the killer died in an explosion."

"I would imagine the list of mourners was a short one."

"I was never satisfied with the convenience of his death, so I sent a team from our explosives unit to Detroit to investigate the blast. Did you know that?"

Devlin shifted uneasily in his seat. "No, I didn't."

"Yes, they found it was a bomb that killed him, command-detonated." August continued to watch Devlin, who didn't say anything. "Laboratory analysis revealed it was the same kind of explosive and detonating device used in an extortion that was going on in the Detroit area at the same time. The target was Seacard Industries. I think at one point you were the agent in charge of that case."

He didn't know how August had found out about his involvement in the Gentkiller's death, but he was impressed that he had. With the exception of his wife, Devlin had never told anyone about it, so admitting it to the Director of the FBI did not seem like the most judicious choice at the moment. "I was assigned to the Seacard case after it was solved and the extortionist was killed trying to pick up the money. I was just the administrative agent. It was meant to be a punishment; there was a ton of evidence and paperwork to process."

August said, "I understand." His tone was conspiratorial. With or without an admission, he was satisfied he knew the truth. "It's just that if someone did have something to do with the resolution of that case, he would certainly have my gratitude."

Devlin studied the Director's face and then said, "And if someone was responsible for the killer's death, he or she would have at least an equal amount of my gratitude if they never told me about it."

A wry smile slanted across the Director's face. He stood up and shook Devlin's hand. "Go find this guy for us, Mike."

An hour later, four people sat working in room 511: Devlin, Bonelli, O'Hare, and a young female agent from Legal Counsel. Bonelli was on the phone with various car rental agencies. O'Hare was calling individual Bureau field offices, where the airplanes in question now sat, waiting to be searched. And Devlin was carefully explaining to the Legal Counsel agent what probable cause existed for the rental car search warrants.

Bonelli had expanded Devlin's wall chart, writing in each aircraft's location, connecting it with an arrow to its original "Blake" flight. Six of the seven planes had been grounded and isolated, but one, the 747 that William Blake had flown from Los Angeles back to Washington, was somewhere over the Rockies, completing its trip west.

Devlin finished discussing the last details with the Legal Counsel agent, and she hurried off to a waiting stenographer. O'Hare hung up. "Okay. We've got teams on the way to search all seven planes. The last one is scheduled to land in L.A. within fifteen minutes. They're going to get it down and unloaded as quickly as possible."

Realizing the massive manpower that was being used to respond to what amounted to no more than a hunch on his part, Devlin said, "I hope for the Director's sake we're right."

"If not, I'm afraid this guy is going to have a much better day tomorrow than we are," O'Hare said.

"Maybe we can do something about that. Tony, what did you get on William Blake and Martin Rich?"

"From the car rental, I got William Blake's credit card number and a home address. It's in Baltimore. I had it checked in the criss-cross, and it's phony."

"What about the credit card company? They might have a good address."

Bonelli had written WILLIAM BLAKE and VISA 773 1730 1121 073 on the wall above the rest of the notes. "I tried to call Visa security, but it doesn't look like we'll be able to get anything until tomorrow morning. And it looks like Martin Rich is probably a phony name. I made a call to the phone number he used, and it's a bar in Annapolis. Whoever answered said they'd never heard of him."

"What about driver's licenses or vehicles for both men?"

"I haven't had a chance to run them yet."

The phone rang. "O'Hare . . . yeah . . . okay, good." He hung up. "The last plane has landed and everybody's off. They've also completed the first two searches—both negative." He looked at Devlin uneasily.

"Tom, even if all seven of them are negative, we're doing the right thing. But while we're waiting, let's see if we can't narrow down the search for Martin Rich and William Blake. Tony, call Baltimore and have them run statewide for DMV."

"Just Maryland? Couldn't those addresses be a decoy? He could be living here in Washington, or in Virginia."

"Do you remember where the driver who was killed in Washington lived?"

Bonelli queried the computer. "Laurel, Maryland."

"Right. And where is Laurel?"

"It's just off 95, between Baltimore and Washington."

"See if this sounds logical. Because the bomber didn't rent a car in Washington, we're pretty sure he lives in the D.C. area. We also know he set a bomb here. If you were him, would you set it before leaving or drag it along on all those planes, through all those cities, and plant it after you got back?"

"I'd set it before I left."

"And what time did he catch that flight to New York?"

Bonelli checked the wall. "Sometime around eight A.M."

"With all he had to do before that plane took off, do you think he would have chanced planting it that morning, or would he have done it the night before?"

"Sure, with those day-date timers, the night before makes a lot more sense."

"That's right. And if he's going to do it under those conditions, he'd want to do it someplace close to home, because if he's stopped for any reason, he can explain being in the area. See how many names in Maryland we're talking about. Have them give you all vehicles registered to William A. Blake and Martin Rich. Also get their DOBs." Devlin said to O'Hare, "Let's see if we can find a coffee machine. I'll buy."

Thirty minutes later they returned, and Devlin handed Bonelli a cup of coffee. The clerk said, "While you were gone, the Director called. They've finished searching all the planes except for the one in L.A. Nothing yet."

"Since that was the last plane we know he was on, I think it's the most likely. It would be the big finish to this phase of his plan. He'd want to plant it at the last possible moment, so there would be less time for it to be discovered."

O'Hare said, "If there is a bomb."

"Sure, Tom, scam me for a cup of coffee and then jump ship."

O'Hare laughed. "Don't worry. If you're wrong, I won't say a word. You can go to the White House all by yourself and explain."

"Thanks," he said. "Tony, I hope you had better luck than I'm having."

"Not much better. There are a total of eight William A. Blakes in Maryland who have cars or driver's licenses. Only two of them have ballpark DOBs: one, twenty-five years old, and one, twenty-nine. Martin Rich was a big zero. There are no driver's licenses or vehicles registered in that name in Maryland."

The phone rang. Everyone sensed what the call was and hesitated to answer it. Finally, Bonelli picked it up. "Anthony Bonelli . . . one moment, sir." He handed it to O'Hare. "It's the Director."

O'Hare put it to his ear. "Yes, sir . . . yes, sir." His face relaxed. He put his hand over the mouthpiece. "The 747 in L.A. In the rear bathroom, taped against the inside wall of the trash bin, about two and a half pounds of C-4, primed and ready to rock and roll."

Without the use of his canes, Bonelli stood, leaned against the desk, and shook his fists in the air victoriously.

||| CHAPTER 27 |||

It was almost 9:00 A.M. when Devlin got in the next morning. Bonelli was not there yet.

The night before, O'Hare had insisted that the three of them meet at the local FBI watering hole after they finished their paperwork. Attempting to be prudent, Devlin timed his entrance around midnight, thinking there would be only an hour or two to drink before the bar closed. But the bartender was a friend of O'Hare's, and after 2:00 A.M., he locked the door and joined them.

Devlin got back to his hotel at 4:30. Although he had been up for almost twenty-four hours, he couldn't sleep. He called Knox.

"Hi," she answered, her voice full of throaty sleep. He could hear her rolling over to check the clock. "You sound end-of-a-day instead of beginning."

"We've been doing a little celebrating."

Her tone focused. "Did you get him?"

"I said a *little* celebrating. When we find this guy, I'm gonna be missing for three days. But we did finally win a skirmish."

"Did you have a part in it?"

"Never left the office."

"That's what the women and children like to hear."

"How *are* the little Devlins?"

"They're great."

"Are their grandparents coming to spend some time with them?"

"They'll be here tomorrow."

"And when will their mother be coming to Washington?"

"Tomorrow afternoon."

For the first time, Devlin realized what had been accomplished by finding that bomb. They had stolen back some freedom from the killer. People could again fly without fear. "Let me get the flight information."

"No need to. Cindy's picking me up. We're going to have a late lunch and catch up. She'll drop me at the hotel."

"Then I'll see you here tomorrow after work."

She hung up, and he was reminded of the distance between him and his family. He leaned over, dropped the receiver on the floor, and fell asleep.

Devlin looked through the notes Bonelli had left on his desk. He found the information from the Maryland Department of Motor Vehicles regarding the two William A. Blakes who had birthdates close to what they thought the subject's was. One lived in Baltimore, the other in Annapolis.

But before either could be interviewed, the credit card information would have to be more fully developed. In the notes, he found the credit card company's phone number.

After being transferred twice, he was connected to someone in the investigative division. He had dealt with similar financial institutions in the past and knew, because of lawsuits, that they were reluctant, like everyone else, to release customer information. But when they thought they were being defrauded, their cooperation was usually offered with more enthusiasm. Devlin explained that he was looking for a murder fugitive who he believed had obtained, and was using illegally, one of their cards. Because he was afraid someone might tip off the media, he did not tell them that William Blake was suspected of being the infamous Freedom Killer. Finally, the FBI was apparently one step ahead of the killer, and he wanted to keep it that way.

While Devlin and the credit card investigator waited for the company's computer to come on-line, Bonelli arrived. The excitement of the night before was still in his eyes. Devlin could hear the Visa investigator typing on the keyboard now. "We show an address in Annapolis, Maryland. Do you have that?"

"I don't know. What is it?" He wrote it down and looked at the two driver's license addresses Bonelli had obtained the night before. He felt his heart beat three hard strokes. The credit card address matched one of them. "That sounds like our boy. Can you fax us the rest of the information you have on him?"

"Sure. Do you want us to cancel the card?"

"No. We may need it to trace him. What's the latest charge?"

"Uh, he rented a car at the Los Angeles airport, looks like four days ago."

"When we get him, I'll give you a call so you can cancel it."

"We appreciate the help."

"So do we."

Bonelli had been looking over Devlin's shoulder and saw the matching addresses. "That's got to be him."

"It sure looks like it. I'm going to let O'Hare know. How about calling all your airline contacts and putting stops with them in case Blake books another flight under that name. And you'd better do the same with the car rental agencies."

The Freedom Killer sat in front of his television, scanning the channels. He stared at the wall clock and made sure its second hand was moving at a normal rate. He pressed the remote button faster than it could change channels.

There should have been something by now. The bomb was set for ten o'clock. He calmed himself and pressed seven, *The Real Deal*'s station. Patience, he told himself. It takes time to get reporters on the scene. With closed eyes, he reviewed installing and arming the bomb. His hands connected the battery to the watch and then to the blasting cap. No, that was fine. Then he turned over the watch and waited thirty seconds. The minute hand was moving. The time—had he set the right time? He studied the dial again: day, date, hour, and minute. Yes, they were all fine.

He picked up the phone and dialed. "American Airlines passenger information—" the recording started. He pressed the necessary buttons to talk to a customer representative. "This is Sheila, how may I help you?"

"Hi, Sheila. My aunt's on her way to Washington and I was wondering if her flight into National is on time."

"Could I have the flight number please?"

"754."

There was a short delay, and then she said, "Yes, sir. I show that flight is actually running ahead of schedule; it's due to land in Washington at ten-twenty A.M."

The Freedom Killer slammed the phone down.

"Good morning, Sharon."

"Good morning, Mr. Devlin. Congratulations on last night."

"If you mean getting Tom to buy the beer, thanks. I am rather proud of that. Is he in?"

She looked down at her phone and saw one of the lines lit. "He's on the phone, but I'm sure he won't mind if you go in."

When O'Hare saw Devlin, he hurried to end his conversation. "Thank you. Let me know." He hung up. "Good morning."

"No thanks to you and that radiator flush you were buying last night."

"You should be thankful it was payday, otherwise I would have ordered the cheap radiator flush." O'Hare's phone rang. "Yes, sir," he said. He fired the remote at the TV and switched to CNN. It was showing stock shots of LAX and an American Airlines 747. The reporter said he had learned that the Los Angeles Police bomb squad had found and dismantled a bomb aboard an American Airlines jet the night before. It was believed to be the work of the cataclysmist. The authorities would not speculate how the killer had gotten the bomb on board or if other planes were being searched for similar devices. O'Hare shut the set off.

"Well, that should piss our boy off," O'Hare said.

"Let's call Hagstrom and find out." Devlin dialed on the speaker phone. "Bill, did you see the news?"

"Yes, I was just watching it."

Devlin asked, "Which way do you think this guy is going to jump?"

"Remember what I told you about powerlessness? Well, with every success he was overcoming that, but he's just been dealt a major blow. He's probably feeling more powerless than ever. If I'm reading him right, he will try to do something more spectacularly destructive than ever."

O'Hare asked, "Any idea what?"

"I can only guess, but something on a larger scale—something with national or international repercussions."

"Can you get more specific than that?"

"I don't think I can. Like I said before, every time he does something, it's a new technique. And I would be surprised if he doesn't have a few contingency plans in case something goes wrong, like it did this time. But whatever he's going to do, I don't think it will be long."

"Okay, Bill. Thanks."

After Hagstrom hung up, Devlin said, "How's that trap-and-trace look in New York?"

"They got the equipment in place, but he has to call first."

"If what Hag says is true about his growing need to humiliate those who take his power away, he'll be calling."

"Do you think he'll try to blow up another plane?"

"I doubt if he'll chance it. He probably thinks we know how he did it, and we're waiting for him. Like Hagstrom says, one of the things that makes him hard to stop is his creativity. I'm fairly certain he'll move on to something else."

"Okay, let's concentrate on what we do have. Did you get anything on that credit card?"

"He used the same Annapolis address that came up on one of the Maryland driver's licenses."

"Is it him?"

Devlin sat down. "I don't know. It seems too easy."

"Easy? If it was so easy, why were you the only one who came up with all this?"

"I think we've only penetrated the top layer of his identity. Why don't you get some loose surveillance on his Annapolis address, and I'll go up there and talk to the neighbors."

"Loose surveillance? How about we call out every available agent and do a frontal assault?"

"If you get more than a handful of people around him, he'll be gone before we can get out of the cars. It's better if a couple of us can sneak up on him. I'll take Tony with me and carry a briefcase. No one will know we're the law."

"Okay, give me the address and I'll call the Annapolis Resident Agency and get some surveillance on his residence." O'Hare checked his watch. "I'm late for a meeting." He handed Devlin a stack of teletypes. "Here are the responses to those license plate leads you sent out to the field. All the white males twenty-five to thirty years old have been interviewed and eliminated."

"What about the ones who didn't meet the profile?"

"Everyone's buried in tips. We're going with the high-percentage leads. We'll get to the others when we get a chance."

Devlin went back to his room and handed Bonelli the stack of teletypes. "How about loading the pertinent information off of these into the computer, then we'll head for Annapolis."

Bonelli smiled in anticipation.

III CHAPTER 28 III

They were halfway to Annapolis when Devlin asked Bonelli, "Ever been here before?"

"Sure, when I was a kid. My father took my brother and me on a tour of the Naval Academy." He laughed. "I think he was trying to inspire us to work hard. He would have loved it if one of us went there. It's an impressive place."

"I'd like to see it sometime," Devlin said. "How about getting out your map and see if you can get us close to Welles Avenue."

Bonelli's finger searched the map. "Here it is. Take the next exit."

Being careful not to drive down Welles Avenue, Devlin cruised the surrounding streets. A block from the target house, he saw a man wearing a suit, slouched down in the front seat of the kind of nondescript car the Bureau usually bought. He pulled up next to him and said, "John Dillinger shot first."

The man smiled as if he were an old friend. "You Devlin?"

"Yep."

"Joe LoFranco."

Even though he sat low in the seat, it was difficult not to notice how big LoFranco was. Devlin estimated the Annapolis agent was at least six feet four and 230 pounds. His hair was jet-black, and he wore a neatly trimmed mustache.

"This is Tony Bonelli, from headquarters." Devlin said. "How many units do you have out here?"

"With some help from Baltimore, six all together."

"Six? That's what I call service."

"Well, it's not like it's golf season."

Devlin laughed. "Someone got the back?"

"Yeah. We even got the plane up."

"Good. Let everyone know you've got the green light to grab this guy if he boogies."

"You got a picture of him?"

"We don't even have a good description. But you'll know him when you see him—he'll be the one coming out of the back door doing Mach four. We're going to talk to the neighbor."

LoFranco nodded. "See you at the Senate hearings."

Watching the house numbers, Devlin said, "Okay, it's going to be on your side. I'm going to drive past it and park in front of the first residence past it. When we go by, don't look at his house. Look straight ahead or look at me. If he's looking out the window—and these people do spend a lot of time doing that—and you're eyeballing him, he'll be gone. When we go by, he'll be looking at you because you're on his side, so I'll sneak a peek at the house. And the same thing when we get out at the neighbor's—neither one of us looks at his place." Their car slowed as it passed William Blake's address, and Devlin glanced quickly at the well-maintained brick bungalow. He pulled up in front of the next house. He could hear Bonelli inhale a little deeper and a little more often. "Nervous?"

"Hell no, I'm scared."

"Good scared or bad scared?"

He looked at Devlin incredulously. "I don't know about Detroit, but in Maryland we only have one."

Devlin's briefcase was on the seat between them. He opened it and took out a Smith & Wesson snub-nose. "Ever fire one of these? It's like the mouse on your computer—just point and click."

"Once a year, they take some of the clerks out to firearms. As long as I can sit or lean against one of the barricades, I do pretty well."

"Just remember, this has a two-inch barrel. It's not for trick shooting; it's basically a defensive weapon." Devlin broke open the cylinder and dumped the five cartridges into his right hand. "Here, aim it at the floor and squeeze off a couple of shots to get the feel of it." Bonelli closed the cylinder, took a sight picture somewhere between his feet, and pulled the trigger three times slowly, memorizing the length and resistance of the gun's trigger pull. He handed it back to Devlin, who loaded it. "These are plus-P hollow-points, so if you have to touch one off, hold on, because with this small frame, it'll take you for a ride." Devlin handed it back. Intrigued, Bonelli stared at the deadly instrument. "It's to be used only if our position is about to be overrun. Don't start slappin' leather because somebody looks at us funny."

Devlin took his Sig Sauer 9-millimeter out of the briefcase and jammed it into his belt below his right kidney. Watching him carefully, Bonelli did the same with the snub-nose.

They got out of the car, and Devlin walked patiently alongside Bonelli as he struggled up the walkway. The entire time, Devlin fought the urge to steal a glance at Blake's residence. Once Bonelli made it up the porch steps, Devlin rang the doorbell. A white-haired woman in her seventies answered. Using Bonelli as a screen from the house next door, Devlin opened his credentials to identify himself. After a moment of bewilderment, she invited them in.

"We're looking for an individual we know only as William Blake. One of the possibilities that came up was your next door neighbor."

"Has he done something wrong?"

"The man we're looking for has. But we're not sure your neighbor is the William Blake we want."

"I can't imagine he is. He's such a nice young man."

"Is he home now?"

"I saw him leave for work this morning."

"Do you know where he works?"

"Yes. The Army ordnance depot just outside of Baltimore."

"Is he in the Army?"

"Oh no, he's a civilian employee. Something to do with computers."

When Devlin and Bonelli got back to the car, they drove to where Joe LoFranco was parked and told him what the neighbor had said. "Do you want to go up to the depot or wait until he comes home?"

"How far is it?" Devlin asked.

"Less than half an hour."

"No need to waste everyone's time out here. Can you come with us?"

"Sure." LoFranco picked up his radio handset. "All units, the man from the zoo is calling it a day. Thanks very much."

Devlin watched the small surveillance plane a mile to the northwest break its lazy circle and head due north. The "zoo," Devlin assumed, was what the local agents called FBI headquarters. Since Devlin was going to work with LoFranco, he wanted it understood that he was not a headquarters manager, out on a whim, trying to collect promotion points. "When they called, did anyone tell you I was sent here from Detroit at gunpoint?"

"Don't worry, Mike. I spent twelve years commuting three hours a day in the Apple. I know a hump when I see one."

The New York office had always been the real test of how badly someone wanted to be an FBI agent. A substantial number of men and women, once they were given orders to report there, simply quit. Those who took on the difficult working and living conditions were given upperclassmen respect by the rest of the agent population. "What did you work there?" Devlin asked.

"Most of the time, the frequent-flyer program."

For New York agents, the frequent-flyer program meant surviving long enough to collect the necessary seniority, or, as they referred to it, mileage, to be transferred to the greener grass that began immediately beyond the boundaries of the City Where Felons Never Sleep. "What about the rest of the time?"

"I minored in TFIS."

Theft From Interstate Shipment in most FBI field offices was not considered a major problem, but in New York it meant one thing—truck hijackings, a federal violation that organized crime had helped elevate to an art form. And for the agents who were called out day and night to reduce its astronomical statistics, TFIS became a badge of honor. When New York agents were allowed a transfer to escape the hardships of trying to raise a family there, they were usually assigned the most difficult cases in their new offices, which, after the Apple, were rarely considered heart-stopping. "How long have you been here in Sleepy Hollow?"

"Two and a half years." LoFranco checked his rearview mirror protectively. It was a habit big-city agents found hard to break. Then, playfully, he said, "You ready to go give this mutt a toss?" and for effect, a little bit of a New York accent was slipped into his voice.

Devlin turned to Bonelli and, without the enhancing brogue, said, "Let's go give this mutt a toss."

Bonelli just shrugged his shoulders.

LoFranco led the way through the security checkpoints. After they had explained their problem to a series of officers of increasing rank, a colonel finally offered his office and dispatched two MPs to bring William Blake in for an interview.

Understandably, when Blake was escorted into the conference room by the two cautious men, he looked confused.
Devlin introduced himself, and Blake asked the question that
people in his position always asked whether they were guilty
or innocent, "What's this all about?"

"Have a seat," Devlin said.

Devlin sat down in front of him. He looked at Blake for
a while until the Army employee became uncomfortable.
"What?"

"Do you know who the Freedom Killer is?"

Blake's head snapped side to side, anxiously, measuring
the reaction of the others around him, hoping someone in the
room would find this equally bizarre. "The one with the
poison and the bombs? Yeah, sure, who doesn't?"

"We think he's using the name William Blake."

Full of nervous bravado, the civilian employee sat back and
put his hands in his pockets. "Well, he's not this William
Blake."

"He's also using your address."

Blake lurched forward. "What!"

"Let me see your driver's license and credit cards."

He took out his wallet. "This is ridiculous." He handed
everything to Devlin.

After looking at each of the items, Devlin asked, "No
Visa?"

"No."

"Ever had one?"

"Never."

Besides the fear Blake was failing to hide, Devlin detected a
trace of indignation, which, in his experience, was usually
brought on by innocence. He was also displaying a patience
with the interrogation that indicated he had a history of relying
on the truth to resolve difficulty. "The man we're looking for

used his Visa in New York, Miami, Chicago, and Los Angeles. When was the last time you were in any of those cities?"

"I've never been to Miami or Los Angeles. And I haven't been out of town in six months."

"When did you last miss work?"

"It's got to be eight or nine weeks ago. I took half a day off for a doctor's appointment. I don't like missing work."

Devlin gave an almost unnoticed nod to LoFranco, who left the room to check on Blake's work attendance. Devlin was not picking up any verbal or nonverbal deception indicators. "Has anyone been staying at your house who could be receiving mail there?"

"Occasionally my girlfriend will stay over, but that's it."

"This person also has a driver's license with your address on it."

"Someone's setting me up?"

"Does anyone dislike you that much?"

"Not that I'm aware of. I get along with everybody."

"Do you know anyone who would be capable of committing murders like these?"

"God, no."

A few minutes later, LoFranco came back in and confirmed that Blake had not missed a day of work in almost three months. Devlin wrote down his name and number at headquarters and handed it to him. "If you can think of anyone, please call me."

"I can go?"

"Sorry for all the drama, but somebody wanted us to think you were involved."

Blake released a deep sigh. "Well, he couldn't have been too smart if I was this easy to clear. Right?"

"That's what's bothering me—he's *very* smart."

III CHAPTER 29 III

Devlin and Bonelli followed LoFranco back to the Annapolis Resident Agency. It was on the second floor of a modest office building in the city's downtown section.

LoFranco used his key to let them in. Devlin said, "Tony, can you call and find out which bank issued that credit card?" Bonelli sat down at a desk, took his computer out, and queried it for the phone number.

LoFranco said, "Mike, do you think this guy is around here?"

"We know he flies in and out of Washington. Every one of these killings has had some connection with the area. He used one alias, Martin Rich, with an Annapolis phone number. And now he's using Blake's identity."

"Is it someone trying to pin it on Blake?"

"I don't think so."

"Then why use his identity?"

"I don't know, but I have a feeling that he and Blake have crossed paths. He didn't pick his name, date of birth, and address out of the air."

Bonelli hung up the phone and said, "The card was issued here in Annapolis by the Chesapeake National Bank on Bay Ridge."

"Do you have a contact there?" Devlin asked LoFranco.

"Why do you think they put FBI agents in small towns? What do you need?"

"See if you can get the original application. We'll have it processed for prints. What I'd really like to find out is how the card was delivered. It doesn't look like it was mailed to Blake's address."

LoFranco said, "There's a decent restaurant across the street if you want lunch. I should be back here by the time you're done."

An hour later everyone was back in the resident agency. LoFranco handed copies of the credit card application to Devlin and Bonelli and said, "It was applied for by mail. If they still have it, the original is at their main office in Baltimore. I'll have someone pick it up."

"I see he listed Blake's address on the application. Is that where they mailed it?" Devlin asked.

"No. My contact said a couple of days before it was to be sent out, he called and said there had been a fire at his house and he was temporarily staying at 1118 Front Street, and they should reroute the card to that address. It was sent by registered mail on December seventeenth. At that time of the year, the bank issues thousands of cards for the Christmas rush, so they didn't have time to get curious. The return receipt shows it was signed for by a Lloyd Franklin. Before you got back, I ran him. According to his driver's license, he's forty-seven. No prior arrests."

"Let's go."

During the drive to 1118 Front Street, Devlin realized they were gaining ground on the killer. They had successfully swerved through much of his deception, and locating Lloyd Franklin was about to bring them considerably closer. Although the killer would have used another alias, Franklin would be able to physically identify the person they were looking for. And he would know what kind of vehicle the killer drove.

Maybe something had slipped out unintentionally during a conversation: where he worked, his family, his bank. Anything. Until now, the Freedom Killer had that Viet Cong invisibility that Devlin had learned to be so cautious of in Southeast Asia. He would always fear untouchable enemies, because they seemingly could not be defeated. But with a little luck, and Lloyd Franklin's help, this enemy was about to materialize. He suspected that LoFranco was filled with the same anticipation but, like Devlin, did not want to provoke the major case jinx by mentioning it.

As though it were intended to warn off his optimism, Devlin became vaguely aware of a siren in the distance as LoFranco's Bureau car turned up Front Street. Ahead, they could see filthy gray smoke rushing above the housetops.

Bonelli started checking house numbers, but by the way LoFranco increased his speed, Devlin knew that the two agents were afraid of the same thing: Lloyd Franklin's house was the one on fire. They pulled up in front of the burning structure—1118 Front Street. Devlin and LoFranco bailed out. "That siren's probably the fire department, but call it in anyhow!" Devlin yelled to Bonelli.

Both men ran to the front door and tried it; it was locked. Before Devlin could do anything, LoFranco reared back and kicked at the dead-bolt lock above the doorknob. It gave, but not completely. LoFranco backed up two quick steps, then leaped up and forward, bringing his considerable weight onto the lock through his foot. The jamb shattered and the door flew open. The same angry gray flannel that streaked from the roof billowed out the sucking doorway. LoFranco rushed in, and Devlin followed.

LoFranco yelled, "I'll take upstairs!"

Devlin could smell gasoline as he worked his way toward the back of the house.

"Anyone in here?" He was in the living room, and his visibility was cut in half by the increasing smoke. There was a small bedroom to the right. He opened the door. The smoke hadn't reached it yet, and he could see it was empty. He got to the kitchen and could hear the fire's roar. Out past the kitchen, on a small back porch, the fire burned intensely. Off to one side was a bathroom with the door closed. Devlin opened it and found Lloyd Franklin. A thin nylon cord, apparently from the window blinds that had been ripped from the wall above the bathtub, cut deep into the skin at the front of his neck. His face bulged red and blue. Devlin unwound the cord from around his neck. The smoke was suffocating. Devlin could hear LoFranco's coughing above the noise from the fire's growing victory. He threw the body over his shoulder and headed for the door, now coughing smoke himself. As he got to the foot of the staircase, he yelled up, "Joe, I got him! Get out of there!"

He heard more coughing. "One more . . . room!"

Devlin walked out on the porch and saw Bonelli standing as close to the house as he dared, his anxiety obvious.

Devlin brought the corpse to the sidewalk and put it down. He turned and ran up the porch stairs as LoFranco ran out of the house and stumbled to his knees, trying to clear his lungs with spasmatic coughing. Devlin helped him to the sidewalk.

A fire truck pulled up. "Anyone inside?" the first fireman off the truck asked.

LoFranco was bent over coughing, so Devlin answered for both of them. "We don't think so; we went through both floors." The fireman glanced briefly at Lloyd Franklin's corpse, then turned back to the truck yelling instructions.

The paramedics arrived in their vehicle, followed by an Annapolis Police Department car. "Tony, have them check Joe; I'll talk to this officer," Devlin said.

Bonelli turned and started toward the ambulance, but both of the attendants were already coming toward LoFranco, who

was starting to control his coughing. The first medical technician took him by the arm and led him to the rear of the emergency vehicle. The second knelt over Franklin's body, took
out a stethoscope, and held it against his chest for twenty
seconds.

With the police officer in tow, Devlin walked up to the
body. The technician looked up at the cop. "Looks like you've
got a homicide."

Devlin did not like lying to the police, especially about a
homicide. But there was no one worse at keeping secrets than
a cop. One mention of the Freedom Killer and it would be on
the news before they could get back to Washington. And any
chance of surprising the killer would be gone. Besides, once
he was caught, the murder of Lloyd Franklin would be solved.
Devlin turned to the officer and said, "We were just driving
by and saw the smoke." After a few standard questions, the
policeman seemed satisfied with Devlin's story and left to talk
to Franklin's neighbors.

Devlin found Bonelli at the rear of the ambulance. The
doors were being closed and the siren was activated. "How
is he?"

"They say he's fine. They're going to have a doctor give
him the okay at the hospital and then release him. He's hardly
coughing now."

"Good. We'll take his car and pick him up." Another police
car pulled up. One of the firemen walked over to it and told the
officer that a search of the house had failed to locate any other
victims and the fire appeared to be arson, with gasoline used
as the accelerant.

Devlin watched the firemen for a moment. Their thick,
bucking hoses jetted water on the few flames that were visible.
The house, which only a few minutes before had seemed so
deadly, so inescapable, now seemed inconsequential. Similarly, Devlin knew that once the killer was caught, history

would treat him with equal contempt, but right now, he was one dangerous son of a bitch.

Devlin had Bonelli wait in the car while he went in the hospital's emergency entrance. He was directed to the treatment room LoFranco had been taken to. A doctor pressed a stethoscope against the agent's bare back and listened to his lungs. After LoFranco took a few more deep breaths, he was told, "You're all right. You may experience some pulmonary discomfort for a while, but you're good for another ten thousand miles or one fire, whichever comes first."

LoFranco coughed lightly. "I'll take the ten thousand miles, Doc." He looked at Devlin apprehensively. "They didn't find anyone else in there, did they?"

"No, I think you made sure of that."

"Sounds like you think I made an error in judgment."

"My wife is always telling me there's nothing wrong with running into a burning building—the trick is knowing when to run out."

"If I remember right, you were coming back in to find me."

"If you think holding up my actions as some sort of safety standard is the way to go, you really are making an error in judgment."

"I'm beginning to see that." LoFranco stood up and clapped Devlin on the shoulder. "But I think I'm about to make one more. Do you drink?"

The three men sat in a bar just outside Annapolis. By the time the first round of beers arrived, fatigue had started to set in. It had been a day in which two promising leads had literally disappeared in smoke. Devlin decided that one beer and a little small talk was going to be enough for him. He asked LoFranco, "You married?"

"Not anymore. It was an easy decision for her; she disliked

New York as much as she disliked me, so the Bureau gave her an opportunity to kill two birds with one divorce."

"Why'd you transfer here? Is this your home?"

"My ex-wife's. I'm originally from Pittsburgh. After the divorce, I moved here as soon as I could get out of New York."

"You do realize that Maryland has stalking laws, don't you?"

LoFranco laughed. "I have a seven-year-old daughter. They live about fifteen minutes south of here. Actually, my ex has been real decent about letting me spend time with her; I get to see her three or four times a week."

"Sounds like she's pretty lucky."

"Maybe for a divorced kid. It's funny—the older she gets, the more I need to be around her. I must be carrying around a couple of megatons of guilt; I would have left the Bureau to be close to her. The need for family—it must be the Italian in me. Right, Tony?" LoFranco then asked the clerk, "You married?"

Bonelli was a little embarrassed by the unexpected question. "No. Uh, no."

"Why not? A young, good-looking guy like you."

"I guess because I keep meeting guys like you, who make it sound so magical."

"What, you don't want to be miserable like the rest of us?"

"Hey, I have to work with Mike Devlin, how much more miserable do you want me to be?"

Everyone laughed, and Devlin said to LoFranco, "After New York, you must find it a little slow here."

"I work a lot, and when I'm really feeling sorry for myself, I've got a friend who owns a restaurant downtown; he lets me come in and cook for him. It's something I've done since I was a kid. It's therapeutic. I've thought about doing it full-time, if I ever get around to retiring." He glanced at Devlin and Bonelli. "Pretty exciting, huh?"

Bonelli smirked. "Compared to my life, it sounds like the Mardi Gras."

Devlin said, "Man, do I know who to party with or what?" He downed the rest of his beer. "Joseph, as much fun as this is, I'd better get going. My wife's in town, and one brush with death a day is pretty much my limit."

After dropping off Bonelli at his apartment, Devlin drove back to his hotel. Although he knew Knox would smell the fire on his suit, which would undoubtedly begin another debate, he was anxious to see her.

"Hi," he said as soon as he opened the door.

"Hi," she responded, and moved toward him. Almost immediately, her right eyebrow and nostril cocked suspiciously.

"We were out on a lead today and this house was on fire."

"What are you doing, Mike?"

"What do you mean? I'm doing my job."

"Do you think that's what your life is about, *just doing your job?*"

"No, I—"

"Normal people have jobs to support their lives. But for you, life is an inconvenience your job has to put up with. Mike, *we're* your job. We're your life. Me and Katie and Patrick."

"Knox, I'm sorry. I—"

"This is exactly why you were sent here—to slow down—but you haven't lost a step. This is not fair to us. How much longer can this go on before something happens?"

"You don't think this guy needs to be caught?"

"Of course I want him caught. And I would be extremely proud if you were the one who did it. I know you are good at this and that taking chances is part of it, but you have a tendency to start slapping the lion in the face after your head goes in his mouth. I'm just asking that . . . I don't know what I'm asking."

"That I consider you and the kids before I stick my neck out?"

"The problem is you don't know when your neck is out."

Devlin flashed back to the noisy men at the Purple Camel and realized she was right. "Knox, I'm sorry, but I'm doing my damnedest to figure this out."

Knox recognized more than sincerity in his voice; there was that same vulnerability she had heard that night on the phone before deciding to fly to Washington.

"Do you think I'm being selfish?" she asked softly.

"I don't think there's anything wrong with being a little selfish. It's always worked for me."

He pulled her into his arms and held her close. She said, "I'm not going to think any less of you if you don't single-handedly solve this case."

"Maybe the problem is, I will."

||| CHAPTER 30 |||

He had not slept in two days. The reporter on *The Real Deal* said the FBI was able to determine that a bomb had been planted on one of at least seven airplanes. Each had been searched, and on an American Airlines flight from Washington to Los Angeles, a device had been found and disarmed. He was extremely angry at himself for being lazy; he should have booby-trapped the bomb.

The report also said that the FBI refused to comment on how they had narrowed the search to those seven specific aircraft, but he knew they had analyzed the flights through his use of the Blake credit card. Choosing Blake had been a good decision. He knew if the FBI discovered that identity, they would confront the Army depot employee and he would hear about it through the base grapevine. But he had to hand it to the FBI. They had found the tiniest flaw and then used it to disrupt his plan. And once they found Blake, he knew it was just a matter of time before they found Lloyd Franklin, who could have identified him. He had had no choice but to kill him.

That mistake had damaged his credibility. Now everybody knew that his *gasoline additive* was actually a series of bombs. It was a shame. If he could have convinced the country that the gasoline supply was potentially lethal, he would have ground America to a halt. As it was, the television reported that almost 30 percent of airline reservations had been canceled, and it was directly attributable to the Cataclysmist's actions. If that bomb had exploded, it would have been 100 percent.

But there were other ways to shut down this selfish, unforgiving society. What he was about to do had become necessary.

It now occurred to him that the FBI was able to detect his plan because he had been repetitive, using the credit card numerous times, establishing a pattern. He vowed not to do anything more than once from now on. Suddenly, he realized he had been at this hotel before. But it was all right because he would be there only two more hours, just until he E-mailed his new message.

He sat down at his computer and started typing. The message would be sent from his Washington hotel room at 6:00 A.M.—long enough in advance of his act to humiliate the FBI, but not long enough for them to stop him. He finished typing and proofread the communiqué:

America,

Freedom can only truly be understood when it is lost. The emptiness it leaves behind becomes its greatest measure, its loudest advocate. Do not think that the FBI has won. Today when the war starts, ask them why they did not stop what is about to happen. They know about it, just as they knew about the bomb on the plane. But this time, because of who is involved, they will let it happen.

This will demonstrate to you that I am willing to use whatever tactics necessary to bring about compliance with my leadership. Maybe then you will understand just how important my mission is. This is my sworn duty. Three days remain.

Devlin hadn't gotten through the door to their office the next morning when Bonelli said, "O'Hare needs to see you."

Devlin checked the time. It was 6:25 A.M. "While I'm up there, can you print out all the airline passengers from your lists that have Maryland addresses or phone numbers?"

"It'll take a little while. What do you expect to get from that?"

"Probably nothing. We don't know what additional aliases he used on the other flights, but he likes using Maryland as his residence. Maybe we'll get lucky and one of them will be his true name. Or maybe there'll be a good address or phone number in the bunch."

As Devlin left, Bonelli switched the printer on and started typing.

"You wanted to see me, Tom?"

O'Hare handed Devlin a fax. "He sent this a half hour ago."

Devlin read the message. "What about the trace?"

"The goddamn equipment malfunctioned. They traced it back through a local Internet service, U.S. Net, but then it would print out only four digits: six-zero-zero-zero. It looks like a commercial number, but we can't be sure. What about the message—can you make anything of it?"

"Whatever he's going to do, it's going to be our fault. Pretty smart how he used our finding the bomb against us. 'Today when the war starts' doesn't sound especially promising."

"Nor does 'who is involved.' "

"Let me check something downstairs. I'll get back to you."

On the elevator, Devlin reread the message. Hagstrom had been right about what the killer would want to accomplish. It seemed that whatever his next act was going to be, humiliating the FBI was going to be its main byproduct.

Devlin had penciled in the four digits at the bottom of the fax. Bonelli was busy at the computer when he came in. "Tony, can you run four digits of a phone number against all that data you've loaded?"

"Sure, that's the way I set this up, for quick reference. What's the number?"

"Six-zero-zero-zero."

Bonelli punched in the number and waited. "Where did you get this?"

"The subject sent another message this morning. Technical Services was using some experimental equipment. They traced it back through an on-line service, U.S. Net, but then it malfunctioned and only picked up these four digits. They're not even sure they're the *last* four."

A single typed line appeared on Bonelli's monitor. "We got a hit—888-6000. A Robert Jones used it as a contact number when he booked a flight from Washington to Kansas City on January seventh. The area code is 703. That's in Virginia."

Devlin dialed and hit the speaker-phone button. A woman answered. "Addison Hotel. How may I direct your call?"

Devlin said, "Robert Jones's room, please."

After a moment she said, "I don't show Mr. Jones staying here."

"Where are you located?"

As soon as she gave him the address in Alexandria, he hung up. Bonelli said, "Do you think that's it?"

"I don't know. But if it isn't, someone is about to die."

III CHAPTER 31 III

Traffic was good, so it took them only ten minutes to reach the hotel. As the doorman started toward the car, Devlin jumped out and said to Bonelli, "Show this guy your ID. I'll meet you in the manager's office." He hurried past the doorman and asked a bellman where the administrative offices were. Sensing the urgency, the bellman quickly led Devlin through a door with a combination lock into the hotel's corporate offices. The manager was startled when he looked up and saw a set of FBI credentials. "I'm Mike Devlin, and we have an emergency."

"Just tell me what you need."

There was a knock at the door and the bellman let Bonelli in. Devlin introduced him and said, "We think there was an E-mail message sent from one of your rooms about an hour and a half ago. How can we track it down?"

"I'm not sure. I've never had this request before."

Bonelli said, "Do you have computerized billing for the rooms?"

"Yes we do—for everything, even the mini-bar."

"If we know the phone number that was called and scan the individual guest bills room by room, would we be able to pick up that number on one of them?" Bonelli asked.

"Yes, you would, but we have over four hundred guests staying here right now."

"How about if we helped you?" Devlin asked.

"Follow me." The manager, now seeming to understand how to accomplish the request, was on his feet. "It'll be quicker in the billing office. There are two terminals." He led them into the next room and sat down at one of the stations, motioning Bonelli to the other. He gave both men a brief lesson in the use of the hotel's computer system, most of which Bonelli seemed to be a step ahead of. "Mike, call directory assistance and get the local number for U.S. Net."

After writing the number down, Devlin placed it between the two men. Anxiously, he watched over their shoulders. Within a few minutes, he realized that Bonelli was scanning the room records almost three times faster than the manager.

The manager, noticing Bonelli's speed, said, "I'm afraid I'm not very good at this." Slowly, he leaned sideways to look again at the phone number Devlin had written down. Bonelli continued to review room bills.

Devlin said to the manager, "I know the number. Let me watch for it over your shoulder."

After a few more minutes, Bonelli said, "There it is! Room 1462."

Spinning the manager's chair around, Devlin said, "I need a master key." While he went to get one from his desk, Devlin told Bonelli, "Call O'Hare. Tell him what we got and to get some people over here. I'm going up."

As the elevator sped toward the fourteenth floor, Devlin drew his automatic and jacked a round into the chamber. As the doors opened, he held the gun behind his thigh and cautiously headed down the hallway.

He reached the room and stood next to the door, placing his left palm lightly against it in an effort to feel any sounds inside. Nothing. He put his ear against the door and listened. The only thing he could hear was his accelerating heartbeat.

With the speed of a glacier, he inched the master key into the lock. He could feel each pin inside as the key pushed past them. When it was fully seated, he leaned back against the wall. He thought of Knox. Why was he doing this? He could wait. Help was coming. The only way out of the room was past him, so the killer couldn't get away. Then he turned and quietly opened the door.

Before taking a step, he listened. Nothing. He moved in and checked the bathroom, the closet—even under the bed.

Someone was coming down the hall. He hurried to the door and swung out into the hallway in a low silhouette, gun pointed toward the movement. It was Bonelli. Devlin straightened up and holstered his gun. "He's gone."

"O'Hare's got some people on the way."

They both walked back into the room. "Be careful not to touch any surface that might have a print on it."

Bonelli sat down hard on the bed. His breathing was heavy. "How about I don't touch anything but this bedspread and let you do the searching."

Devlin searched all the drawers, pulling them out by the bottoms, and then the waste baskets. "He didn't even leave a Q-Tip."

"The manager said he hasn't checked out yet."

"He's probably not going to."

"Said he paid cash up front."

"So he wouldn't have to come up with a credit card."

The door suddenly burst open. Devlin looked up at the

muzzles of two guns pointed at him. One of the men yelled. "FBI!"

Devlin flipped open his credentials. "Me, too."

"You Devlin?"

"Yeah. You from WMFO?"

"Yeah. We were on our way into the office. I'm sure there are others responding."

"Have the room processed for prints. Also have them check the bed and bathroom for hair. Maybe we can get some DNA on this guy. Come on, Tony, let's go down and see what the hotel has on him."

Devlin sat behind the manager's desk studying the bill for Room 1462. It had been rented the evening before in the name of Phillip King. He had listed his address as 2346 Oakmont, Annapolis, Maryland. The manager came in and handed Devlin back the plastic evidence envelope that held the original registration. Devlin examined it for additional information, but there was nothing that wasn't already in the computer. He picked up the printout of the bill and looked at the phone calls. There were two: one to U.S. Net, and one across the river to a number in Washington, D.C. "Tony, check this number and see if we have it."

Bonelli was already working on his laptop, loading in the Phillip King information. A few seconds later he said, "Nothing."

Devlin dialed the number. "This is the Reverend Epps's room. May I help you?"

The name surprised Devlin. "Reverend *Jonathan* Epps?"

"That's right. Who's calling, please?"

Three years earlier, the Reverend Jonathan Epps had been catapulted into the national headlines when he settled a growing dispute between CyberWorld, a national billion-dollar-a-year chain of retail computer stores, and a number of black rights groups. The problem started with a routine business magazine interview, during which the CEO was asked why the corporation never used African-Americans in its very hip, very popular television commercials. Thinking like a businessman instead of a corporate executive, he gave a quick, bottom-line answer: Blacks were a negligible portion of their consumers, so there was no economic need to target them.

When the comment was reported, a number of black groups responded with charges of racism and demanded that black actors be put in the commercials immediately. CyberWorld took offense at being called racist and offered figures in its defense, showing that it employed a higher percentage of blacks than most corporations its size. The executives dug their heels in and said they would not give in to the extortionistic demands of the groups. For weeks, angry rhetoric was traded back and forth in the media. Finally, the Reverend Epps stepped in.

The sixty-year-old minister had spent many of his years negotiating similar disputes and, by his own design, managed to remain outside the public eye. He preferred the easy access that anonymity had given him. He had seen how confrontations intensified once well-known black leaders announced they were getting involved. He liked the role of the unknown peacemaker, and that was exactly how he had entered the CyberWorld controversy.

Probably his greatest strength was his ability to remain emotionally detached. He had discovered during decades of mediation that it was the key to unraveling most arguments.

When he calmly offered to help the beleaguered corporation with their problem, its executives were receptive. Here seemed to be a black religious leader who did not carry the irrational weight of celebrity and was eager to help. As he sat down with the executives, they expected the offer of some sort of compromise position on the use of blacks in the commercials, but the solution Epps offered went much further.

With him, he had brought an impressive set of statistics, showing the growing number of young black people becoming involved with computers. More and more, they were being accepted into prestigious universities throughout the country, not only in computer science, but in fields that were becoming increasingly dependent on computers—everything from astronomy to accounting to writing. He also cited projections of how many of these young people would be purchasing their own computers in the next ten years. The biggest reason blacks were not buying more of their products, he explained, was their lack of exposure to them in their formative years, especially in the inner city. He concluded that the corporation should have the demographic foresight to start planting the seeds in this untapped but very developable market.

The arguments had been presented in CyberWorld's favorite language—profits. The company needed no further convincing. The corporate officers agreed immediately to start cultivating the new market. They announced plans for an advertising campaign and pledged to donate 1 percent of annual profits in the form of their products to inner-city schools and community centers. Also, a corporate volunteer program to instruct the inner-city children was to be initiated. And finally, CyberWorld, wanting to preclude any similar public relations problems in the future, offered Epps a position on its board of directors. He shocked everyone by deciding he would, in order to help the young people, be a consultant and nothing more. He asked for a salary of one dollar a year.

When it was all over, Epps attempted to leave as he had arrived—unnoticed—but the CEO, at a news conference, went into great detail about what the minister had done, including the refusal of a large salary.

That was the end of his anonymity. The reverend's popularity among blacks soared. As more became known about him, it was discovered that he was a man of simple needs. He wore inexpensive suits, didn't own a car, and when traveling, he tried to stay at the homes of people who offered their hospitality, usually insisting on washing the dishes for his supper. If he did stay in a hotel, it was inexpensive. To black America, he was becoming a symbol of unity.

"You said this is the Reverend Epps's room?"

"Yes. At the Shelby Congress Hotel. Who is this, please?"

An icy fist tightened in Devlin's chest. The killer had somehow gotten the direct dial number to the minister's room. That meant he had been tracking Epps's movements. "This is Mike Devlin. I'm with the FBI. Is the Reverend there?"

"FBI! Is there a problem?"

"I don't know. *Is he there?*"

"No, he's already left for the prayer breakfast."

"Where's that at?"

"The Convention Center."

"What time?"

"Eight-thirty."

"Do you know if the Reverend received a call this morning from a Phillip King?"

"There's a couple of messages on the desk. Let me look," the voice said. "Two calls—one from a Mrs. Harding and, yes, a Mr. Phillip King."

"What did King want?"

"Just like you—he wanted to know what time the breakfast was."

Devlin slammed the phone down. It was almost eight-thirty. He turned to Bonelli. "Get O'Hare. Tell him I think the target is Jonathan Epps. He's speaking at the Convention Center. *Now!*"

III CHAPTER 32 III

Devlin raced toward the Convention Center, weaving in and out of traffic, pounding on his horn.

His tires squealed as he stopped outside the center's main entrance. He got out and ran inside. A cardboard sign on an easel said that the reverend's breakfast was being held in the main ballroom. Devlin started running down the tiled corridor in the direction of the arrow.

He rounded a corner and saw an elderly black man, who was wearing a suit that was a little too big on him, sitting at a card table collecting tickets. He looked up at Devlin through thick glasses. "Are you here for the breakfast, sir?"

Devlin held up his credentials and was through the door before the man could react. There were over five hundred people sitting around white-linen-covered tables set with dishes and utensils. The meal had not been served yet. Epps had just been introduced and was stepping up to the podium, which was on a small stage.

Devlin started scanning the crowd. He estimated that there were about three dozen white people in the room. He looked from one to the next, quickly eliminating the women and measuring the men, looking for eyes filled with a purpose other than fellowship. Seeing that Epps would be more exposed as he mounted the stage, Devlin started walking toward him.

Somewhere behind Epps a door burst open. Devlin pulled

his jacket back and hit the thumb release on his holster. A stream of waiters and waitresses started coming out carrying large serving trays piled with food. Devlin watched them. There were only a few white men. They busied themselves getting their tables served.

Devlin walked briskly to the stage and Epps now noticed him approaching. As the agent started slowly up the stairs, the minister smiled curiously. The room grew quiet. Then as Devlin moved toward Epps, an incredulous murmur started.

For the first time, Devlin noticed that the room was two stories high. He searched the second level for windows and skylights. There were none. But then he saw it.

Back above the doors he had come through, on the second floor, were six small square openings, apparently for movie projectors and spotlights. Something moved slightly. Devlin focused on it. Another even less visible movement made him realize what it was—the barrel of a rifle. He turned and ran toward the minister. Epps saw him coming and froze. Devlin hit him an instant before he heard the rifle's explosion. The round hit the wall somewhere behind them, and Devlin knew they were still exposed. People started screaming. Plates and utensils hit the floor. Devlin looked up and could still see the rifle barrel. Now it was tilted up. Then he saw a couple of short, jerky movements. Devlin recognized the sequence: The killer was chambering another round.

Keeping himself between the gunman and Epps, Devlin forced the minister off the back of the platform. "Stay down," Devlin ordered. Another round splintered the wooden floor of the stage in front of him. He drew his automatic and fired a four-round burst at the small opening. The rifle was already gone.

Watching all six of the small, square apertures for a reappearance of the rifle, Devlin skirted the stage and ran back through the entrance. The old man taking tickets pointed and said, "He went that way!"

Devlin started running down the hall but had to slow down for every recess and alcove for fear of being ambushed. He replayed the timing sequence of the shooting in his head, trying to calculate how far ahead the killer was. Enough time had elapsed that he would not need an ambush to effect an escape, so Devlin decided to run at full speed.

The Freedom Killer would not have parked his vehicle anywhere that it might have been ticketed or, worse, towed. Also he was too smart to be trapped inside the building, and would have a well-planned escape route. His car had to be somewhere it would not be bothered.

Devlin spotted a sign marked DELIVERIES. That made sense: It was a place where transient vehicles could park temporarily without undue notice. He headed in the direction of the sign. As he came around a turn, he thought he heard the heavy steel door in front of him click shut. A small wire-reinforced opaque glass window was centered in the upper half of the door. As Devlin turned the knob, the window exploded, knocking him back. The gunshot echoed up the corridor in front of him, and he thought the report sounded like a handgun. He could feel a couple of small cuts on his face bleeding. Fortunately, he had been standing next to the door instead of in front of it, an old fugitive agent's precaution.

Carefully now, he looked through the hole where the window used to be and heard footsteps disappearing into the distance.

Running again, he tried to listen for the killer, to gauge his lead, but because of his own steps and breathing, it was impossible to hear anything. He stopped, held his breath, and listened. Nothing.

He was moving again. Every twenty-five yards, the corridor was interrupted by another steel door like the one that had been shot through. The first one he opened cautiously, then ran to the next. With each succeeding door, he took a little less time getting through it. Finally, he found himself in the shipping-receiving area of the Convention Center. Several wooden pallets were stacked high with cardboard boxes. At the far end was a double metal door. One of them was just closing.

Since Devlin had not actually seen the killer exit, he moved past the pallets cautiously in case the closing door was a diversion. When he finally reached it, he pushed it open an inch and looked out. The delivery area of the building was one floor below street level. A wide concrete ramp, thirty yards in length, rose up to an exterior loading zone.

Everything was quiet, so he stepped out and started up the ramp slowly. He heard the door lock shut behind him. At the top of the incline was a steel garbage Dumpster that was almost as wide as the ramp. It sat off the ground on wheels. Devlin thought he saw something move behind it. Instinctively, he flattened out as a shot ripped through the air and hit the cement wall behind him. He had no place to go, so he fired a round at the metal container as he got to his feet.

The "Bouncing Bullets" lecture from New Agent Training school flashed through his head: Rounds fired at low angles, whether into a wall or the ground, have a tendency not to ricochet at a similar angle but rather to travel in a line hugging the surface fired into. Walking up the ramp carefully, Devlin fired at the ground in front of the black steel receptacle, trying to skip his shots under it and catch the killer in the foot. The human foot contained twenty-six bones, and next to the hand, it was the most complicated mechanism in the body. It also contained a high concentration of nerve endings and, while a difficult target, was usually incapacitated once hit.

Judging the distance to the top of the incline, Devlin timed his rate of fire so he would have a few rounds left when he reached the top.

He got three quarters of the way up the ramp, and thought he saw the huge container move. Suddenly, it was coming at him. There was no room to get around either side of it. As it was about to hit him, he jumped up and grabbed the top edge. He was rolling backward and then felt the speed accelerate. The son of a bitch was in front pushing. It hit a bump, and Devlin could tell it was almost full; its weight made it that much more deadly. He glanced back at the cement wall that was coming at him quickly and knew he was about to be crushed by the container's force.

As he was about to hit the wall, Devlin pulled himself up onto the edge of the Dumpster and somersaulted into it. He landed on his back just as the Dumpster smashed into the wall, and his head was driven into its steel side behind him with enough force to knock him unconscious.

It was cold, and Devlin was under water. His oxygen was waning. This had happened to him before, so he didn't panic. He stroked a little harder toward the surface until he hit his head. The surface was frozen over. He must have fallen through the ice. Now he swam side to side, looking for his entry hole. The lack of air started to burn his lungs. Tiny exploding lights swirled through his window of vision; the edges shrank and grew dark. He tried to swim faster, but he couldn't. The natural painkillers in his body began kicking in. This is not a bad way to die, he decided.

Then he heard a voice. Where had he heard it before? With the little bit of consciousness he had left, he swam toward the sound. A great column of light lowered itself through the water and he swam through its warmth; the voice now calling his name. *Mike, where are you?* Mike—that was his name, wasn't it? His head broke through the surface, and he saw he was surrounded by the walls of the Dumpster.

"Mike, where are you?"

Devlin sat up. "Tom?"

O'Hare could see the disorientation in Devlin's expression. "Are you okay?"

His confusion continued a few moments longer until his mind untangled itself and then raced back, gathering the facts that explained how he had gotten to his present location.

"Yeah. Yeah, I'm fine." Retrieving his gun, he holstered it and climbed down out of the trash container clumsily. "I can't tell you what a lousy place that is to take a nap."

O'Hare put his arm around Devlin's shoulder and guided him toward the building. "I think we need to talk."

||| CHAPTER 33 |||

One thing Devlin thought he would never get used to was the drastic changing of gears an agent was sometimes asked to go through. One moment, with a great burst of violence, he might have to kick a door in and disarm a fugitive. Then, while the acrid air of battle was still fresh in his nostrils, he would be asked to spend hours in an agonizing search of the suspect's apartment for some particle of evidence that might link him to the crime. Ever since Vietnam, combat's rare opportunity had been Devlin's escape from the daily treadmill, and he hated when its brief afterglow was interrupted by an insistence that he return to the very tedium he was attempting to avoid.

The ideal sequence in an investigation was to collect the evidence and then become involved in the demands of arrest.

But the attempt on the Reverend Epps's life had demonstrated that was not always possible. Immediately after O'Hare returned to the Convention Center's ballroom with Devlin, the section chief started directing the crime scene investigation. Two dozen Washington Metropolitan Field Office agents had responded to the emergency call. Most of them were waiting to interview the people who were at the breakfast when the shooting erupted. Because there were more than five hundred people present, most of whom had not seen anything of significance, the task of taking statements from every one of them would have been not only too time-consuming but probably counterproductive. With that many people, each agent had to conduct in excess of twenty-five interviews. In a given time period, anything beyond five tended to quickly dampen the most tenacious interrogator's resolve. Agents, especially if receiving a preponderance of negative responses as they would have in the Epps case, start looking for shortcuts to quicken the pace. When being questioned by the FBI, witnesses try to be as thorough as possible, but if agents are trying to cut corners by not asking exhaustive enough questions, it quickly becomes apparent to them. They then have a tendency to believe that the importance of their evidence was overestimated and that it need not be passed along. The end result is lost information.

O'Hare was well aware of the shortcomings of such mass interrogations, so he went to the podium and asked those who thought they had seen something that might help the investigation to pick up their chairs and move to one side of the room. A relatively small number of people did so. The Washington agents moved in and began their interviews.

Clerks from WMFO arrived with additional evidence kits, and although he was still a little shaky, Devlin led a smaller group of agents along the shooter's escape route, showing them likely places, including the Dumpster, that they might dust for fingerprints.

In the projection booth, two agents found the rifle the Freedom Killer had abandoned. After photographing exactly where it had been found, the weapon was brought to O'Hare. He called over another agent he seemed to know. "Get the full description on this weapon and call it over to ATF. Don't let anyone breathe until they've completed the factory trace." Then he told the agent who was holding the rifle with evidence gloves, "Find some plastic to wrap it in and then *you* hand-carry it up to Latent Prints. Have them do the dusting. Tell the examiner it's a priority."

Devlin returned to the room and found a quiet corner to sit. It was almost a half hour before O'Hare came over to him. "There's someone who wants to meet you—formally." He stepped aside so Devlin could see Reverend Epps. As they shook hands, the minister glanced at the scattered cuts on Devlin's face. "I want to thank you for what you did."

"Well, I would hope so." They both laughed.

Suddenly there was a clamor of voices at the door. A group of reporters had arrived and insisted they be allowed into the room. O'Hare hurried over to the single agent who held them back and explained that no one would be allowed in until the Bureau had completed its investigation.

Devlin stared into Epps's weathered face. "This was not about killing you."

"I understand. I'm sure he wanted to start some sort of racial conflict, but I think he was underestimating us." O'Hare came back, and Epps asked, "Do you think he will try again?"

"Would you?" the section chief asked.

"I suppose not, but then I doubt if we answer to the same God."

"Because his plan was exposed," O'Hare said, "the public now understands what he is trying to do. He's smart enough to realize if anything happens to you from here on out, it would unify everyone against him, and that's the last thing he wants."

"Is there anything I can do to help?"

"There may be. Since he wants to use fear to make everyone change the way they live, the best thing you can do is to carry on as if nothing has happened. As soon as we are done here, let's invite the media in and you can conduct your prayer breakfast as if nothing has happened."

"It will be my pleasure. In fact, how about if I change the subject of my sermon to Don't Let a Pinprick of Hate Infect an Entire Society."

"Sounds perfect. And we'll have some agents stick around to make sure there are no more problems."

Epps offered his hand to both men. "Thanks again."

O'Hare took Devlin by the arm and led him toward the kitchen door. "Someone has told these reporters what happened. Right now they know an agent prevented the murder, but they have no idea who it was. So unless you want to spend a couple of hours being molested, you'd better get out of here."

"Talk about a perfect morning."

"Was there anything at the Addison that might identify this guy?"

"I didn't see anything before I left. WMFO was supposed to process the room. Maybe Tony found something. Do you know what happened to him after he called you?"

"I had him take a cab back to the office."

"I'd better get back there and see if there isn't something we shouldn't be doing."

"Are you sure you're all right? Why don't you take the rest of the day off?"

"I'm fine. The important thing is this guy's rhythm is broken. If we can keep the pressure on him, he'll unravel. But there's only three days left to do it."

III CHAPTER 34 III

As soon as Devlin got into his car, he twisted the rearview mirror so he could look at his face. He wasn't particularly worried about the cuts but rather about how his wife would view them. They were minor, but some blood on his collar made them appear more serious than they were. Knox was out for the day, so he decided to go back to his hotel and change.

He stood in the bathroom and carefully let the tips of his fingers test the size of the lump on the top of his head. It was not as big as he expected. He showered, changed clothes, and headed back to the Bureau headquarters.

He stopped to see O'Hare. "Did you find anything after I left?"

"We got a number of partial lifts, but we don't know if any of them are his."

"How about the man taking the tickets? He ran right by him."

"Between the excitement and those Coke bottles he calls glasses, he didn't know if the shooter was white or black. Latent has dusted the rifle, and there's not even a *smudge* on it. I doubt if he took time to wipe it down while you were shooting at him. The lab people think he must have sprayed his hands with something beforehand—something clear, so it wouldn't be noticed."

"If he did, then none of those partials were his, either. What about the factory trace on the rifle?"

"ATF said it was shipped to a Baltimore gun dealer. There are agents on the way to interview him right now, but I suspect it'll be another dead end."

"Speaking of dead ends, this guy used the name Phillip King at the Addison Hotel, with a home address in Annapolis. I was thinking Tony and I could get together with LoFranco and see if we can't get someone to burn *that* house down."

"From now on, the only time you're going to leave this building during work hours is when I personally take you to National and put you on a plane back to Motown."

"Come on, Tom. This is no big—"

"Yes, it *is* big. As far as this case is concerned, you're under house arrest. I've been sitting here trying to figure out how you always become the crash dummy, and I can't. So I'm going to take the time-tested management approach and over-react: *No more street time.*" O'Hare waited for a reaction. "Is there any part of that you don't understand?"

"I understand the overreacting part."

"Let me put it a different way. I've got lots of other people I can send out there to get hurt, but I have only one agent with a mind twisted enough to outguess this maniac. You've done it twice, and I need you around to figure out his next move."

"The last two times, he warned us. This time he won't. The answer is out there, and I got a feel for this guy. I'll be able to spot him if I get within a hundred yards of him. If you'll let me go look for him, maybe he won't get to his next move."

O'Hare's frustration was evident in his voice. "Mike, it's time to pass the baton. You're not going out there. Do you understand?" Devlin didn't answer. *"Mike?"*

The thing that was bothering Devlin the most was not the seemingly unanimous opinion that he was no longer capable of deciding what was dangerous, but that he was starting to believe it himself. He reached up and touched one of the cuts on his cheek. He thought about Frankie Butler, the Detroit bank robber, and the stunt at the Purple Camel. And then today at the Convention Center. Every one of those confrontations could have cost him his life. Somehow he always seemed to wind up going one-on-one with these people, and the first rule of survival he had learned in the Bureau was to never go one-on-one with anybody. And having these reservations was starting to worry him, because the most destructive weapon an agent could carry onto the street was self-doubt. He needed time to think. "Okay, Tom, you can sign me up for the rubber gun squad."

Although surprised, O'Hare was pleased at the resignation in Devlin's voice. "Good. I'll have LoFranco handle that lead. Right now I've got enough problems. Our friends at the White House want to make some political yardage with the attempt on Epps's life. They've directed us to interview all known members of white supremacy groups."

"That doesn't make any sense. This guy is incapable of belonging to anything."

"No one said it had to make good sense, just good copy."

"So there's a couple of hundred more agents not looking for the killer," Devlin said.

"At least. The latest Bureau-wide figures show that over a thousand new suspects are being phoned into the field offices each day. God knows how many more they'll be receiving after this is announced."

"It's like the Unabomb case—we could have the subject's name sitting in those tips and never get to it."

"That's why I want to see if we can go proactive," O'Hare said. "Be here at eight A.M. tomorrow morning. I've set up a meeting with Bill Hagstrom to see if there's something we can do to make the killer come to us."

*   *   *

After Bonelli had returned to the office from the Addison Hotel, he had reexamined a copy of Phillip King's bill. It showed a home address of 2346 Oakmont Avenue in Annapolis. Then he queried his computer for Robert Jones, the name that had first come up in conjunction with the hotel's phone number. Apparently the Freedom Killer had stayed at the Addison twice, each time using a different alias.

A week earlier, Bonelli would have found the King address in Annapolis encouraging, but after experiencing the bitter aftertaste of disappointment caused by the killer's ability to leave a false trail, he proceeded unemotionally. Since the name Robert Jones was so common and had been given without a corresponding phone number, he held little hope that it would be productive. But he called the Maryland Department of Motor Vehicles and queried it, along with the name Phillip King. There were eight pages of Robert Joneses, fourteen of which were in the killer's age range, but not one Phillip King with the right year of birth. Then Bonelli called FBI Baltimore and asked them to check credit and criminal on both names. While he was waiting for the results, Devlin walked in.

The cuts on the agent's face startled him. Bonelli tried not to stare at them, but there they were—finally offering proof that the phantom they had been chasing through telephone calls and computers was real. "I heard about the shooting. You all right?"

"Until my wife sees me. Have you had a chance to run those aliases he used at the hotel?"

Bonelli told him about the DMV checks. "Baltimore's running credit and criminal."

"That's nice work."

"Do you think this is another dead end?"

"Probably. I wouldn't waste any more time on 'Robert Jones.' But if Baltimore comes up with anything, call it up to LoFranco."

"We aren't going up there?"

"I'd like to, but O'Hare has taken away my belt and shoelaces."

"I don't understand."

"He doesn't want me covering any leads on this unless it's from this room."

"Because you got hurt?"

"I think that had something to do with it."

"So what do we do now?"

"Try to find another way into this guy."

"How?"

"Since I haven't got the slightest idea, let's start at the beginning and go through everything again."

Bonelli turned off his monitor, picked up a stack of teletypes, and, under his breath, said, "I'm sorry I asked."

"No need to mumble. I've heard it before."

When Devlin entered his hotel room that night, Knox was watching the news and didn't hear him come in. The lead story was just finishing. It was about the attempt on Epps's life. "It is suspected that the Cataclysmist was hoping the assassination of the civil rights leader would cause racial strife across the country."

The anchorwoman then asked, "John, do we have any idea how the FBI was able to discover this plot in time?"

"Diane, I talked to someone who told me that the FBI had discovered the Cataclysmist had stayed at an area hotel and they were then able to trace the plot from there to the Convention Center."

"You reported that one FBI agent had exchanged shots with the killer. Do you know if either of them was injured?"

"We don't know about the would-be assassin, but the agent received minor cuts from flying glass. We've asked FBI officials here at the scene if we could interview that agent, but they are refusing to identify him."

Finally, Knox noticed her husband and shut off the television. "I was just listening to—" She saw his face.

She did not show any compassion—or guilt because of the lack of it. Anger, controlled but threatening, removed all compromise from her tone. "I can't do this anymore."

"You can't do what anymore?"

"Welcome home the conquering hero."

"Is that why you think I do this?"

She laughed coldly. "Mike, that's why you do everything. It's been your whole reason for getting up in the morning ever since I've known you. Lifeguard, Marine, FBI agent, each a bigger hero than the one before. Where does it end?"

Devlin felt his own anger rise. "What I do has to be done."

"What has to be done! . . . For the case or for yourself?"

"We almost caught the killer today."

"We? I'll bet you your credentials there wasn't another agent in sight."

"There wasn't time. Should I have waited and let him shoot that man?"

"Let me explain something. Your father was an alcoholic, and he deserted you at the age of twelve. Since then your life has had one driving force—to prove you're better and tougher than he was. Now, I don't know if you're tougher, but let me put this on the official record: You are better than he was. You're a good man. I love you; the kids love you. And that's enough—trust me. You don't need to prove anything more."

"I like what I do," he said defensively.

"That's good, that's healthy, but the problem is the way you do it."

"Look at me. I'm okay, just a few scratches. There are no broken bones, no stitches, no bullet holes."

"No *new* ones."

Devlin sat down on the bed. "Okay, tell me how we can resolve this."

"No, Mike, there is no resolution. You are not going to change, and I, unlike the ASAC in Detroit or Tom O'Hare, am no longer going to worry about you. You know the risks you're taking, and I'm telling you it's not fair." She got up, went the closet, and started packing a small bag.

"Where are you going?"

"To spend the night at Cindy's. It'll give you some time to think."

As she walked to the door, he said, "I don't need any time to think."

"You don't? Then answer me this: Katie is going to be twelve in three months. I want to know what I should tell her if something happens to you and she no longer has a father around." She stared at him, waiting for an answer. When none came, she opened the door. "Never mind, I just figured it out. I'll tell her, 'Like father, like son.' "

||| CHAPTER 35 |||

He listened to the mocking echo of his own laughter. Ever since being denied entrance to the Academy, he laughed when he became severely frustrated. And that happened only when he failed. Now he had failed twice—first the plane and then the assassination. Despite everything he had accomplished, his power was again being taken away. For a while, that authority had given his life form, even density. Now everything was disintegrating amid the taunts of that damn laughter.

But even though he had failed, he would not allow himself to be a failure. Three days remained. Time for one more act—something more deadly than all the rest of it put together—and then their punishment. He had warned them, given every opportunity to comply. Now they would finally understand who he was.

He heard his father's key turn in the lock. *No, not now! Not when he had finally convinced himself that he could overcome all obstacles.*

"Hello, son."

"Father, you didn't call." His answer was curt and uncontrollably rude.

"I had a meeting in Baltimore and we finished early. How are you?"

"I'm fine."

"You seem upset. Did that job you told me about not pan out? I warned you to have more than one iron in the fire."

One corner of his mouth turned up viciously. He wanted to tell his father, *No, that's not it. However, today I was unsuccessful while trying to kill a civil rights leader. Are you disappointed I failed at that?* Of course he couldn't tell his father that, but there were other ways to hurt him. "They didn't turn me down. I turned them down. I decided I didn't want to work there."

"Why? Any job is better than this."

"You mean me taking handouts from you."

"I don't think I'm encouraging your success by paying you to lie around all day. I didn't mind doing it until you got on your feet, but it's been six months, and now you're turning down jobs."

"In other words, get a job or the money stops."

"In other words, get a job, period." He took out a check. "This is the last money you'll get from me."

The son took the check and laughed. "You have no idea what is going on in my life." Slowly, so as to prolong its effect on his father, he tore the check into small pieces. "You can take all your money, buy barbed wire with it, and shove it up your ass."

His son had never talked to him like this before. He was confused and hurt, but most of all afraid. Afraid of his own child. He had to leave. When he reached the door, his son said, "Father, wait."

Thank God, he thought, he wants to apologize. He turned and faced his son.

"You can't go until you use *failure* in a motivational sentence." He could see the hurt in the old man's eyes as he ripped the door open and stormed out.

He thought he would feel better after battering the man who had breathed this miserable life into his lungs, but he didn't. There was only more aching laughter.

The girl's skin, he decided, was the color of cinnamon, a light yellowish brown. It gave the impression of health, very unusual in prostitutes. He drove up next to her and rolled down the window. She said, "Hey, baby, what're you looking for?"

He smiled disarmingly. "Something my father wouldn't approve of."

"I don't know about your daddy, but I definitely got something your mama wouldn't go for."

With mock formality, he said, "May I see the menu?"

She grabbed her large unbridled breasts playfully and said, "If you like dark meat, baby, this is the place."

"And price?"

"For you, a half and half, if we use your van, will cost you twenty-five."

"Hop in."

She got in and directed him to a nearby warehouse district. He parked in the shadow of an abandoned building and turned off the headlights. She said, "I need to see those presidents first, baby." He took out two tens and two fives and handed them to her. She counted them quickly and didn't say anything about the extra five dollars. He started fondling her breasts. "Hold on while I get your pants down." With practiced hands, she unbuckled his belt and opened his fly.

As soon as she lowered her head toward him, he clamped his hands around her throat and let them tighten mechanically. Her arms began to flail immediately, but her blows were at best glancing. He pushed her face down deeper and squeezed harder. Another two minutes passed before she stopped struggling. Then he shoved her into an upright position and looked at her. "What have I done?"

Lowering her onto the seat, he leaned over and closed his mouth around hers and blew air into her lungs. Again and again. Harder and harder. Finally he saw her chest rise without his help. Then he felt her jerk to life. A short cough, followed by a deep, frightened breath. She was disoriented, as if in an unsettling dream, her limbs incapable of response. She desperately wanted to get out of the vehicle but couldn't. His fingers found their way around her throat again and closed off her air. He sneered at her. "I gave you five extra dollars so you will die five times. Keep count now—this is two."

Vaguely aware of his words, she did not resist, wanting only to return to her dream's mending sleep. For her, like for so many prostitutes, death was simply another drug.

||| CHAPTER 36 |||

Bill Hagstrom was the last to arrive at O'Hare's office. Devlin introduced him to Bonelli and Ernie Latimer, one of the Bureau's top technical agents.

O'Hare said, "Last night Baltimore located the owner of the rifle used in yesterday's attempt on Epps. He reported it stolen in a B and E the night before last. They're going to do some more work, but right now it looks like another dead end." Hagstrom was taking notes in a small green book.

O'Hare said, "Ernie, tell us about the trap-and-trace problems."

"It's simple—an E-mail message takes only a few seconds to send. Since he's calling from this area to New York, it's long distance, and long distance takes a great deal more time to trace. It's a miracle we got those four digits yesterday. The new equipment isn't working like we hoped it would. We'll be lucky to get anything the next time he calls."

Hagstrom said, "I seriously doubt if he is going to send us a warning next time."

"That's what Mike said," O'Hare said. "I thought the killer had this overwhelming need to humiliate us."

"Right now, he's the one being humiliated. Put yourself in his position. He has huge feelings of inadequacy, but for a while he is able to overcome them through these acts. Then he

196

tries to take it one level higher and humiliate us with a warning, but instead, the last two times out, we beat *him*."

O'Hare said, "Please tell me you think we've scared him off."

"No one is going to scare him off. He's very good at making adjustments. Look at the Lloyd Franklin murder. He waited until Mike was on to him before doing it. And since he stole the rifle only after killing his landlord, it means the assassination attempt of Epps was, at best, a contingency plan. He probably decided on it after his grand design was interrupted by us finding that bomb on the plane. But whatever he does next, he'll go back to what has worked in the past, and in the past, he gave us no warning."

"Have you got any general ideas at all what he'll try to do?" O'Hare asked.

"I can see some patterns shifting. After he failed to blow up the plane, his emphasis went from terrorizing the country to punishing whoever he could. He knows that the killing of Reverend Epps would not have furthered his cause. In fact, he probably realized that it would have made him a criminal rather than the savior he wanted to be. So I think his motivation has become one strictly of vengeance. I talked to Dr. Craven last night about the latest message, and we're both in agreement about the shift in motivation. In the first three communiqués, he is threatening the country. In the last one, he is specifically targeting the FBI. One of his primary reasons for the attack on Epps was to get even with the FBI for stopping the airplane bombing. Remember how he said we knew who the target was and implied because he was black we weren't going to do anything about it? After his failure with Epps, his desire for revenge, especially against the FBI, will be pretty intense."

O'Hare said, "I guess it's fortunate he doesn't know who Mike is."

"To this point, his hate has been pointed at institutions, nothing smaller. People like him need that large, vague umbrella under which they can lay blame for all the problems in their life. If his target is narrowed down to one person whose innocence can be demonstrated, he risks discovery, by others as well as by himself, and that might cause him to realize that the fault lies with him. Deep down inside, I don't think he wants to take that chance."

O'Hare asked, "Did Craven see anything in the last message that might help us identify him?"

"We both felt his return to the military language was important. His stress level is up, and one of the ways he deals with that is by returning to something that is reassuring for him. It's a natural instinct. Somewhere in his past, military regimentation has given his life order, and now that he is in difficulty, his language indicates he is reverting to it. When we find him, the military will be a prominent part of his background."

"Can we go proactive?" O'Hare asked.

"I don't think the things we've done in the past to make the killers come to us, like staking out the victims' gravesites or running phony ads in the paper, would work with him. He's too disciplined, too cold-blooded."

"There is one thing we could do," Devlin said.

O'Hare looked at him cautiously. "What?"

"Let the media interview me as the agent in charge of the investigation. I'll describe him as a coward on a power trip. I'll finish it by asking anyone who has information regarding this case to call or E-mail us here, and we'll give out the numbers. Because we know he's calling from Maryland, Ernie should be able to get a local trace on him."

Everyone was silent. Finally, O'Hare said, "Mike, I can't let you do that."

"The alternative is to wait and see how many people he can kill the next time."

After a few seconds, O'Hare asked Hagstrom, "Will he go for it?"

"Absolutely, but it would work better if we said that Mike is the one who prevented the Epps assassination."

"I don't like it," O'Hare said.

"What's the problem? He can't get at Mike here. It's not like you're staking him out in the open. Once he sends that message, he should be an easy pop."

O'Hare said, "Maybe we could get another agent and say it was him."

"You can't. This guy has traded shots with Mike. There's a chance he'll recognize him."

"I still don't like it."

Hagstrom said, "Listen, Tom, his grand plan has been destroyed. His rage is growing exponentially. When that plane didn't blow up, he still benefited, because a lot of people refused to fly. But this failed attempt on Epps has gained him nothing. In fact, I think everyone's fear of him is turning to disdain. His clock is running down and he needs a big win. If you let Mike do this, I assure you he'll call in."

O'Hare asked, "Ernie, can you guarantee a trace?"

"Are you sure he's in Maryland?"

Everyone looked at Devlin. "That's where all the footprints keep disappearing."

"If he is, I can set up the lines to immediately trap his call. I'll need twenty-four hours to set it up and do some simulations. I want to be sure it's going to work."

O'Hare stared at Devlin and gave a short, sarcastic laugh. "And Detroit called me to make sure you didn't get involved in anything dangerous."

Devlin smiled. "I'm going to be answering phones. How dangerous can that be?"

As Joe Lofranco pushed his key into the door of the Annapolis Resident Agency, he heard the phone. It was Devlin. "Hello, Mike."

"I was wondering if you got anything on the Phillip King address."

"I just got back. It's a small restaurant right outside the main entrance to the Naval Academy."

"I don't suppose Mr. King was working there."

"No, I talked to the owner, and he wasn't familiar with anyone by that name."

"Do you think our boy chose the name and address randomly, or did he have some reason, like he did with William Blake at the ordnance depot?" Devlin asked.

"I don't know. In fact, I ate dinner there last night and breakfast this morning. If there's a connection, I couldn't find it. The place is called the Twin Anchors. A lot of the midshipmen frequent it. As soon as I check my messages, I'll head over to the Academy and see if there are any Phillip Kings there, past or present."

"Let me know, will you?"

"O'Hare still won't cut you loose?"

"Not even if I put a gun to his head. Besides, we've got a small subplot we're working on here." Devlin told him about the proactive plan to get the killer to call or E-mail a message to FBI headquarters. He also explained Hagstrom's and Craven's observations regarding the fourth communiqué and its reversion to military language.

"You know, I never saw the last message. Can you fax it to me?"

"I'll send it right now. And I wouldn't get too far from your radio. Everyone's betting their paycheck this guy is going to call in, and when he does, they think it's going to be from your zip code."

"Good. I'd like to see if I can still hit the fastball."

III CHAPTER 37 III

Something was going wrong in his son's life, and he needed to know what it was. The boy had had his problems growing up, but being disrespectful to his father was never one of them. Maybe it was drugs. Hopefully not, but he had to find out. Parked a half a mile away, he dialed his son's number. There was no answer, so he drove to the house and let himself in. As he looked around, he suddenly realized how orderly the house was kept. He supposed it had always been that way; he had just never noticed. Was he that insensitive to who his son was? It was not a good sign. He was evidently failing as a father.

The only two rooms that showed any sign of personal activity were a small office in the rear and the lone bedroom. He decided to search the bedroom first. In the nightstand drawer, he was surprised to find a loaded revolver. But then he reasoned that it was probably for protection, a normal precaution in this day and age. Next he started searching the two dressers.

As soon as he pulled up in front of the house, he saw his father's car. He took a moment and sat meditatively, calming his disdain so he could act rationally and respectfully. But as soon as he came through the door, he could hear drawers being searched. His self-control dissolved as he hurried to the bedroom. His father didn't hear him enter. As he watched, his rage became uncontrollable. "What are you doing here?"

Startled, his father jerked upright. "I, uh—"

Calmly, without the slightest trace of remorse for the night before, he repeated his question. "What are you doing here?"

"I'm worried about you. Yesterday, that wasn't like you."

"Wasn't it? Then what is like me?"

There was a coldness he had never seen in his son before. "What is wrong with you?"

He laughed—almost insanely, his father thought. "Trust me, you can't handle this. Hell, you're still in denial about Grandfather."

"I want to know what's wrong, son."

"*Son?* Maybe *you're* what's wrong."

Anger started to rise in the old man. "If I am, it's because I've given you too much, but right now I demand to know what's going on here."

"You demand?" he hissed through his teeth. He stared at him for the moment it took to make a decision. "Okay, you want to know. I'll show you. It's down in the basement." He turned on the light and led the way down the stairs. As soon as they reached the bottom, the lone bulb fizzled and went out. But there was enough light coming through the small ground-level windows for them to see. At one end of the gray concrete chamber were a series of doors. The son took out his keys and opened one of them. Both men walked into the small room, and the father was stunned at its contents. Arranged neatly on a large metal table were several handguns, boxes of different caliber ammunition, and what looked like explosives. The son picked up a .45 automatic and chambered a round.

"What the hell is all this?"

"This is who I really am." The confusion on his father's face pleased him.

"What, you're a gun nut . . . you've joined a militia, what?"

A cruelness distorted the son's face. "No. But you'll be pleased to know that I'm finally the best at something—I'm the Freedom Killer."

For a moment the father was paralyzed, but then his index finger started to move disapprovingly toward his son's chest.

The .45 exploded.

Before Devlin was allowed to go on camera at the news conference, approval from the Director of the FBI, the attorney general, and the White House had to be obtained. While everyone understood the appearance was necessary if the Freedom Killer was to be caught, there was a reluctance to let someone who had not been taught how to comb and curry his responses be exposed to the risks of such intense media scrutiny. Image, in the upper reaches of the government, wasn't as important as stopping the killer, but it was a very close second.

Bob August had no such reservations and quickly persuaded the attorney general that the unprecedented action was indeed a necessary evil. The White House was the final obstacle. And the man he had to talk to was Ralph Larsen, the staffer who had refused to make a decision when the seven airplanes needed to be grounded and searched for a bomb. "Ralph, Bob August. I think we've got a good chance to catch the Freedom Killer, and I need to run something by you." The Director then explained why it was necessary for Devlin to appear on live network TV.

"Wouldn't this work just as well if *you* gave the conference and had this agent stand behind you?"

"The Behavioral Science people feel that the killer is so self-controlled that nobody but the man who has stopped him twice will be able to provoke him into making that call."

"My gut reaction is to say no. The media will eat him alive. He could make a mistake up there and destroy any investigative advantage we have."

"Mike Devlin *is* our investigative advantage. He's an unusual agent, and I have complete confidence in him."

"I'm sorry, Bob, but I have to say no."

August waited a moment before speaking and then in a predictive tone said, "Why don't you give it some more thought. We've got about an hour before we need a final decision. Then, if we still can't agree, I'll have to seek a less palatable alternative."

"Less palatable for who?"

"For whom," he corrected. "For all of us."

After the Director hung up on him, Larsen sat with the disconnected phone in his hand, trying to figure out if August's threat was valid. What could he possibly do? He worked for the attorney general, who served at the pleasure of the White House. But there was something in his voice that had sounded confident. Larsen knew how to find out. He dialed a number at FBI headquarters. "Scott Adler."

"Scott, Ralph Larsen." He lowered his voice. "Can you talk?"

Adler returned his cautious tone. "Let me close my door." Larsen had met Adler after the Freedom Murders had started and Larsen was sent over from the White House to act as liaison with the Bureau. Adler was a special assistant to the Director and was getting ready to retire. The second day Larsen was there, Adler came up and introduced himself. He had seemed overfriendly until he mentioned that he was eligible to retire and was looking for something else in government, possibly up on the Hill. Apparently, he saw the White House staffer as his next meal ticket. So Larsen strung him along, hinting he could probably find him something worthy of his talents. In the following days, he tested the agent's shift in loyalty by asking him to provide small, confidential details about the Bureau's investigation, which Adler did unhesitatingly. "Yeah, Ralph, what's up?"

"You know about August wanting to put this guy Devlin on the news?"

"Yes."

"When I told him no, he said he was going to do something none of us would like. Any idea what that might be?"

"No, but let me try and find out. I have to take a couple of communications in for his signature anyway. Will you be there for a few minutes?"

"I'm not going anywhere until I hear from you."

Twenty-five minutes later, Adler called back. "Did August ask you to approve the searching of those planes for the bomb and you never gave him an answer?"

"That's not the way it happened—"

"Ralph, you don't owe me any explanations. But he's going to leak it to the media that the White House has been obstructing the Bureau's investigation, that the plane would have been blown up if the searches had depended on your cooperation. And, without anything too specific, there will also be some questions raised about a recent opportunity to solve the case, meaning this news conference, but again you refuse to accept any responsibility."

"That son of a bitch!"

"Just let me know if you need anything else."

Larsen hung up. He had thirty minutes left of the hour August had given him. Thirty minutes to convince someone above him to take the responsibility for allowing Mike Devlin to appear before the media.

Thirty-five minutes later Larsen called the Director. "Bob, I've talked this over with my boss, and he feels it would be in everybody's best interest if you did go ahead with the news conference."

"Just out of curiosity, Ralph, how do you feel about it?"

Larsen suspected August was gloating. "It doesn't matter how I feel, but you'd better hope you're right about this."

"Good-bye, Ralph." August disconnected the call and smiled. Across his desk sat Scott Adler. "Evidently, you were very convincing, Scott. He didn't seem very happy."

"Just following orders. You're the one who had the foresight to plant me in his camp."

"The first day I saw him, I knew he was going to be a problem," the Director said.

"But why didn't you just threaten him with the leak yourself?"

"It wouldn't do for the Director of the FBI to threaten the White House."

"It'd be your word against his."

"I hope you didn't say anything to him you might regret." Adler looked at August questioningly. "He records all his calls."

By the time LoFranco finished reviewing his phone-mail messages, Devlin had faxed the Freedom Killer's latest message to him. Without taking the time to read it, he pushed it into his briefcase and headed for the Naval Academy.

At the main gate, he flashed his credentials at the sentry and was waved through. The building that housed the base personnel office was all too familiar to him. He had been there many times, conducting background investigations for government applicants—the bane of every resident agent's career. After being shown into the head of personnel's office, he was told the commander would be there shortly.

Remembering the killer's last message, he took it out of his briefcase. He circled the military buzzwords Devlin had alluded to. The commander came in, and they shook hands. "What can I do for you, Joe?"

"I'm working on the Freedom Murders, and we're getting a lot of tangents intersecting in Annapolis. From the profile we've developed for the killer, there are indications he was in the military."

"You're thinking he's one of our graduates?"

"I doubt it. More likely someone who got tossed. Or maybe an enlisted man who used to be stationed here."

"Can you give me some parameters?"

"White male, mid- to late twenties. Bright, but probably with low self-esteem. Possibly a traumatic event in his personal life started his military demise. And our Behavioral Science people believe he's a very rigid person."

"That last trait won't narrow it down much. This is the Naval Academy—we like to think we invented rigidity."

LoFranco laughed. "How about the rest of it then?"

"I hope I'm not going to sound defensive, but I can't see us accepting a person like this in the first place. As you know, we not only have stringent academic and physical fitness requirements, but we also conduct extensive psychological tests beforehand."

"I guess that leaves only the enlisted men who were stationed here."

"Maybe it was someone who applied to the Academy but was rejected," the commander offered.

"How many of those are we talking about?"

"There are literally thousands each year."

"Is there some way we can narrow that number down? How about applicants from the enlisted ranks?"

"I suppose it's a possibility, but we usually have a good look at them before we ask them to consider the Academy."

"That's a good point. If not getting in here is what set this individual off, then it would stand to reason that the Naval Academy is something he wanted for a while. But I guess that wouldn't be the case with enlisted men, since you seek them out. Where else do applicants come from?"

"The largest number are high school graduates."

"But this person has had some exposure to the military." LoFranco handed him the fax of the killer's message. "See the language I circled?"

"Definitely military."

"Okay, if he's not an enlisted man and probably not a high schooler but has had exposure to the military, what does that leave?"

The commander thought for a moment and then said, "How about private military academies? We do accept a small number from those each year."

"Are there any that have a reputation for making it easier to get in here?"

"Officially we treat them all the same, but I think because of their proximity, we accept a few more from the Maryland Military Institute than anywhere else."

"I guess I'd better head over there then. I was there once before, on a bank robbery, but I don't really know anybody. Do you have the name of someone I can talk to in personnel?"

The commander opened his desk drawer and took out a stack of business cards that were held together with a rubber band. He shuffled through them and then handed LoFranco one.

The agent copied down the name and telephone number and was about to hand it back when he noticed the Maryland Military Institute's motto inscribed across the top of the card: LEADERSHIP, DUTY, COUNTRY.

LoFranco looked back at the seven circled words on the fax he had shown the commander. Three of them were LEADERSHIP, DUTY, COUNTRY.

III CHAPTER 38 III

Bonelli was surprised to see Bill Hagstrom walk into room 511. "Get used to it, Tony," Devlin said. "Once they find out you're going to be on TV, they all want to be your friend."

"Believe me, this isn't my idea. O'Hare thought you might need some help with preparing your insults for the killer, but obviously the man has no idea where your natural talents lie."

"Shouldn't you be off somewhere swapping boyhood stories with a pedophile?"

Hagstrom turned to Bonelli. "I rest my case."

"You think this is really going to work?" Bonelli asked.

"The whole key is if we can get under this guy's skin. You've been subjected to Agent Devlin for a while; wouldn't you like to send him a nasty message?" Bonelli smiled. "Michael, do you have any idea what you're going to say?"

"I hadn't really thought about it."

"Well, I have. We know it's the need to overcome his powerlessness that's driving him. Through his initial acts he was defeating those feelings, but with his last two attempts failing, I think he will be more susceptible than ever to criticism. He should be vulnerable to any verbal attack. I would get on him about his incompetence not only as a man but now as a killer. Because he is a coward, he killed children to feel better about himself, but now he can't even do that successfully."

"Bill, we just want him to send E-mail, not a nuclear device."

"Let's really put him away. How about if we pump a little misinformation up his shorts, too. Tell the media that because of his obvious low intelligence, we believe he is a high school dropout. Also that he's probably physically unattractive and a recent releasee from a mental institution. He's incapable of any kind of personal relationship, but especially those with women."

"I assume I shouldn't directly challenge him to send me a message."

"No, he might sense what we're trying to do. Just give the numbers at the end. Make sure you give it a lot of *'me'* when you do. 'You can contact *me* if you have any information.' He'll do the rest."

"Anything else?"

"You should have this attitude of omnipotence. Try to sound like he does in his messages. The things we dislike most about others are the weaknesses we suspect within ourselves. First you're defeating his plan and now you're taking over his power. It'll drive him crazy."

"Are you going to be here for the news conference?"

"No, I'm overdue at the unit now, but good luck."

"Hopefully, this won't be one of those luck things."

"How long have you been an agent?"

LoFranco had been to the Maryland Military Institute once before, a year and a half earlier to arrest a bank robber. One of the eighteen-year-old cadets, for reasons that had never become clear, went into a local bank and presented the stunned teller with a demand note, asking for two thousand dollars in twenties. He was quickly given the money and, being an amateur, fled, leaving the demand note behind. LoFranco had responded to the bank and, after questioning the victim teller, examined the note. It was written on the back of one of the cadet's own deposit slips from a different bank. Someone trained in television psychology made the comment that for an individual to do something so stupid, he must have had a hidden desire to be caught. But LoFranco talked to an old, salty bank-robbery agent in Baltimore who told him that it was fairly common. Thank God, he said, bank robbers made such wonderful mistakes. As a general rule of thumb, you don't want to be looking for anyone smarter than you.

LoFranco remembered driving onto the grounds of MMI that day and thinking what a strange setting it was to make an arrest. There, all the rules and discipline of military life had but a single purpose: to draw and darken the line between authorized and unauthorized, to simplify the decision-making process so that even those of the lowest rank could understand what they were expected to do and, more important, what not to do. But evidently, the eighteen-year-old bank robber had failed to adapt to the simple black-white guidelines of the military. Hell, LoFranco thought, maybe he wanted to get caught; maybe it was his way out of this sterilizing regimentation. Maybe it was the Freedom Killer's way out, too. He pulled up to a building that was marked ADMINISTRATIVE OFFICES and got out.

Inside, he was directed to the office of a civilian counselor. He knocked and walked in. After LoFranco identified himself, the man extended his hand. "I'm Tom Watts." He appeared to be in his fifties and had thick close-cropped steel-gray hair. His erect carriage and obvious military bearing told LoFranco that he was retired from one of the services. "What can I do for the FBI, Agent LoFranco?"

"Please call me Joe. I assume you've heard of the Freedom Killer." LoFranco then explained what had led him to MMI.

"God, I hope you're wrong."

"That's a distinct possibility," he said, although he felt it wasn't.

"What exactly can I provide you with?"

"Our profile indicates that this person is in his mid-twenties and probably never graduated from college. Through investigation, we have determined he lives in Maryland and possibly had a strong desire to go to the Naval Academy. Would it be possible to put together a list of people who fit those guidelines?"

"Identifying those who didn't graduate in the last five years is easy enough. From that, we can determine who has Maryland ties. The only thing that we won't have is who was desirous of going to Annapolis. But I can tell you there's probably never been a cadet here who wouldn't accept an appointment in a heartbeat."

"I guess that's where we'll start, then. I'm sure you understand how urgent this is, so the sooner I can get the list, the better."

"If it's urgent enough for you to help me, we can get started right now."

"You've got yourself a clerk."

For the better part of three hours, the two men reviewed files. The majority of the dropouts were eliminated because they did not meet one or more of the characteristics of the Behavioral Science profile. When they finished, there were seventeen names on their list. "What do you do now, Joe?"

"We'll run some background checks on them—see if they've had problems in the past or if their names have come up previously in this case."

"And then?"

"We'll go talk to them and, if we think it's warranted, offer them a polygraph."

"Would this individual take a polygraph?"

"If he thought he could beat it, he might. Anyway, we usually like to concentrate on those who won't."

"If you need anything else here, you've got my number," Watts said.

LoFranco thanked him and left.

All seventeen of the men listed had Maryland addresses. Three of them lived in the western extremes of the state, but the rest were within easy driving distance of Washington. LoFranco decided to return to the resident agency in Annapolis and get the names to Devlin so he could run background checks on them, but he noticed that two of the ex-cadets lived just south of Baltimore, at addresses which were directly on his route back.

He looked again at the fax Devlin had sent him. The last line on it warned there were three days left to comply, and LoFranco knew the killer could strike anytime before then. The intervals between his acts were getting shorter. LoFranco weighed the problems of interviewing suspects by himself against the urgency of the situation. He felt if there was one chance in a thousand of interrupting the killer's plans, it was worth the risk. Besides, there was no guarantee the killer's name was on the list, and if it was, LoFranco knew how to back off when conditions became risky.

The first of the two former MMI cadets was Harrison Langston. He had left the school in his second year. The file had not given a reason, but his grades were far below average. One annual rating had described him as "lacking the focus and motivation necessary to adapt to the traditions and goals of this institution."

LoFranco found the house easily. It was in a clearly middle-class suburb of Baltimore. Before getting out of the car, he took out his two-inch revolver and placed it in his right-hand overcoat pocket. He opened his briefcase and searched through the fifteen or so case folders he normally carried with him until he found a grainy black-and-white bank robbery surveillance photo. It had been taken a year ago during a robbery of an Annapolis bank. LoFranco had solved it six months earlier, and the subject of the case was in jail awaiting sentencing. Tucking it into his inside suit coat pocket, he got out of the car. Carefully, he gripped the gun in his pocket, keeping its weight from hanging obviously, and walked to the door.

Faintly, he could hear the doorbell ring inside the house. A few seconds later a man in his mid-twenties came to the door and looked at LoFranco without offering a greeting.

With as disarming a smile as he could muster, LoFranco said, "Hi, how are you? I'm investigating a bank robbery that took place yesterday in Annapolis. Did you hear about it?"

"And you are?"

"Oh, sorry." He held up his credentials. Then he pulled out the surveillance photo and handed it to the man. "That's the person we feel is responsible. The getaway car was found a block away, so we're checking with people in the area. Do you recognize him?"

Without any emotion, the man said no and handed the photo back.

"Appreciate your looking." LoFranco pulled out a small notebook and pen. "Could I have your name, please?"

"What for?"

"So we know who we've talked to. You know, so we don't forget and come back and bother you again."

The man seemed to consider the logic of the request with some suspicion, but then answered, "Harrison Langston."

During those years in New York, LoFranco had developed some pretty reliable warning systems, and right now they were going off. He decided not to push this interview any further. "Sorry to bother you."

The next house was ten minutes away. This time a woman in her late forties answered the door. After LoFranco flashed his identification, she invited him in. Because she was present, he decided to be a little more straightforward. "I'm looking for"— he looked at his list absentmindedly to give the impression that the person he wanted to talk to was not all that important— "Edward Quigley."

"That's my son. Is there a problem?"

"Oh no, ma'am. Someone has applied for a government clearance and has given your son's name as a reference. Nothing more than that."

"You gave me a start there for a minute. Eddie's in the Army now, a sergeant. He's stationed in Germany."

"Lucky guy. I always wanted to see Germany—not bad enough to join the Army, though." He smiled. "How long has he been over there?"

"A little over a year. We haven't seen him since the Christmas before last."

"I guess that's the downside. Would you have his address? We'll probably just send him a form to fill out."

"Sure, hold on while I get it."

As soon as LoFranco got back to his office, he called Devlin at headquarters and explained how the words in the killer's message had led him to MMI.

"I guess you still *can* hit the fastball, Joe."

"Thanks. I just got back from MMI with a list of dropouts that meet the profile."

"Great. How many are we talking about?"

"Seventeen, but I eliminated one on the way back here. He's been in the Army overseas for the last year."

"How did you find that out?"

"I stopped by his house and talked to his mother."

"By yourself?"

"I used a pretext."

"Isn't there someone in the RA to give you a hand?"

"They're all handling other leads on the case—you know, call-in tips, plus the supervisor has them interviewing everyone with white-supremacy connections. I'll be fine. Don't forget, I survived New York."

"Are you doing more interviews tonight?"

"As soon as I fax you this list and get a sandwich."

"Go ahead and send it. Which one did you eliminate?"

"Edward Quigley. I also pretexted Harrison Langston. He made the hair stand up on the back of my neck, so I pulled off. How about taking a little closer look at him?"

"I assume you're not going back to reinterview him," Devlin said.

"Not by myself."

"Just be careful."

LoFranco laughed. "Easy money. What time are you on the tube tonight?"

"They're trying to get it done in time for the network news. The trace lines have been set up and tested. In fact, I better get going."

"I'm putting the list in the machine now," LoFranco said. "If I get anything interesting, I'll call."

||| CHAPTER 39 |||

Joe LoFranco had a decision to make. With fifteen suspects to go, there were two possible investigative approaches available: He could take the least likely ones and eliminate them, leaving the strong suspects for later interrogations when more help was available, or he could do whatever was necessary to identify the Freedom Killer as quickly as possible and hopefully stop his next crime. Experience had taught him that if an agent was not aggressively investigating a case, it would remain unsolved. Invariably, crimes were resolved by those who were willing to put their heads down and charge up the middle.

Since Annapolis had become the unofficial center point of the killer's activities, LoFranco made a list, ranking the suspects by their proximity to the town. The first one lived in Annapolis. He would start with him and interview as many as possible tonight.

He checked the time. It was a little after seven, and he was alone in the office. A strange emptiness came over him. It felt like the night his wife had told him she wanted a divorce. He thought about it for a few minutes longer and then attempted to shrug it off. When the feeling wouldn't leave, he unlocked his desk and took out his large-frame magnum. He had not felt the need to carry it since leaving New York. He broke open the cylinder and found it was not loaded. Opening another drawer, he pulled out a box of Bureau issue hollow points and loaded the weapon. Then he counted out another twelve additional rounds and dropped them into his right-hand suit coat pocket. The snub-nose he usually carried in his briefcase went into his left-hand overcoat pocket as a backup. As he stood and felt the two uncomfortable weights hanging on him, he decided they would be a good reminder to be cautious. He stopped when he got to the door, and turned to survey the space that had been more than his place of work for the last two years. It seemed unusually pleasant.

The first address was a five-minute drive. LoFranco sat a half a block away and watched the house. There were lights on in almost every window of the small frame Cape Cod. Three cars were parked in the narrow driveway that ran alongside the house. He could see people occasionally move past the window.

When he got out of his car, he noticed that the temperature was dropping and the wind was picking up. The top edge of his ears began to burn with the cold. Knowing he shouldn't button his coat over the holstered gun on his hip, he placed both hands in the outer pockets and used them to wrap the coat around himself.

Quietly, he walked up the driveway, placing a hand briefly on the hoods of the cars. The two closest to the street were warm, reassuring him that there were other people in the house. Witnesses—he would go straight up the middle.

When LoFranco knocked on the door, he heard someone yell, "I'll get it, John." The door opened and the man answering it got an eyeful of FBI credentials. "John, I think you'd better get this one." He waved LoFranco in with a smile and retreated back to the small dining room. On a table were the usual poker staples: cards, chips, snacks, and beer.

John Sprague walked in from the kitchen holding two open beer cans in each hand. He was twenty-four or twenty-five years old, with a thick auburn beard that hung along bloated cheeks cracked by webs of thin red veins—a drinker's face.

"Yeah, can I help you?" His speech had an alcohol-softened texture to it. LoFranco doubted if Sprague was receiving words any better than he was transmitting them, so he held his credentials up to improve the ex-cadet's focus. "FBI? This is a penny-ante game."

The other players were letting intermittent drunken snorts of laughter escape. "Is there somewhere we can talk?"

"Uh, sure." Keeping one of the cans of beer in his hand, he led the way into the kitchen and shut the door.

Sprague was now visibly nervous and his attention span had improved noticeably.

"You went to MMI?" LoFranco asked.

"Yeah, three years."

"Why didn't you graduate from there?"

"What's this about?" Sprague asked, trying to sound angry.

"This is about you answering questions without the artificial indignation." LoFranco stared at him unemotionally.

"Sure, sure. It's just that I'm not used to the FBI coming in here asking questions."

"This can be a short ride, or if you insist, much longer."

Sprague smiled. "Okay, what do you need to know?"

"MMI."

"They threw me out my last year."

"For?"

"They thought I had a drinking problem."

LoFranco looked down at the beer in Sprague's hand and then at the brimming trash can near the refrigerator. "Imagine that."

Sprague blushed slightly. "It's my life."

"Has your life ever taken you to Los Angeles?"

"No."

"San Francisco?"

"No."

"Dallas?"

"I've been to Florida and Chicago. Other than that, I've never really traveled much."

"Where were you yesterday morning between eight and ten?"

"At work."

"Which is?"

"I'm a plumber. I was doing a job over on Union, uh, 721. I was there all morning. They had a pipe burst."

LoFranco was suddenly aware of the weight of the two guns and extra ammunition he was carrying, indicating that the edge caused by his caution was waning. "I'll let you get back to your game."

"That's it?"

"You wanted the short ride."

The next suspect's house was at the far end of a dead end

street. The house stood alone a good half a block from the closest neighbor. LoFranco could see only a hint of light coming through one of the windows facing the street. Driving slowly, he got to the far side of the house and could see a light in a rear room. He parked in the driveway and sat for a moment, feeling his caution return. "Great place for an ambush," he heard himself whisper. He made sure he had his bank robbery photo and got out.

After he knocked on the door, he noticed the house was surrounded by a discomforting stillness. Something was telling him to leave. As he was about to retreat to his car, a pleasant voice came through the door, "Could you come around to the back, please?"

The side of the house was unlighted. LoFranco reached inside his pocket and gripped his snub-nose. Cautiously, he walked toward the rear, and as he did, stepped in a puddle of water, soaking his shoes.

He reached the back door and gave it two light raps. It opened and a handsome face stared up at him from a wheelchair. "Yes, sir, can I help you?"

LoFranco's hand relaxed from around the snub-nose and he let it settle at the bottom of his coat pocket. After he identified himself, the man in the wheelchair introduced himself as the next person on the list of ex-cadets. "Come on in, I've got something on the stove." He turned and wheeled himself toward the kitchen. Because of the man's lack of mobility, LoFranco decided a pretext wouldn't be needed and followed him.

"Please, have a seat."

LoFranco sat down at the table. "I'm checking on some cadets from MMI."

The man pushed himself to the stove behind LoFranco, and the agent heard a lid being lifted from one of the pans on the stove. "Guilty—I attended school there for three years."

"I just have a few questions, and then I'll let you eat your dinner in peace." LoFranco noticed a newspaper spread on the floor in the corner. A pair of shoes sat on top. The paper around them was soaked. "Do you live here alone?"

Before the question was out of his mouth, LoFranco realized it was a mistake. Immediately, he could feel the man moving behind him. Firearms training kicked in—the pivot course. LoFranco stood and spun away, protecting his right side from the threat behind him. He felt his thumb unsnap the safety release on his holster, then his palm found the grips of his magnum.

The Freedom Killer was on his feet and three quarters of the way through a baseball swing with a four-foot length of steel pipe when LoFranco's gun cleared its holster. His finger clawed at the trigger as the pipe caught him just below the temple, crushing his eye socket. LoFranco felt an electric shock run down his arm. The last thing he saw before he blacked out was his gun falling to the floor.

||| CHAPTER 40 |||

When the media heard that a rank-and-file agent would be allowed to answer their questions unguardedly during live network coverage, they gathered with the enthusiastic community of piranha at the rumor of beef Wellington.

The attorney general, who is, at least organizationally, the FBI Director's superior, ordered that the event should take place at the Department of Justice building. As it was about to start, Tom O'Hare led Devlin through the maze of security.

Even though Devlin hadn't yet entered the room, the cameras started flashing as soon as the door opened. Solemnly, he stepped inside. There seemed to be one long continuous flash; cameras clicked and whirred. Devlin headed to the podium and stood to the right of the Director, who stood to the right of the attorney general.

The three men stood there for the better part of a minute while the photographers snapped away. When a lull finally became audible, the attorney general said, "I'd like to thank the ladies and gentlemen of the media for coming on such short notice. Our purpose in asking you here is to announce a new investigative thrust in our efforts to identify and apprehend the individual who has been referred to as the Freedom Killer. We are asking for the public's cooperation. It is our belief someone out there has information that could help us with this case. To provide some of the specifics, I'll turn the microphone over to the Director of the FBI, Bob August."

The attorney general stepped to the side, and August moved behind the podium, bringing a fresh eruption of flashes. He waited a moment and then started speaking. "The FBI has established a hotline for any citizens who may want to phone in information about these crimes. In the event someone is worried about their voice being recorded, we have also set up an E-mail terminal for the same purpose. All information, whether phoned in or sent via E-mail, will be handled in the strictest confidence." The Department of Justice media representative walked up next to the Director, holding a large white cardboard sign with both numbers printed on it. August continued, "Now I'd like to introduce you to the agent who was able to stop the attempt on Reverend Epps's life yesterday. He'll be able to take some of your questions. Ladies and gentlemen, Special Agent Mike Devlin."

The flashes strobed for a full minute. A number of the photographers moved closer, trying to get the full detail of the unhealed cuts on Devlin's face. Although he was ill at ease with all the attention, Devlin stood stoically through the neoburlesque moment, dutifully posing as the steely-eyed FBI agent the nation was expecting to see.

When things finally settled down, the media representative placed the sign he had been holding on an easel, stepped up next to Devlin, and pointed at a female reporter. She stood up and asked, "How did the FBI uncover the plot to kill Reverend Epps?"

That figures, Devlin thought—the one question that could destroy the plan to have the Freedom Killer send an electronic message would be the first one asked. The assassination had been prevented by tracing the killer's E-mail, but if that was to come out now, he would never send another. Devlin had constructed a lie that he felt would stand up under cursory examination, but if the media became curious enough, it probably wouldn't last forty-eight hours. However, if all went well, that would be long enough. "Previously, we were able to identify one of the aliases this individual was using. Further investigation determined that the name was used on a flight from Los Angeles to Washington, D.C. The plane involved in that particular flight was the one in which the Los Angeles police found a bomb. Interviews of the passengers and entire flight crew identified a number of people who remembered the person we believe planted the bomb. Two days ago, that same flight crew had a layover in Washington, and as luck would have it, one of the flight attendants was checking out of the hotel yesterday morning and thought she recognized the same individual getting off an elevator in the lobby. She called us, and working backwards, we were able to determine that Reverend Epps was the target."

The same reporter asked, "How did you find one person among all of those guests? Did he use the same alias?"

"The first thing we checked was the alias, but no one by that name was registered there. During his previous acts, we had learned that he would use a false identity once and never return to it. We were also able to find out that he did not have credit cards for each of his other aliases, so we asked the hotel who had registered without using a credit card. There was only one person who hadn't. Subsequent investigation of that individual led us to the plot against Reverend Epps."

"Could you elaborate on your subsequent investigation?"

"I'm sorry, I've been as specific as I can until this phase of the investigation is completed."

The media rep pointed at someone else.

"Could you give us the alias and the name of the hotel?"

Devlin flashed a courteous smile at the reporter for a moment, and the room grew quiet as everyone waited for the answer. "You didn't really think your job was going to be that easy today, did you?" A ripple of polite laughter broke out. "I'm sorry, we're still working on that."

Another reporter was picked. "Do you think this killer will strike again?"

The *killer*? Even the attorney general had called him that. Whatever happened to *cataclysmist*? Devlin wondered. He had felt certain the term would endure. It was original and unusual and, most important, was a one-word explanation of the story. Fashion, he decided, would never be his calling. "I don't know, but that's why we've established these numbers, so someone can contact us and we can stop him—hopefully before he attempts anything else."

Another reporter stood up. "Agent Devlin, what will your role now be in this investigation?"

Devlin glanced at O'Hare. "I've been ordered to remain at FBI headquarters, coordinating the investigation from there."

"From your tone, it doesn't sound like being confined to the Hoover Building would be your first choice."

"I'd rather be working leads than creating them, but this is what I've been assigned to do."

The media rep recognized another reporter. "Has there been an update of the Freedom Killer's profile?"

"Yes, there has. We now think that in our initial profile, this individual's intellect and ability were overestimated. From the way he has bungled the last two crimes he has attempted, we realize he couldn't be as smart as he first appeared. More than likely, he is an academic dropout, and may even be a recent releasee from a mental institution. Additionally, this type of individual is usually unattractive and incapable of any kind of social interaction, especially with women. He is using these acts to prove his manhood to everyone, especially himself, but in reality he is simply a coward, who kills men, women, and children so he can feel better about himself."

Then another reporter asked, "The last two times he sent warnings and you were able to stop him. Do you think he will next time?"

"I don't think he has that kind of confidence in himself any longer."

A somber-faced reporter got to his feet. "I'm still not satisfied with your explanation of how the assassination attempt on Reverend Epps was prevented. Could you be more specific?"

Once again, the thing Devlin had tried to downplay the most was threatening their plan. He had to find a way out. Quickly, he went through a mental checklist of the points Hagstrom had wanted him to make and was satisfied he had covered the important ones. Smiling, he said, "I think I've already evaded that question once. Anyone else?"

"What do you think this guy's goal is?"

"Ultimately"—Devlin reflected thoughtfully for a moment—"an erection."

The roar of laughter that went up launched the media coordinator forward to the microphone. "I'm sorry, we don't have time for any more questions."

Someone from the crowd yelled back, "Don't worry. After that, we won't need any more answers."

Devlin glanced at O'Hare, who shook his head in disbelief. The Detroit street agent didn't have the courage to look at the Director. If he had, he would have seen a small smile of understanding hiding in Bob August's eyes.

Just before Joe LoFranco regained consciousness, he had the sensation of riding through the darkness on a Tilt-a-Whirl. He kept trying to sit up straight, but the centrifugal force held him in check. All his organs—his brain, and even his testicles—were swept to one side. A rushing silence slammed shut somewhere inside of him, and his eyes opened. Pain clamped onto the left side of his head, and the more awake he became, the deeper it bit into him. Something cool was draining from his aching left eye, and as he attempted to wipe it away, he realized that his hands were taped to the arms of a thick oak chair. Suddenly, he heard Devlin's voice. "Thank God," he mumbled.

But then people started laughing. What the hell was going on? He forced his mind to focus. Next to him sat the Freedom Killer, watching the news.

A vicious sneer curved his lips as he realized the FBI agent had come to. "You don't think I'm that unattractive, do you, Joseph?" There was no reply. "I'll bet it wouldn't take me long to get you to tell me how handsome I am."

From his crooked perspective, LoFranco spit at the sadistic face, but missed.

The killer turned back to the television and watched the end of the news conference. Devlin stepped away from the podium, exposing the card with the two hotline numbers on it. Immediately above it was the Department of Justice seal.

"Joseph, I knew what I wanted to do next, but not where. Now I do. And with your help, I think we'll be able to involve Special Agent Devlin."

||| CHAPTER 41 |||

Devlin looked around room 511 to make sure he hadn't forgotten anything. The only remaining evidence of his and Bonelli's days and nights there were the markings on the wall that had helped them decipher the killer's movements. Devlin felt as if he were abandoning something trustworthy and, more important, something lucky. He hoped the new space would be as accommodating.

O'Hare had told Devlin that ten agents would man the phones at another location in the building, and when they received a worthwhile call, it was to be transferred to room 621. There, two more agents, experienced in handling tips, would further filter any calls before passing them on to Devlin. It was a two-tier screening system designed to ensure Devlin's availability. If instead he became tied up in meaningless conversations and the killer happened to phone in instead of E-mailing him, Devlin might miss the call. Twelve-hour shifts had been set up for the two agents who shared the room with Devlin and Bonelli. As soon as he walked in, Devlin noticed that both the jacketless agents had Browning 9-millimeters in their holsters. The only agents allowed to carry those weapons were members of the Hostage Rescue Team. Evidently, O'Hare felt Devlin needed a little extra protection. "Any calls?" he asked them.

"A few from the usual full-moon worshipers, but there was one I think you'll find interesting." As the agent started leafing through a small stack of chits, Devlin noticed that the second agent, although reading the newspaper, was absentmindedly using the speed dial on one of his telephones over and over. "Here it is," the first agent said. "This woman called and said she saw you on TV and liked all your macho talk about erections, and if you're man enough, she'd like you to meet her at the Still and Grill in Georgetown at eight o'clock tonight. Said to ask for Knox." He handed Devlin the message and gave him a single, conspiratorial eyebrow salute acknowledging his good fortune.

Devlin folded the paper and put it in his pocket. "Sounds promising." The speed dialer was still at it. Devlin nodded toward him. "What's with him?"

"Jack just transferred in from L.A. Took major pipe on a divorce. I tried to talk to him because I've been there myself, but the lad's in denial. Blames the whole thing on his ex's lawyer, one of those slip-and-fall pukes who advertises on TV. So Jack waits until there is no one in the law office and calls the guy's machine on the eight hundred number and then hangs up. He does this as many times as he can, and the way he figures it, next month when the phone bill comes, there'll be an extra ten grand in coast-to-coast charges. You've got to admit, it is poetic."

Bonelli was sitting at a desk at the opposite end of the room. Surrounding him were several stacks of folders, arranged neatly on the floor. Pinned to the wall at eye level was a collage made up of several pieces of paper taped together. The wall markings from room 511 had been carefully copied on them. The letters and numbers were even the same size. Evidently, Bonelli also found them reassuring. Devlin wondered if the clerk hadn't placed them there as his own personal Rosetta stone, to interpret any future intentions of the Freedom Killer. "Are you all settled in?" Devlin asked.

"In, and ready for *the* call."

"Have we heard from LoFranco?"

"He hasn't called me."

Devlin turned around. "Either of you guys get a call from the Annapolis RA?" Both agents shook their heads. Devlin dialed the resident agency. After the third ring, an answering machine identified the number as FBI Annapolis. Once the beep sounded, Devlin left a message for LoFranco to call him. Then he turned to Bonelli. "Have you finished running that list of MMI dropouts?"

"I checked them through my database and got nothing. I'm still waiting on some criminal histories and automobile registrations."

Devlin checked his watch. "How much longer are you going to be here?"

"If nothing comes up, probably an hour or so."

"If LoFranco calls while you're here, get a number where I can reach him in a couple of hours. I want to see how he's doing with those interviews."

"Anything else?"

Devlin stabbed his thumb over his shoulder in the direction of the monitoring agents. "Give each of those guys a copy of the MMI list. If someone calls in with one of those names, they'll be able to match it up." Devlin picked up the list and scanned it. "I know it's a long shot, but there's something that feels right about this."

"Where will you be?"

"At the Still and Grill in Georgetown, but I'm going to see O'Hare first."

"After that television performance, he'll probably want to offer you the Bureau spokesman job."

Devlin laughed. "Right now I think the Freedom Killer would be more welcome in his office."

O'Hare was seated at his desk writing when Devlin entered and said, "I thought I'd turn myself in."

"Christ, Mike, I know you had to stop the questions before they blew up our plan, but you're supposed to do it with a little diplomacy."

"I guess I offended the wrong people, because our guy hasn't called yet."

"I assumed that. The agents doing the monitoring in your room have strict orders to notify me as soon as he does."

"Speaking of those agents, when did the Hostage Rescue Team start taking tips?"

The section chief blushed slightly. "Okay, you caught me. I just wanted to be safe."

"How about the rest of HRT?"

"They're saddled up and ready to go."

"Where are they staged?"

"The Baltimore Washington International Airport. It's between Baltimore, Annapolis, and Laurel. We've got helicopters and vehicles standing by, depending on where they have to go."

"Sounds like all we need now is a little cooperation from the killer."

"Why do you think he hasn't called?" O'Hare asked.

"Maybe he hasn't seen the news yet."

"Maybe he's had enough."

"I'll believe that when his two-week deadline passes without anything else happening," Devlin said.

"I've lost track; when is that?"

"In two days."

"You don't think he's quit?"

"He's got too much time, money, and hate invested in this to leave without saying good-bye."

"I hope you're right, at least about calling. We've got a lot of people, in and outside the Bureau, holding their breath," O'Hare said.

"Give him a little time. That attempt on Epps was just yesterday morning."

"God, it seems like a week ago."

"That's because we've done a week's worth of work since then."

"Okay. I've got to go see your new best friend right now."

"Who's that?" Devlin asked.

"The Director."

"The Director?"

"Why do you think you're not on a plane back to Detroit? He actually liked the way you handled the press conference—considering your primary assignment was to piss the killer off."

"No kidding. When you get up there, tell Bob that Mike says, Hey."

The Still and Grill was located in one of those trendy Georgetown buildings that was supposed to look like the nineteenth century on the outside and the twenty-first on the inside. The exterior consisted of ancient brick walls, sandblasted into a second life, which rose up to restored ornate cornices, while the interior use of acrylics, patterned laminates, and neon lighting was designed to transport the customers two hundred years forward once they stepped across the threshold.

Devlin found Knox at a small, dark table in the back. He kissed her carefully, hoping her mood was not as somber as the table she had chosen. She responded with equal caution.

He sat down, and they looked at one another tentatively. Finally she said, "I guess last night got a little out of hand."

"I should have called and told you what happened instead of just walking in and scaring you like that."

"Mike, that did frighten me, but there's something else about this whole thing that scares me even more."

"What's that?"

"That you'll turn this into another vendetta like Gentkill."

"That man executed four FBI agents, all very decent people."

"And you killed him."

"He tried to kill me."

"You could have arrested him." Devlin didn't say anything. "I think I understand why you did it, but it scares the hell out of me that there's this vigilante hidden inside you."

"This case is different. It's not personal."

"Among others, four children were murdered, and it's not personal? I know you better than that, Mike."

"Okay, *I'm different.* Sometimes you have to do something insane, and as much as it seems necessary at the time, you eventually realize you could never do it again. I can still feel my thumb pushing that detonator button and then the concussion from the blast. It's like Vietnam—I went there because I felt I had to at the time, but I could never do it again. There's only so much of that in a man, and I'm afraid all mine is used up."

"Then why are you on television insulting this maniac?"

Devlin glanced around to make sure that no one was within earshot and then lowered his voice as a further precaution. "We're trying to make him angry enough to send a message so we can trace him. I'm just the messenger."

"You stand up on the national news and tell the world that he is an impotent escapee from a mental institution, and you think he'll take it out on the government and not you?"

"Do you remember my answer about not being able to leave the headquarters building? That's the only place he knows where to find me. He's smart enough to figure out he'll never get past security, so the only way he can strike back at me is by sending a message. It was my job to get him so frustrated he couldn't help but do that."

"Mike, one thing is clear: This person is clever. Couldn't he find out our hotel or follow you to a restaurant? He could be here right now."

"I'm very surveillance-conscious. If he tried to follow me, this case would be over." Devlin reached into his suit jacket, took out a key, and handed it to her. "Here."

"What's this?"

"On the way over here, I moved us to another hotel, the Avalon, just to be safe. We're now Mr. and Mrs. Lawson. And you're right—this guy *is* clever. That's what gives him his power. But what makes him so smart is orchestrating all this death at a distance, which is exactly why he doesn't want to go one-on-one with me, or anyone else. Distance is important to him. Through it, he can commit murder while avoiding the dangers of being close to the crime. He relies on cleverness to avoid confrontation, not to cause it. For him, it proves his superiority."

"So, once again, you see no danger for yourself."

"O'Hare won't let me out, and this guy can't get in. You tell me where the danger is."

"The problem isn't keeping him from you; it's keeping you away from him."

The waiter came, and Devlin ordered a glass of wine for Knox and a beer for himself.

"Don't underestimate your power of persuasion," he said. "I've given what you said last night a lot of thought. That's why I didn't argue with O'Hare when he grounded me." He reached across the table and took her hand. "Knox, for the first time since I became an agent, I have no desire to trade punches with this guy—or anyone else."

Her eyes softened. "It's just that I worry about you."

"I'm glad you do."

"Does that mean you're going to be more careful?"

"That thing with Epps scared the hell out of me, if that answers your question."

She smiled sincerely. "It does."

"So, how did I look on TV?"

"Very mythical."

"You can't do any better than that."

She put her other hand over his. "Seeing all of that on the national news did make me realize the importance of what you're doing. I am very proud of you."

The waiter brought their drinks.

She held up her glass to him. "Here's to fear. May you grow old to enjoy it."

||| CHAPTER 42 |||

The guard looked at the FBI identification and said, "What brings you to the Department of Justice this morning, Agent LoFranco?"

Joseph LoFranco's credentials had not been difficult to alter. The killer needed to take only three Polaroids of himself before he was able to duplicate the size of the ID photo. Then, with a little glue on the back, he positioned it over LoFranco's picture. Under the protective plastic of the ID case, the telltale edges of the new photograph were virtually impossible to detect.

"I'm with the Bureau's Technical Services Unit." He patted an oversize briefcase that looked like it could be a toolbox. "Someone called and said there were some strange noises on the phones down in the heating plant. I guess in a building so full of lawyers, you'd have to figure sooner or later the paranoia would find its way even to the basement."

The guard laughed. "I'll have to remember that one."

"Anyway, I got the short straw. They told me to come over here and sweep the lines."

The guard pointed at a bank of elevators. "Any of those will get you down there." The guard winked. "Who do you suppose it is, the Mafia or the KGB?"

"I would hope that both of them have better things to do. I know I have." The guard chuckled and watched as the Freedom Killer walked to the elevators and pressed the DOWN button.

When Devlin arrived at the monitoring room that morning, he introduced himself to the two midnight-to-noon agents. "Oh, yeah," one of them said, "the hard-on guy."

He smiled and shook hands. Yes, he thought, I have taken the Devlin name about as far as it can go.

"Here's the calls we've taken," the agent said as he handed over a thick stack of papers. "And here's what the day crew left." Devlin took the second set from him.

He sat down at his desk and started reading the tips, not only for "good-looking" suspects, but to determine if the killer had called in himself, posing as a helpful citizen. Although the agents working the hotlines had been warned about the tactic, Devlin thought it was still a possibility. It was not unusual for a serial offender to attempt to insert himself into an ongoing investigation to gain information. Someone who was clever could pump an unsuspecting agent and obtain details that would not normally be available to people outside of law enforcement.

And there was one other ploy the killer might try: He could phone in an innocent-looking tip to set up whatever he intended to do next. Devlin had no idea what that might be, but he thought if that was the case, it might be discoverable by a thorough analysis of the calls.

For the next hour, he read and reread the tip sheets, trying each time to probe deeper and deeper into the twisted maze of the killer's mind, searching for a possible target. During the fourth time through, he realized he had lost his objectivity. A woman who had been at the Reverend Epps's breakfast called in and said she had recently seen an individual who resembled the man who had fired the shots. During the previous reading, Devlin had written across the top of her tip, *Was this caller really a woman?* Obviously, it was time to stop. Shuffling the pages into a neat pile, he put them on Bonelli's desk.

Twenty minutes later the computer specialist arrived. The sight of Devlin and the two other agents sitting lethargically at their desks told him the case status. "I guess he didn't call."

Devlin nodded at the new stack of papers on the clerk's desk. "Everybody *but* him. When you get settled, how about running the names of both the callers and the suspects. Let's see if anyone is fibbing to us." Devlin picked up the phone and dialed.

"FBI Annapolis."

"This is Mike Devlin down at headquarters. Is Joe Lo-Franco there?"

"No he's not, Mike."

"I left a message for him last night and he never called back."

"He probably hasn't been back here yet. This thing has us all buried. In fact, I'm the only one here and I'm on my way out the door. I haven't seen Joe in two or three days."

"Is that normal for him?"

"If he's working on something hot, he can get pretty intense."

"Does he live alone?"

"Yeah, he has an apartment in town."

"Could you give me his home phone? I'll try him there." After receiving the number, Devlin disconnected the line and redialed.

On the third ring, LoFranco's recorded voice told Devlin to leave a name and number. He left a message and hung up. "Tony, what time did we get that fax from Joe yesterday, the one with the MMI suspects?"

Bonelli picked up one of the folders on the floor and after searching through it briefly, pulled out a piece of paper. "Uh, four forty-seven."

"And you never talked to him after that?"

"No."

One of the monitoring agents put half a dozen new tips on Devlin's desk. "You can just about tell when they're running sound bites from your news conference last night—they get a surge in calls downstairs."

The pattern for the rest of the morning was the same. After the television in the room was switched on, the tips came in small, predictable clumps. The majority were telephonic, but a few were sent via computer. Devlin scrutinized them all, but the one they wanted still hadn't come.

At noon, the monitoring agents were relieved by the same two noon-to-midnight men from the day before. The mandatory low-voltage insults that usually occur during an FBI guard change were exchanged. "You're late, bitch."

"I'd rather be late than a *sniveling* bitch."

"See you tomorrow."

With that accomplished, Jack unfolded his newspaper, put his feet up, and went to work on the speed dial.

A little before one o'clock, O'Hare and Hagstrom walked

in. After being briefed on the tips, O'Hare asked Hagstrom, "Why hasn't he called?"

"He's going to do something. What worries me is how long he's taking. We were hoping for a quick, emotional blunder, but that hasn't happened. He's more controlled than I had hoped. I'm afraid he's working on something above average."

"Why hasn't he at least sent Mike a fuck-you?"

"Maybe he's tailoring this next one to make Mikey look especially foolish." Hagstrom smiled at Devlin. "Maybe he's going to demand you do another press conference."

Devlin was relieved to hear laughter about anything connected with his television appearance, even if it was at his expense. "Maybe he thinks he's already won," O'Hare offered.

Hagstrom said, "Not if he's seen the morning papers. They're carrying front-page articles about amusement park attendance, airline reservations, and over-the-counter pharmaceutical sales all being up, higher than when all this started. I think everybody has decided to send *him* a fuck-you. This country may have its problems, but being willing to be kicked around is never going to be one of them."

||| CHAPTER 43 |||

Less than fifteen minutes after O'Hare and Hagstrom left, one of the monitoring agents' voices sawed through the air with unmistakable gravity: "Mike, I think this is him."

Devlin vaulted from his chair and hurried to the computer screen. The message read:

Agent Devlin—

Sorry I missed you the other day at the Convention Center. But I've found a substitute—the previous owner of the credentials numbered 9817.

From across the room, Bonelli could see the anguish on Devlin's face. He grabbed his canes and struggled to his feet. "What is it, Mike, some nut?" Instead of answering, Devlin just stared at the screen.

The other agent held up his phone. "Mike, this one's asking for you by name. Sounds like he's got a problem."

Devlin was afraid he knew what the message meant. If he was right, the last thing he wanted to do was answer the phone. A terrible certainty came over him that 9817 was Joe LoFranco's credential number. "Hello."

"Mike!" The voice, torn with pain, was barely recognizable, but it was LoFranco's. His words were released slowly, as if each one was being censored under the penalty of death. "He's got me, Mike. He cut one of my fingers off. Said he's going to call back every fifteen minutes. Each time you're not there, he's going to cut off another one. Wants to make sure you stay there so you can't stop him." There was a violent scream, and then the line went dead.

O'Hare, who had been called by Bonelli, came running in. Devlin yelled at the agents, "Did you get it?"

Jack hung up the phone. "Yeah, they got it downstairs. Comes back to a William Packard at an address just outside of Annapolis." He handed a slip of paper to Devlin.

Devlin said to O'Hare, "He's got Joe LoFranco," and then told him what he had said.

Bonelli had queried his computer. "Mike, William Packard

is one of the names on LoFranco's list of MMI cadets. It all fits."

O'Hare said, "Okay, I'll have HRT up there in no time. I'm going, too." O'Hare looked at the monitoring agents. "Both of you come with me; we're going to need all the manpower we can get. Mike, you have to stay here and stall him if he calls back." Moving toward the door, he said, "Don't worry, we'll get Joe out of there."

As soon as Devlin looked at him, O'Hare diverted his eyes, revealing the frailty of his promise.

A half hour later, as O'Hare led a speeding convoy of agents and equipment along Route 301, another message appeared on the monitoring room screen:

Devlin—
   There might be a sarin bomb in the DOJ building. I don't think anyone but you is clever enough to deal with it. If it is there, it will go off at 3 P.M. However, Joseph and I will be calling in a few minutes, and if you're not there, instead of his finger, I will take his life. What a quandary. My dick is getting hard.

Bonelli said, "Is this for real, or is it more of his gasoline bullshit?"

Devlin checked his watch: It was two-fifteen. Forty-five minutes to go! *Was* this another ruse? Was there really a bomb? If not and he ran off to the Department of Justice, he would be responsible for LoFranco's death. But if he stayed to protect LoFranco's life and there was a bomb, thousands of people could be killed. He had to find out. "Tony, do you have a DOJ phone list?"

Bonelli opened a desk drawer and quickly leafed through a dozen different phone directories until he found it.

Devlin grabbed it and found the number for the front security desk. "This is Mike Devlin with the FBI. We have an emergency. Can you tell me if an agent by the name Joseph LoFranco logged in last night or today?"

"Hold on while I check." Thirty seconds later, he came back on the line. "Yeah, at 10:05 A.M. this morning."

"You've got to evacuate. There may be a bomb in your building."

"Who is this again?"

Devlin handed the phone to Bonelli. "Try and convince him. It won't be easy. I'm going over there."

"What about Joe?"

Devlin had made two decisions. First, a bomb had been planted. Since LoFranco had his own U.S. Attorney in Maryland, he would have had no reason to meet with anyone from DOJ in Washington, so the killer must have used his identification to gain access to wherever he had planted the device. Second, because LoFranco now knew the identity of the killer, he was going to be murdered no matter what Devlin did. Unless O'Hare could get there in time.

There was no question about the Freedom Killer's brilliance. Most of the legal arm of the federal government was in that building, and there would not be enough time to convince anyone else to respond to the threat. It was all so logical: He had to go. But he couldn't desert LoFranco. He stood staring at Bonelli.

One of the hotline phones rang. Both men, sensing something, froze. It rang again.

Devlin pulled the phone off its cradle. "Devlin."

One of the agents taking calls downstairs said, "I think this is the same guy that just called you."

Reluctantly, Devlin said, "Joe?"

"Mike, you're *still* there?" Although LoFranco's voice was

still filled with pain, it held a certain resolve, as if he understood that nothing could be done. Devlin remembered him kicking down the door of the burning house and racing in. He had seemed so indestructible. More than anything, Devlin wanted to tell him to hold on, to remind him that the call was being traced and that help was on the way. But the killer was listening. He allowed himself to say only, "I'm here, Joe."

"You've got to go get that bomb," LoFranco urged.

Devlin was certain the killer was standing over LoFranco, willing to kill him at the utterance of the first syllable of the first wrong word. "I'm staying right here," he lied, hoping to buy LoFranco some time.

The tortured agent answered with a short, peaceful laugh. Then his speech became broken, its rhythm disjointed, Devlin supposed, by pain. "Don't be stupid. *Mike,* you've got it— *backwards.* Don't worry about me. This son of a bitch can kiss my *buttsss*—" LoFranco's voice trailed off in a hiss of agony, and then the call was disconnected.

In a low, pleading tone, Bonelli continued to talk into his phone. He shrugged his shoulders at Devlin to tell him he wasn't making any progress with the security guard. Then he said to Devlin, "Isn't there some sort of emergency code I can give this guy?"

"There may be, but I'm from Detroit, I wouldn't know it."

"Can't you call the attorney general's office?"

"If we can't convince a guard, by the time we got through to anybody higher up, it would be too late. Call the Director's office. Maybe they can do something," Devlin said as he ran out the door.

||| CHAPTER 44 |||

Devlin ran down the street. The Department of Justice was one block away. Involuntarily, LoFranco's last words replayed themselves. Incredibly, he had used them to sign his own death warrant, forcing Devlin to deal with the bomb.

He made himself stop thinking about LoFranco. Sarin gas, according to a counterterrorism squad memo he had read in Detroit, had been used by domestic terrorists in Japan and could be produced from common insecticides. It was a hydrogen-cyanide gas, and the last bomb the group had planted was found unexploded near a ventilation duct. According to experts, the device, although relatively small, was potent enough to kill as many as ten thousand people. Devlin couldn't remember its long chemical name, but he did recall the gas was an extremely lethal substance that short-circuited the nervous system. Within seconds of exposure, muscles all over the body went into spasms, causing vomiting, choking, convulsion, and death. At room temperature, sarin was a liquid, so the killer, by attaching it to a bomb, had indicated how it was to be used: The purpose of the explosive was not to kill or maim but to vaporize the liquid and disperse the gas into the air. Because the DOJ building was so layered and compartmentalized, Devlin figured that the killer, following the lead of the Japanese terrorists, would have to go for the ventilation system, which meant the basement.

As he got to the front entrance, he didn't see many people leaving, which meant Bonelli still hadn't convinced anyone that an emergency existed. Bomb threats had become so common at federal buildings, officials tended to demand more than a phone call before taking action.

The lobby of the huge stone building was tall and gray, reflecting its architectural intention to be as cold and dispassionate as ideal justice. Devlin ran up to the nearest guard and held up his credentials. "There's a bomb in the building and you've got"—he looked at his watch—"twenty-five minutes until it goes off." Security people behind a long desk picked up their phones and started dialing frantically. A startled murmur rose from the people within earshot, and they started streaming toward the door. The guard took a cautious step toward Devlin. "Let me see that ID again."

Devlin pushed the identification into his hands. "Which way to the basement?"

While still studying the photograph on the ID, the guard unconsciously pointed to the elevators. When Devlin turned to go, he said, "Hold it!"

Devlin took off his coat and let it drop to the floor. The guard seemed more convinced by the sight of his 9-millimeter than the identification. Calmly, Devlin said, "You now have twenty-four minutes. Evacuate this building and call the Metro bomb squad."

The guard ran to his desk as Devlin disappeared into the elevator.

In the basement, the doors opened and he could see people streaming past, their eyes full of controlled panic, focused on escape. Most of them were headed for the stairs, but some stopped short when they saw the elevator arrive. A black man in a suit got on. Devlin asked him, "Which way to the physical plant?"

"Man, you better get out of the building—there's supposed to be a bomb in here."

Grabbing hold of the automatic door, Devlin repeated his question: "Which way?"

"Straight down, past the double doors, on the left," he said, and ripped Devlin's hand away.

Once he was past the double doors, the vibration of the huge furnaces combating the January weather led Devlin quickly to the heating plant. He was amazed by the amount of machinery and ductwork that was there. The air was filled with the oily, metallic odor of electrical machinery working. He glanced at his watch—nineteen minutes to go. "It has to be in the ducts," he reasoned out loud, as if asking for confirmation from the unconcerned furnaces. "Somewhere it wouldn't be easy to find." He scanned the impenetrable forest of huge knotted cylinders hanging from the ceiling and decided on a plan of attack.

Squeezing along a side wall, he started walking to the rear of the plant. Halfway back, he noticed thick dust on the seldom-traveled floor. He looked behind him and saw his own footprints. Bisecting the room, he swung under some low ductwork and started searching for another set of prints. Careful not to come up on his own tracks, he kept changing directions, narrowing down his search area. Finally, there they were— one set going, one coming. He had lost track of where the door was, so he knelt down and looked under the massive pipes. Once he spotted the entrance, he followed the killer's footprints in the opposite direction.

He didn't have to go far to find where they ended. A small trampled space on the floor showed where the killer had stood and labored.

Directly above, Devlin found the bomb taped to one of the large ducts.

The immediate area was well lighted, and Devlin found that

puzzling, considering the killer's usual concern for conceal-ment. But then he noticed the surface above the device. In thick black letters, a message had been left on the duct work, obviously for him. DID I SAY 3:00? MY MISTAKE. He checked the bomb's timer—only four minutes left!

Devlin now realized he was standing in front of certain death. Knox and everyone else had been right. Apparently, he had been so glaringly self-destructive that even the killer had figured him out. His entire plan had depended on it. LoFranco's second call had been programmed to send Devlin eagerly to the bomb without enough time to defeat it.

He had four minutes to get out, to run. But hundreds of people were still in the building. He couldn't leave; if he did, what Joe LoFranco had done would become meaningless. And he was sure the killer had planned on that, too.

Maybe the answer was not in neutralizing the bomb but in disabling the heating system. If he could turn off the blower on the furnace, the gas produced by the explosion would be con-tained within the basement. After examining the machinery around him briefly, he realized it would take too much time to figure out.

The bomb was more complex than the one that had been dis-covered aboard the plane. But then the killer had expected Devlin to find this one. The timer and battery were set in a thick acrylic case that was positioned deep enough into the plastic explosive to give the impression that it was booby-trapped.

He estimated there was one to one and a half pounds of C-4. Enough to kill him if he made a mistake, especially since he would be the first recipient of the gas.

But something was preventing the device from sitting flush against the pipe. He peered into the tiny telltale crack that separated it from the duct and saw a hint of something metallic. Devlin remembered being surprised that the bomb on the plane hadn't been booby-trapped. But it looked like this one was. Like all serial offenders, the Freedom Killer was evidently improving his craft. Devlin felt certain a secondary triggering mechanism existed and was positioned between the C-4 and the ductwork so that if the entire bomb was pulled free, a pressure-release switch would instantaneously detonate it.

The timer read three and a half minutes!

Devlin closed his eyes and drew in a deep breath. He held it for a few seconds and then, releasing it slowly, he opened his eyes. He studied the device and ignored the dwindling deadline.

Although the timer and blasting cap seemed too risky to disarm, the canister containing the liquid sarin appeared to be strapped to the outside of the C-4 with only the one long continuous strip of heavy gray tape that held the entire bomb to the pipe. The only option left was to separate the canister from the bomb. The damage from the explosive would be minimal compared to what the vaporized sarin would do. But had the killer again anticipated Devlin's analysis and subsequent course of action?

From his pocket, he took a small stainless-steel penknife his daughter and son had given him for Christmas just a couple of weeks before. It had a nail file, scissors, and a single blade.

The blade was still razor-sharp. Carefully, he started sawing through the tape, along the line between the C-4 and the container that was full of liquid. Halfway through, he could not see any problems, so he cut a little faster, until the tape was severed completely. Ever so slowly, he peeled the canister away from the bomb.

Suddenly, he saw the edge of a recess cut into the plastic explosive. Devlin didn't have to go any farther to know it contained another pressure-release booby trap. He rolled the container back over the bomb and held the two parts together firmly. He laughed out loud. The killer had even been able to predict exactly how Devlin would try to disable the device. It was perfect: Devlin couldn't run now, because as soon as he removed his hands, the components would separate and the bomb would detonate. And within seconds, staying would cost him his life, too.

He looked at the knife in his hands and thought of Katie and Pat. And Knox. She knew this day would come, but he had chosen to ignore it. Given another chance, he vowed, things would be different.

He decided he had to do something. Carefully, he started separating the container from the C-4 again until he could see the triggering mechanism. He slipped the knife blade between it and the sarin canister. And then, while keeping pressure on the booby trap with the blade in his left hand, he very gradually unrolled the liquid container from the tape. Although he had not intended to, he looked at the timer—thirty seconds left!

Once the sarin was free from the bomb, he lowered the canister and held it between his knees. With his right hand, he took the dangling tape and tried to wrap it around the booby trap to keep the pressure on it. But the tape seemed to have too much give in it to hold the triggering device by itself, so he pushed the thicker body of the knife against it and held it firmly. Ten seconds!

Now he had to get the tape across the knife and hope it would hold until he got out of there. He pulled the gray strip as tight as he could across the knife and quickly smoothed the tape down on the duct to hold everything together. *Four seconds!*

Holding the sarin with both hands, Devlin ran. He knew he was racing death to the door. He was four feet from it when the bomb exploded.

||| CHAPTER 45 |||

The Hostage Rescue Team never had a more personal mission: to save one of their own. Its leaders were assembled in a grade school parking lot, three blocks from the house where Joe LoFranco was being held and tortured. Tom O'Hare spoke quickly: "Is your perimeter in?"

"Yes, sir, Baltimore SWAT has it locked down," answered the HRT commander.

"Okay. He's already threatened to kill LoFranco, so I want an immediate entry. No telephone, no bullhorn, no negotiation. Just swift and, if need be, deadly entry. William Packard has taken enough lives; don't hesitate to take his." O'Hare's voice avoided the usual emotion of such an order, giving it that much more authority. "Have your people seen anything of him?"

"Let me get an update, sir." The commander turned away from the small group so he could hear better. "This is Hotel Romeo Tango One. Does anyone have any movement?" He pressed his hand tightly over the radio's earpiece. After listening to the responses for a few seconds, he turned back toward O'Hare. "Negative, sir."

"How long until you can make entry?"

The team leader checked his watch. "Ten minutes."

"Okay, let's go get him out of there."

As the HRT commander entered his car, he spoke again into

the radio. "Observers, get up to the doors and see what you can hear. We are going in. Entry in one zero minutes."

Two agents low-crawled up to the small house, one toward each entrance. Warily, they pushed small, flat motion detectors under the doors and listened with special earplugs. Half a block away, their team leader brought his car to a stop out of sight of the house. The motion detectors were to establish where any movement might be within the house. The commander transmitted, "Does anyone have anything?" Both answers were negative. "Who has the rear entry?"

"Team Three here."

"How does it look?"

"It'll go down without a problem."

"Copy. Team One, do you have the front?"

"Affirmative."

"Can you flash-bang it on my signal?"

"That's ten-four."

"All units, we're going in, in zero five minutes. Everyone stand by."

Four additional HRT members, all heavily armed, crept up to the back door and waited.

O'Hare sat in his car, fifty yards away, watching the front of the house while he listened to the tactical radio traffic. Like anyone asked to make life-and-death decisions, he was second-guessing himself. Was sending HRT headlong into the house the right thing to do? If they could get to Packard before he could get to LoFranco, it was. He refused to think of the alternative.

From the front of Packard's residence, O'Hare saw a blinding flash a split second before a startling explosion. He stomped the accelerator.

Within moments, the entry team transmitted, "We're in!" Cars screeched up to the front of the house, trying to further disorient Packard. The Baltimore SWAT team maneuvered closer to the house, tightening the perimeter. They took up firing positions behind any cover available.

O'Hare abandoned the safety of his car and ran to the rear of the structure. He could hear the agents inside barking militarily to one another as they worked their way through the rooms. Another door was kicked in.

As the section chief came through the back door, one of the HRT men swung around and pointed a small black machine gun at him before he realized who it was. Then, on the agent's radio, O'Hare recognized the HRT commander's voice. "The location is secure." O'Hare held his breath, waiting for the rest of the transmission that said LoFranco was safe. It never came. He hurried through the house.

Sitting in a chair with his arms and legs taped down was LoFranco. One hand was wrapped in a bloody rag; his head craned forward uncomfortably. The cause of death was not immediately apparent. The commander said, "He used his knife again, at the base of the skull."

O'Hare walked behind the chair and saw the terrible wound.

"If it's any consolation, sir, he's been dead for a while."

O'Hare looked at the blood on LoFranco's neck and saw it was partially dry. "What about Packard?"

The commander pushed open an adjoining bathroom door. Lying on the stained white tile floor was William Packard, a look of surprise locked into his lifeless face. A very small hole in his right temple oozed a bloody trickle. A small-caliber automatic with a silencer lay on top of his half-open hand. "Because of the silencer, we never heard the shot. He's also been dead for a while. The way I see it, LoFranco was dead before we got here, and Packard probably spotted us or SWAT setting up and knew it was over. He evidently thought he was saving us the trouble."

O'Hare looked back at LoFranco's body. "That's too bad. It wouldn't have been any trouble at all."

||| CHAPTER 46 |||

"Mrs. Devlin?"

"Yes."

"I'm Dr. Nelson, the neurosurgeon on call. How much have you been told?"

"Not enough."

"Well, he appears to be fine. He has suffered a concussion and a badly bruised right hand. We're going to keep him overnight to be sure there are no other problems."

"Do you have any idea what happened?"

"The paramedics who brought him in said it was some sort of explosion. They didn't know what had caused it."

The message she had received from Tom O'Hare's secretary said that a bomb had been involved. She had been an FBI agent's wife long enough to sense when the Bureau was suppressing information. "So he's okay?"

"Fortunately, yes. I'm told he was down in a furnace room and there were a lot of ducts and machinery between him and whatever exploded, which absorbed most of the blast. He apparently leads a charmed life."

With a less than charitable edge to her voice, she said, "We'll see about that."

Knox stood outside her husband's hospital room, trying to determine which of her two emotions she should give in to—anger that he had exposed himself to death or relief that he had

252

survived. As soon as she entered the room and saw him, she knew it was relief.

He was sitting up in bed, but dozing. She touched his hand lightly, and he opened his eyes. "Hi," he said, fighting some mild sedative.

"Nice to see you again."

He blinked hard and sat up. "What about Joe LoFranco— did they get him?"

"I don't know, Mike. Who's Joe LoFranco?"

Devlin explained LoFranco's involvement in the investigation and how the killer had used him to maneuver Devlin to the basement of the Department of Justice building.

"My God, that's awful. Who can I call to find out?"

"O'Hare. If he's not there, Sharon, his secretary, might know."

Knox made the call, spoke briefly, and hung up. "Sharon wasn't there. The woman who answered said Tom was on his way over here."

Devlin grew quiet, afraid that for once, bad news was traveling slowly.

"Mike, wait until Tom gets here. You never know." He remained silent. "Well then, think about all the lives the two of you saved."

He put his head back and stared at the ceiling. "If it's any consolation, I was terrified." He raised his hands as if they were weighing an invisible bomb. "Holding something so close that is going to kill you in a few seconds has a way of cutting through a lot of denial."

"I hope that's true, Mike." He felt the sting of the doubt in her voice.

Bonelli walked in, with O'Hare close behind, and introduced himself to Knox. Devlin said, "Joe didn't make it." The utterance was part question, part affirmation, part protest.

"I'm sorry, Mike," O'Hare said. "It appears he was dead before we got there."

"And Packard?"

"Ten-seven."

"You guys?"

"No, he was considerate enough to do that himself."

"So it's all over."

"It's all over." Knox squeezed Devlin's hand. O'Hare asked him, "How are you feeling?"

"I'm okay."

"That was a helluva thing you did."

Devlin glanced at Knox protectively. "Packard made sure I didn't have a choice."

"He was one smart SOB," O'Hare said.

"Yes, he was. That's one of the reasons I'm surprised he committed suicide."

"Well, remember Hagstrom said he might."

"I know, I just thought he was a little too self-absorbed for such an unspectacular finish," Devlin said.

"In the end, everything fell apart for him. He saw we had him surrounded. Had a dead agent in the house, plus all the other evidence we found. Explosives, day-date watches, the poison he used in the children's aspirin. We even found one of the bottles he had tampered with, but it looked like it leaked, so he never planted it. He knew he was through."

"What about the Lassa virus?"

"In his freezer."

"Sounds like you have everything. Did anyone find out why he left MMI?"

"In his senior year, he applied to Annapolis. After passing all the requirements, he failed the psychological evaluation. So he withdrew academically, and apparently socially."

"Hagstrom will be studying this guy for years."

"He was one of a kind," O'Hare said.

"Let's hope."

Knox said, "Think you'll be up to it if I make flight reservations for tomorrow afternoon?"

Before Devlin could answer, O'Hare said, "I'm sorry, Mike. I'm going to need you to stay another day or two. You and Tony have developed some new techniques that I think Quantico will want to incorporate into their future curriculum. And I'll need your formal statement regarding what happened today."

Devlin said, "Do you mind, Knox? I'd like to stay anyway. I'm sure there'll be a memorial service for Joe."

"That's fine, but I should get home."

"I'll be okay."

"Please, just rest. We'll get out of here now." She stood, and Bonelli pulled himself up on his canes.

O'Hare remained seated. "If you don't mind, I'd like to talk to Mike for a minute."

Knox kissed Devlin. "Come on, Tony. It's secret agent stuff, and believe me, it's not that interesting. How about if I buy you dinner? You deserve it after carrying this guy the last two weeks."

"Then I should buy you dinner—you're married to him."

"I like the way you think. Mike tells me you're not married."

They started toward the door, and Devlin could see the blush on the back of Bonelli's neck. "No, I'm not."

As they disappeared down the hallway, Knox said, "You have got to come to Michigan. I know the perfect girl. You do like redheads?"

O'Hare smiled after them. "There's a young man who will never be the same."

"Do you mean because of the case or because of Knox?"

Still looking toward the door, O'Hare said, "You're a lucky guy, Mike."

"Funny, the last time I saw your wife, I thought the same thing."

"You know, Devlin, as an agent you're not half bad, but as a friend you're really starting to annoy me."

"You said it yourself—Susan is a good person. I just think she deserves a little honesty."

"Thanks, Mike, but maybe I *like* my personal life screwed up."

"That's exactly why you should listen to me."

"I don't want it that screwed up."

Devlin laughed. "I thought it was worth a shot," he said. "So do you have secret agent stuff?"

"I assume Knox knows what happened at Justice."

"The broad strokes, yes."

"That's okay, I know she won't say anything. But the attorney general wants us to deny any reports of a bomb, especially the sarin aspect. They are releasing a statement that the explosion in the basement had some sort of mysterious industrial origin. They're afraid that as hated as the Department of Justice has become, if the details get out, some wacko will see how easy it was and be able to duplicate it. You and a couple of Metro bomb officers are the only eyewitnesses. They're also being sworn to secrecy."

"Sounds reasonable."

"In case you're wondering, they said there was more than enough sarin to take out everyone in the building."

"I guess I was lucky that container didn't break open during the explosion."

"I talked to one of the cops who found you. He said you were wrapped around that thing like it was the winning touchdown. Do you remember what you told the paramedics when they were wheeling you out on a stretcher?"

"No."

"You told them to cover your face because your wife was sick of seeing you on national television." They both laughed.

O'Hare suddenly looked fatigued. "But it's a shame no one will ever know what Joe LoFranco gave his life for."

Devlin thought of the all-consuming camaraderie that takes over some law enforcement officers' lives, individuals who care only about the opinion of their peers. He didn't know if that bond evolved out of necessity or through some arcane social process, but Joe LoFranco, as Devlin had known him, was such a man—proud of who he was and selective about whose respect he gathered. "That's all right," Devlin said. "We know."

||| CHAPTER 47 |||

At midnight, after the nurse had checked on Devlin, he got dressed, called a cab, and had the driver take him to the Vietnam Veterans Memorial.

The air around the wall was cold and exhilarating. Like the celebration of those who had fought the war, the monument had been placed underground, hidden except from those who knew where to search for its dignity and its anger.

Despite the weather and the hour, a dozen or so men stood facing different sections of the wall, their sections, their histories, confronting nightmares, remembering comrades whose only possessions left on earth were the sharp edges of their names chiseled into the smooth black surface. The smell of alcohol softened the air. It served as a prodding companion without whom some of them could not have come. The observation walkway in front of it sloped downward below ground level. Year by year, the height of the sections grew to accommodate the increasing number of casualties.

Devlin walked to 1971 and found PFC Robert Austin, one of his men, who had been awarded the Medal of Honor. He touched the name and thought of Joe LoFranco and how the two men had died while serving the same oath: to defend the country against all enemies. A quote Devlin had heard during a war protest popped into his head: *Fool boys with toys but men with oaths.* Had they been fooled? If they had, so had he.

A tall man in his sixties with a freshly barbered gray crewcut walked up and stood next to Devlin. His eyes, sharpened by too many sad days, looked at Devlin analytically. "Semper Fi?" The simple, universal recognition between Marines was usually more of a greeting than an inquiry.

"Yes, I am."

"Me, too." The man touched the wall softly. "My son. Wanted to be a Marine like his old man. My fault, I guess. When he was a kid, I used to feed him all that boot camp stuff about it being the only branch of service. He was a great kid."

"Most of them were." Devlin pointed to Austin's name. "I had a rifle company over there. He was one of my men. Wanted to be a baseball player so he could buy a house for his parents. Instead, they got a medal."

The man stared straight ahead, his eyes filling up. "They got more than that."

"What about your son, what did he want to do?" Devlin asked.

"More than anything, he wanted to be cop."

Devlin looked at the son's name. "I'm sure he would have been a good one."

"Yes he would have . . . I guess someone has to walk point."

Devlin shook the man's hand and offered, "Semper Fi." Then he took a cab back to his hotel. He needed Knox.

||| CHAPTER 48 |||

The night was spent refighting skirmishes, some as long lost as Vietnam, with others as recent as Annapolis. By 5:00 A.M., with the last traces of the sedative gone, Devlin's aching right hand woke him. His head throbbed with tiny explosions. He pulled himself out of bed and got into the shower.

After he dressed, he woke up Knox. "Are you going to sleep all day?"

Through glazed eyes, she stared at the clock on the night stand. "Is that right, five forty-five?"

"Come on, get up. I'm taking you out for breakfast."

"I don't think I want to eat at any restaurant that's open at this hour."

"I'm going to go downstairs and get some coffee and rolls. Just throw on some jeans. Fifteen minutes."

Knox sat huddled against her husband on the steps of the Jefferson Memorial, sipping lukewarm coffee. She said, "Are you going to take some time off now?"

"Yes. Let's take the kids someplace—"

"Warm?"

He laughed. "Okay, whatever you think we can afford."

They fell silent and watched as winter's distant sunrise turned the surface of the Tidal Basin to a dusty pewter. Knox said, "Tell me a secret about yourself, something you've never told anyone."

"*If* I had such a secret, why would telling you be in my best interest?"

"Because it would make me love you even more."

"Usually, the only thing that's kept *that* secret is some form of ugliness."

"Exactly. You couldn't expose it to someone you weren't completely devoted to."

"I'd prefer to leave a little mystery in our marriage," he protested.

"Trust me."

He hesitated and then said, "I'm eleven years old and it's Christmas Eve. My father hasn't had a drink in a year and a half, so it's been great. I could finally have my friends over. We seemed to have enough money, even a car. We're waiting to open our presents and suddenly I'm aware that he's late. I think maybe I'm just anxious to open my gifts. But as long as I could remember, I was always aware of when he was late— it usually meant one thing. Sure enough, he walks in drunk. My mother started crying, and as tough as he was, he started crying."

"What about you?"

"It didn't seem like the appropriate response. It just wasn't enough. So I told them I was going to bed. My room was in the attic, so I went up and sneaked out a window. Without the slightest idea where I was going, I started walking. It was snowing, and there wasn't anybody on the street. We lived about a mile from the church. Whether that was my destination or not, I don't know, but I found myself in front of it. I stood there with the snow coming down. There was a life-size Nativity scene. Except for the figures, it was made out of wood. A lot of straw was scattered around. I set it on fire and walked home. I never went back to church until Katie was baptized."

Knox was quiet for a long while. "So that's why you wouldn't get married in a church. I'm surprised you agreed to the baptism."

"I guess I felt whatever was taken away from me that Christmas was finally given back." She put her hand around his neck and kissed him. He could taste the salt from her tears. "Okay, it's your turn."

"What I was going to tell you isn't nearly as revealing."

"It doesn't matter, just so it's something despicable."

She laughed. "Okay. Once, in college, I stole a police car."

"What?"

"When I was a freshman, this good-looking jock asked me out. He was a senior and one of his football buddies was a doorman at this bar, so I was able to drink there. About half-way through the evening, it became painfully obvious that Mr. Football was never going to become Mr. Right, so I asked him to take me home. It's snowing and very cold, and we're far enough from the dorm that he knows I can't walk. Being the gentleman he was, he tells me I'll have to wait until he gets done drinking. Knowing how long that might take, I got mad and left. A couple of blocks later I realized that was a mistake. I walked by this little coffee shop, and because of the cold, the police car parked outside had its motor running. I'm a little drunk and figure, What the hell. I jumped in and took off. The only smart thing I did that night was to leave the car a couple of blocks from the dorm so they wouldn't look there first."

Devlin laughed. "Good thing the statute of limitations has expired on both of us. But you were right—I do have a new respect for you."

"And don't you love me more now?"

They had left the hotel so quickly she had not been able to put on makeup or do anything with her hair other than pull it straight back. The morning light touched her face mysteriously, making him realize that of all the things he had neglected in the name of duty, not taking a few moments every day to fall in love with her again was probably the most foolish. "I don't think that will ever be possible."

After taking Knox to the airport, Devlin drove back to headquarters. When he walked in, Bonelli stopped his typing and said, "While you were sleeping in, I started putting this memo together." He handed it to Devlin.

"Absolutely no slack. You really are getting this agent thing down." Devlin looked at the document. "How did you get so much done so fast?"

"I've been keeping a daily diary since we started."

"This is pretty detailed."

"Yeah, but I need you to fill in some of the jumps in logic you made. With a little luck, I think we should be able to finish this late today or early tomorrow."

During the next three hours, they completed the chronology of the investigation up to the prevention of the bombing of the plane. Afterward, for the first time since they had met, they took the full forty-five minutes Bureau employees were allotted to eat their lunch in the Hoover Building cafeteria.

The first thing Devlin did when he returned was to reread the notes he had made that morning. At the bottom of the page were two questions that he had penciled in. Inexplicably, neither of the questions involved the part of the report they had already completed. *Did Packard's phone records show calls to his computer on-line service at the time the E-mail messages were sent to* The Real Deal? *Who else did LoFranco interview from MMI?* Devlin wondered why he had written them until he realized that both questions had to do with LoFranco's death.

"Tony, is anything bothering you about all of this?"

"Like what?"

"Do you see anything that doesn't fit?"

"What is it?"

"Take a look at the solution to this case. Does it make sense?"

Bonelli took several minutes to reread his notes. "Sorry, Mike. It all seems tight to me."

"Okay, what has the killer done throughout this entire case? The thing that was so frightening about him?"

"The way he anticipated every move."

"Exactly. Every move depended on anticipating us. Whether it was the President with the poisonings or me trying to disarm that bomb, his signature was to predict what we would do and use it against us."

"That's true." Bonelli's voice dragged on the second word, indicating he was not sure where Devlin was heading.

"Then why didn't he guess that we would have a trace set up when he called us from Annapolis?"

"That's a good question."

"Yes, it is. And what do you think we should do about it?"

"Find a good answer."

"Everyone's going to think we're crazy."

"What do you need me to do?"

Devlin was heading toward the door. "It's good to see I've been such a bad influence on you. Call MMI, and stay on the phone until someone faxes you Packard's cadet file. Ask them also to send a copy to Bill Hagstrom. Then get a hold of the phone company and see if Packard made calls at the same times those messages were E-mailed to New York."

"Where will you be?"

"Ident. I want to see if his prints were found on any of the evidence in this case."

"And if they weren't?"

"We'll be going to Annapolis."

* * *

Danny Jennings had started his Bureau career immediately after high school as a lowly clerk in the Identification Division. While attending college at night, he worked his way up to the Fingerprint Examiner position, matching latent prints to inked ones for testimony in court. Then he became an agent. His first stop was the Pontiac, Michigan, Resident Agency, where he and Devlin shared the excitement of working first-year cases together. Now Jennings was the head of Latent Prints, a position equal in salary and authority with that of a Special Agent in Charge. Devlin was shown into his office, and Jennings offered his hand. Devlin reached across with his left and shook it. Jennings asked, "A little banged up?"

"A little."

"You did us proud yesterday, Michael."

"I thought that whole thing was supposed to be a secret."

"Inside the Bureau?" Jennings laughed.

"O'Hare has me doing the paper on the investigation, and I need to know if Packard's latents were on any of the lifts from this case."

"Haven't you heard? He's dead. Who cares?"

"Just wrapping up some loose ends."

Jennings looked at him with friendly suspicion. "You haven't changed since we were rookies. And you don't lie much better, either."

"Okay, I'm not sure Packard is our boy."

Jennings laughed cynically. "How many times are you planning to solve this case?" He picked up the phone. "Have Kirsten come in here with his Freemurs notes."

When the fingerprint examiner came in, Jennings introduced him to Devlin and asked, "Neil, have you completed all your comparisons on this?"

"Just about. What are you looking for specifically?"

Devlin said, "On which items have you developed latents?"

Kirsten flipped through a couple of pages and read: "Parking stubs from Raintree Motel—numerous unidentified prints of value. Recovered poison bottles—no prints of value. Components of bomb recovered from American Airlines—one print of value. Numerous partial lifts from car rental agencies, but none of value, and the only prints on the sarin container from DOJ were Mike's."

Devlin asked, "So the only latents you have are the parking stubs and the bomb?"

"That's right."

"The print from the bomb—where was it located?" Devlin asked.

"On the adhesive side of the duct tape that held the device to the wall," Kirsten said.

Jennings asked, "Have you checked it against Packard's?"

"I have checked his prints against those on the stubs, and there were no matches. But not the bomb yet."

Jennings said, "Please go do it now, so I can prove to this hardheaded mick that he's chasing ghosts."

After the examiner left, Devlin said, "Do you remember that deserter case back in Pontiac when we locked up the wrong guy?"

"How was I supposed to know it was his brother? He said he was the fugitive."

"He said that so his brother could get away."

"How could I know that? There were so many deserters back then, and the military never sent photos."

"His name was tattooed on his arm."

Jennings smiled his surrender. "I was young."

Devlin glanced around the office with mock disgust. "I know it's been a while since you've worked for a living, but like with that deserter, it's still just a matter of reading the trail markings."

Jennings shook his head and smiled. "If that's Packard's print on the tape, are you buying drinks?"

"If it is, I'll have nothing but time on my hands. I'll even buy you dinner."

A few minutes later, Kirsten came back in. "That was fast," Jennings said.

"It was easy. Packard is thirty-two over thirty-two, all whorls. This print is a tented arch. They don't match."

||| CHAPTER 49 |||

Bonelli was still on the phone when Devlin returned. After a few more snatches of conversation, he hung up. Devlin handed him a cellular phone, and Bonelli asked, "What's this for?"

"I checked it out of Technical Services, in case we go somewhere. It's too cold outside to be standing in phone booths. Who was that?"

"The telephone company. There were no calls on Packard's bill that coincided with any of the E-mail messages. Maybe he made all the calls from a hotel room, like he did when he tried to kill the minister."

"That brings us back to the same question: Why would he then make those last calls from his home, when it was so critical?"

"It doesn't make any sense. What about the fingerprints?"

"No match, and they do have a quality latent on the airplane bomb that couldn't be anybody's but the killer."

The fax machine rang briefly, and then the receiving light came on. "That should be Packard's MMI record," Bonelli said.

Impatiently, Devlin read each page as soon as it was printed. Fifteen minutes later, he called Hagstrom. "What do you think, Bill?"

"This guy definitely had some problems. Look at page six—the stuff from the school psychologist."

Devlin read:

The subject has demonstrated a volatile personality with feelings of severe rejection, anxiety, and interpersonal deficiencies with a strong underlying negative self-attitude. Also, he appears to have no self-esteem. Thus, because he is only corrected when he is wrong and not rewarded or confirmed when he displays appropriate behavior, the subject feels he "can never do anything right." Since his behavior has always been evaluated negatively, he does not trust his own self-judgment.

Devlin said, "Sounds like the kind of person we're looking for."

"It gets better. Go to page nine."

Devlin found it:

His fears of rejection are apparent in the following projective sentence completion test when he states: I FEEL A FRIEND WILL "not ridicule you." WHEN I WAS A CHILD "it was rotten." MY MOTHER "hates me." MY GREATEST FAULT IS "I can't get along with people." IN SCHOOL, MY TEACHERS "disliked me." MOST OF MY FRIENDS DON'T KNOW I "am afraid of people."

MOST PEOPLE I KNOW "dislike me." THE PEOPLE WHO WORK FOR ME "dislike me." SOMEDAY, I WILL "be big." I WISH I COULD LOSE THE FEAR OF "people being better than me." COMPARED TO OTHERS, I AM "nothing."

Devlin said, "That's the second time I've read that, and I still can't get over the extent of his self-hatred."

"It is extreme. But I think the most telling part of this report, for our purposes, is the concluding paragraph on page sixteen."

His fear of people stems from a fear of being rejected by them and their making negative value judgments about him. Subject's underlying feelings of insecurity precipitate aggressive behavior patterns in him. Feeling insecure, he often acts out. "The best defense is a good offense." Subject often acts precipitously; he has strong needs of group belonging and often acts quickly and inappropriately if he perceives that someone is being done an injustice. And when these acts backfire, his feelings of inadequacy and worthlessness are reinforced. The subject has a tendency to distort reality, feeling that the way he wants things to be is actually the way they are. His tendency to isolate himself is his method of avoiding trouble and especially rejection. It is my opinion that without the strict order and regimentation of this academy, the subject's problems would increase dramatically.

After he had finished rereading the evaluation, Devlin asked, "What do you think, Bill?"

"I think I'd like to know why you're pursuing this. The evidence against Packard is overwhelming, and he's dead."

"Humor me—I've had a head injury. Can you say this is definitely the Freedom Killer?"

"It's a pretty limited analysis, but he is a possible."

"Possible? That's it?"

"I guess I expected more."

"Like what?"

"I don't know. I guess I would have liked him to have been involved in some violent episodes, like brutally beating someone, or maybe a nice soothing arson. Some sort of predictive *actual* behavior."

"Maybe he was just too smart to get caught."

"Maybe. But that brings up another point. Packard's IQ was tested at 114, not as high as I would have thought the killer's to be. Although IQ does not always reflect intelligence, I've read that entire report, and nowhere in it is he ever described as intelligent. Psychologists love to see themselves as involved in mental chess matches with their patients. If someone gives the least hint of being bright, they're going to record it as a key factor to whatever their conclusions are."

"Are you saying William Packard may not be the Freedom Killer?"

"You know, Devlin, there's a rumor going around the Bureau that you're still looking for Abel's killer."

"Could it be someone else?"

"No, Cain killed him."

Devlin lowered his voice and patiently asked his question again: "Bill, could it be someone else?"

"Let me put it this way: If you had shown me this file without any of the other evidence against Packard, I would probably have said it was not him."

"One last question then. If it is someone else, what is his next move?"

"I suppose, one of two possibilities. Because he has gone to all this trouble to lay this off on someone else, an intelligent guess would be that he will completely vanish."

When Hagstrom was quiet for a few seconds, Devlin asked, "Or?"

"Remember, 'Comply or else'?"

"Yes."

"If William Packard is not the killer and if the killer has decided not to vanish, I would think he is about to commit the single most destructive act he can create. Something more devastating than everything else he has done combined. For him, it will be this country's punishment for not acknowledging his power."

"Then I guess someone should start looking for him."

Bonelli, although only hearing one end of the conversation, knew they were leaving for Annapolis. He started loading his laptop and the cellular phone into his backpack. When Devlin hung up, he asked, "Are you going to tell O'Hare about our little *research* trip?"

"I stopped by there on my way back from Ident. Sharon said he's got a major kidnapping in Salt Lake City and a serial murderer in Chicago, who is using scalpels on nurses. Besides, I don't think he wants to hear about my premonitions. If we get something, there'll be plenty of time to bring him in."

III CHAPTER 50 III

It was cold and, as was winter's paradox, sunny and clear. Although Devlin was still in some pain, he felt a rare excitement. He was on his own, trying to solve a mystery the rest of the world didn't know existed. And whether or not that mystery existed at all wasn't as important as the freedom of both time and direction he was experiencing. As though it would prolong his euphoria, he obediently drove at the speed limit through the brilliant January sunshine.

He glanced over at Bonelli. His face seemed younger, more trusting. The last traces of the anger that had defined their early alliance were finally gone. "You look awfully pleased with yourself, Tony."

"If I didn't know better, I'd think I was happy."

Devlin gave a short laugh. "Be careful, this is the Bureau. You don't want anybody to find out."

Bonelli smiled absentmindedly as he stared out his window. "Mike, is this the biggest case you've ever worked?"

"It certainly has the most victims."

"Sitting in front of that computer all those years, I never dreamed that I would get a chance to do something like this. Right now I feel like I could run a marathon."

"That's great, but you'd better pace yourself. We may have a ways to go yet," Devlin said. "How many names are on that MMI list?"

Bonelli lifted the computer out of his bag and placed it on his lap. After typing his way into the Freemurs file, he answered, "Seventeen."

"And two of those we can eliminate: Quigley, who is overseas in the Army, and Langston, who we know Joe backed off of. That leaves fifteen. Pick one out."

"I don't know what order Joe went in."

"That's the point—no one does. He could have used a dozen equally logical approaches. By the time we get done discussing them, we could have interviewed four or five of the ex-cadets. Pick one."

Bonelli considered the list for a few seconds. "There's one in Laurel. Remember, one of the car bombings was there."

"Laurel it is."

It was almost five o'clock when they pulled up to the house. According to LoFranco's list, it belonged to Alfred Grayson. Devlin felt a familiar burning in his stomach. "Do you still have my snub-nose?"

Bonelli patted his backpack. "Do you want me to come with you?"

"No, I've found that these things go better one-on-one," Devlin lied, and Bonelli understood why.

Devlin knocked on the door and unbuttoned his overcoat. The inner door opened, and Grayson stood there shirtless, glaring at what he evidently perceived as the latest intrusion into his life.

"Yeah," he said, his snarl muffled by the storm door. His skin glowed red and blue, and his breathing was accelerated. Seeing that his muscular body was pumped, Devlin guessed he had been lifting weights. He held up his credentials and showed a face that was unintimidated to the point of boredom. "Yeah, what do you want?" Devlin remained silent and stared back into Grayson's discourteous expression. Reluctantly, he opened the door and Devlin stepped in. "What's the goddamn FBI want with me?"

All bullies, Devlin had discovered at an early age, guarded the same secret: They were socially limited people, who relied on the harshness of intimidation because they were so susceptible to it themselves. "Believe me, the last thing the FBI wants is you." Almost instinctively, Grayson's fists knotted. Devlin looked down at them and said, "Save the Rambo sketch for the tourists."

With what seemed like a strange, internal struggle, he forced his hands behind his back as though they had embarrassed him. "Do I need a lawyer?"

"The only thing you're going to need is a little honesty and a lot less attitude."

"I haven't done anything."

"Were you interviewed by anyone from the FBI yesterday?"

"No."

"Did you know an agent named Joe LoFranco?"

"No."

"Have you been doing any traveling lately?"

"Like to where?"

"Detroit, Miami, Chicago, Dallas, San Francisco, Los Angeles?"

"Never."

"Ever been to Atlanta or Disney World?"

"No."

Devlin was not picking up any deception in Grayson's answers. "Did you know William Packard at MMI?"

Understanding flooded Grayson's face. "So that's what this is about. He killed that FBI agent yesterday. Yeah, I knew him," he said, his voice gathering arrogance. "I kicked his ass for him once."

Having no idea how big Packard was, but taking into consideration Grayson's size and the general operating guidelines of people like him, Devlin ventured a guess: "Wasn't he a lot smaller than you?"

"He started it," Grayson said, and jerked his head back, realizing how immature his answer sounded.

A dozen little lights lit up inside Devlin's head, telling him that Grayson couldn't be the killer, not with his lack of subtlety. He left without another word, letting Grayson regret his final words.

As soon as Devlin exited the house, he could see Bonelli's head anxiously craning back and forth watching the house. "How was he?"

Devlin said, "We'll probably be looking for him in a year or so. Who's next?"

Bonelli directed him to the next address, but no one was

home. When they tried a third address with the same results, Devlin said, "This is going to take forever."

"I was wondering how long the *patient* approach would last."

"Let's take a minute to look at this." Devlin pulled the car to the curb and turned off the engine. "Have you got any ideas?"

"I wish I did."

"Okay, if we are right and someone else is the killer, there must be something we're missing. Let's walk our way through the last thing we know he was involved in—LoFranco's murder. Joe obtained a list of seventeen former cadets at MMI and the night before last started interviewing them. He went to the killer's house and was taken hostage."

Bonelli said, "Where did he start from, the RA?"

The question stunned Devlin. "That's a good point, but more important, how did he get there? Where *is* his Bureau car?"

"Wasn't it at Packard's house?"

"I don't know. Let me have that cellular." He dialed the FBI office in Baltimore. "This is Mike Devlin from headquarters. I'd like to talk to whoever is handling the Joe LoFranco case."

"That would be Agent John Woodward. Hold on, I'll connect you."

Devlin heard the extension ring. "John Woodward."

"John, Mike Devlin at headquarters. I imagine you're kind of busy, so let me ask you a quick question—where did you find Joe's Bucar?"

"Maryland State Police recovered it just outside of South Haven in a bank parking lot. Hold on, Mike, I'll get you the exact location."

Thirty seconds later, Woodward came back on the phone and gave Devlin the bank's address. "Has it been processed yet?" Devlin asked.

"This morning. We didn't find a thing—not even a smudge."

"How far away from Packard's house was the bank?"

"Seven, maybe eight miles."

After Devlin hung up, he repeated the conversation to Bonelli, who asked, "I don't understand. So he dumped the car seven or eight miles away. Why is that important?"

"Whoever the killer is, we know he's a loner."

"Right."

"If it was Packard, how did he get home from the bank?"

"That's right. He wouldn't walk seven or eight miles."

"Look at the list and tell me who we should talk to next."

Bonelli thought for a second. "Someone who lives within walking distance of the bank."

"That would get my vote. Now, figure out who that would be."

Bonelli pulled out a small pad of paper and started making notes while he checked addresses of the ex-cadets against his Maryland map. Finally he said, "There are only two within two miles of the bank—Daniel Owens and Rockland Tubbs."

"Who lives the closest?"

"Tubbs. About a mile away."

"Rockland Tubbs—why do I recognize that name?"

Bonelli said, "I don't know. The MMI list is the only time I've seen it before."

"Tubbs?" Devlin asked himself. "Tubbs?" He picked up the phone again and called the FBI headquarters switchboard. After being transferred twice, he got the electronic surveillance clerk on the line and asked her to find the tape of LoFranco's last two calls. While she located them, he tried to remember the dead agent's last words. There was something about them that had never sat right with Devlin. The words, the rhythms—something that now seemed important. She came back on the line. "Did you want to hear them?"

"Please, and play them twice." He took Bonelli's pad of paper and wrote down LoFranco's words.

Don't be stupid. Mike, you've got it—backwards.
Don't worry about me. This son of a bitch can kiss my
butts.

As Devlin listened to it the second time, he underlined *Mike, backwards,* and *butts.* He hung up and studied what he had written.

"What is it, Mike?"

Devlin leaned over to show Bonelli. "These are Joe's final words, the way he said them. See how the pacing is off. It should be, 'Don't be stupid, Mike.' But he said it more like 'Don't be stupid—Mike!' And he emphasized my name. He also emphasized *backwards*; he even hesitated before saying it. And he emphasized *butts.* Why would a tough ex–New Yorker who used *son of a bitch* in the same sentence say *butt* instead of *ass*?" Bonelli shrugged his shoulders. "Take out the two sentences that start with *don't.* It's like he was telling us, 'Don't pay any attention to this sentence.' Then look at the three words he emphasized—*Mike, backwards,* and *butts.*"

Bonelli looked at Devlin questioningly. "I don't get it."

"*Mike—backwards—butts.* He was saying, 'Mike, turn *butts* backwards. Joe was giving us his killer's name. Move the *s* around, and *butts* becomes *Tubbs.*"

III CHAPTER 51 III

"Shouldn't we call somebody?" Bonelli's words were quick, anxious.

Devlin was watching the isolated house at the end of the road. "And what would we tell them? That *Tubbs* spelled backwards is *butts*? The more people we call from now on, the more obstacles we'll have to deal with."

It was dusk, and lights were becoming evident through the windows of other houses. Although they were parked a quarter of a mile up the road, Devlin could see into the garage attached to the Tubbs house. "No lights on, and the garage is empty. Doesn't look like he's home. Seems like a good time for a little reconnaissance."

"I got to tell you, Mike, this is starting to scare the hell out of me."

"There's nothing wrong with being scared as long as you don't let that frighten you."

Bonelli stared at him, trying to judge his seriousness. Of all of Devlin's smiles he had memorized in the past two weeks, he did not recognize the peculiar one that now covered the agent's face. Their car drove slowly toward the house.

Pulling into Tubbs's driveway, Devlin said, "Okay, give me three quick beeps on the horn if you see anyone heading this way." He opened his briefcase, took out a small black metal flashlight, and got out of the car.

After he disappeared around the side of the house, Bonelli unzipped a side compartment on his backpack and took out Devlin's snub-nose. He rolled down the window a couple of inches so he could better listen to the solitude that had suddenly confronted him.

Devlin shined his light in the back door. It was the kitchen. Everything, as best as he could tell, was normal. He didn't see any lights, so he tried the doorknob. It was locked. He moved to the far side of the house and looked in another window. The flashlight beam scanned a room that appeared to be a small study. A computer sat on a large desk under a single bookshelf. He was about to move to the next window when one of the books caught his eye. The colors on the cover were Day-Glo orange and optic-lime; it was Dr. Craven's book *Psycholinguistics and Threat Analysis*. Vaguely recognizing the book next to it, he strained to read its title—*In Search of Serial Offenders*. It was written by an agent who had retired from the Behavioral Science Unit. Devlin had read it himself a year earlier. That's why this guy was one step ahead of us, he thought—we helped train him.

Devlin got back into the car and stared through the windshield.

Bonelli asked, "Well?"

"It's him."

"How do you know?"

Devlin explained about the books.

"Are we going to call for help now?"

Devlin didn't seem to hear Bonelli. "His first message said we had two weeks to comply."

"So?"

"When did he send that?"

Bonelli's fingers flashed over the keyboard. "Fourteen days ago."

"Exactly?"

"Exactly two weeks ago today."

"That means he's out doing it right now."

"Doing what?"

"Punishing the United States of America."

"How are we going to find out what that is?"

Devlin looked at him. "There's only one way. I've got to get inside."

"Without a search warrant?"

"I've got a feeling there isn't enough time, or enough probable cause. Let's go."

"*Let's?* As in you and me?"

"Do you remember Hagstrom's profile that this guy would be a record keeper, documenting his activities?"

Bonelli's reluctance was obvious. "I thought reading was a prerequisite to becoming an agent."

"Not computers."

Using his flashlight, Devlin led Bonelli to the rear door. Once there, he took off his overcoat and used it to cover one of the four small panes of glass in the door. He drew his 9-millimeter and jabbed it into the coat, breaking the window. The cloth muffled the sound of the broken glass hitting the floor inside. Devlin shook the glass fragments from his coat, and put it back on. "Wait here a minute." He disappeared inside.

Bonelli turned around and anxiously watched the road for headlights.

After a couple of minutes, Devlin reappeared. "Come on."

Bonelli followed him to the study, which was a converted bedroom, and sat down in front of the computer. Devlin switched on a small reading lamp. "You're sure there's no one here?" Bonelli whispered.

Devlin started flipping through the books on the shelf. "I've checked the whole house except for the basement."

"Don't you think you should?"

"Okay."

"Before you go, have you seen any computer disks?"

"No."

"Keep an eye out for some. Otherwise I guess everything's on the hard drive." He switched the computer on and the monitor lit up. After watching the screen for a few seconds, he said, "Good, his files aren't protected."

"Isn't that unusual?"

"No. A lot of people don't bother." Then his voice took on a sarcastic edge: "The fool probably thought locking his doors was enough."

Funny, Devlin thought, how the most prolific lawbreakers always thought of themselves as the least likely to become the victims of crimes. Equally amusing was serving these individuals with search warrants. They invariably became indignant at the "violation" of their rights. Whatever the reason Tubbs had not encoded his files, Devlin took it as a sign that whoever was pulling the big strings was issuing him further license to *expedite* the investigation. He said, "I'll go check the basement." But Bonelli, whose hands and eyes were locked combatively on the computer, did not seem to hear him.

Devlin opened the basement door and tried the switch, but the lights didn't work. He flipped the switch again. Nothing. Suddenly, a chill of apprehension ran down his spine. Drawing his 9-millimeter, he started down the stairs.

III CHAPTER 52 III

Trained by years of forcing his way into places where he
had not been invited, Devlin sensed a familiar foreboding as
he entered the basement's sunken darkness. It was usually
caused by something as subtle as the lingering odor of a fugitive, who had run through the room, sweating fearfully, to hide
in a closet, or a woman who swore her boyfriend was not there
and then held her breath as Devlin started to look under the
bed. Although he couldn't identify the cause of his apprehension, it hovered over him, guarding whatever secret he was
about to discover.

He wheeled his flashlight 360 degrees. The basement was
as large as the house above it. At one end, the furnace and hot-
water heater sat amid a couple dozen large cardboard boxes,
all sealed. There were three smaller rooms at the other end.
Devlin walked to them cautiously and tried the doorknobs. All
three were locked.

An ancient workbench stood against a side wall. On it were
the usual homeowner tools, but nothing with enough prying
capability to open the doors. Then he noticed a pair of Channellocks. Holstering his automatic, he adjusted the jaws of the
plierlike device so he could get a good bite on the doorknobs'
stems. He set the flashlight down and used both hands to rotate
the tool. The lock resisted for a few seconds before something
inside snapped. He picked up the flashlight, drew his gun

again, and stood to the side as he pulled open the door of the first room.

It was completely empty. Devlin wondered if it had contained the boxes of incriminating evidence before they were planted at William Packard's house.

The second door, in addition to the doorknob lock, had a deadbolt, so he went to the third room and, using the same technique, forced it open. It contained a table, the top of which held several guns, ammunition, and explosives. Devlin took a quick inventory of the ammunition and saw that several boxes contained .45-caliber bullets. But there was no corresponding weapon. He had to assume that Tubbs, wherever he was, had it with him.

He went back to the second door and, using the Channellocks, forced the doorknob. But the deadbolt held fast.

On the workbench, he found an electrical circular saw with an extension cord. He plugged it in and took it over to the door, on which he made three cuts around the lock. One yank on the knob ripped the door away from the notched-out deadbolt. The wooden square containing the lock fell to the floor.

As soon as it was open, Devlin realized what subliminal sensation had made him cautious when he entered the basement. The majority of the room was taken up by a freezer chest. With the door open, its hum now became louder. Although the electrical light had not worked, subconsciously he had heard the hum of the freezer. It was an inconsistency that he knew would not be explained until he opened it.

Slowly, Devlin lifted the lid. Lying at the bottom was the body of a man. He was about sixty years old and was dressed in a suit. Blood covered his chest, and Devlin could see small crystal spikes where the oozing liquid had frozen. Searching the man's clothing, he found a wallet containing a driver's license, which identified him as Roland Tubbs, with a Chevy Chase, Maryland, address. Devlin assumed he was Rockland

Tubbs's father and, from the impatient scowl frozen on his face, that he had chosen to give his son one last lecture rather than beg for his life.

Bonelli's voice carried down into the basement urgently: "Mike, you'd better get up here!"

||| CHAPTER 53 |||

Bonelli could hear Devlin hurrying up the stairs and yelled to him before he was in the room. "I've got his diary. Hagstrom was right. It's all in here." Devlin looked at the screen. "Here's where he's talking about killing the research tech from the Centers for Disease Control. And here, about the break-in at the drug company in Kansas City"

Devlin read a few lines and then said, "Skip to the end. Let's see the last entry."

Bonelli scrolled rapidly to the end. "It's dated today."

It read:

This shall be the only entry I have logged before the fact. I do not know if I will live after tonight, but it is of no consequence because history will write my final chapter. The unforgiving have refused to forget my grandfather's name. In return, I will never let Washington, nor the world, forget mine.

—Rockland Tubbs

Bonelli looked back at Devlin. "What's he going to do?"

"I don't know, but we better get back to Washington. How long will it take to transfer everything on his hard drive to disks?"

"Not long."

"I'm going to call O'Hare and let him know." Devlin picked up the phone and dialed. There was no answer; he hung up and called the headquarters switchboard. "This is Mike Devlin. Can you put me through to Tom O'Hare's house?"

"O'Hare."

"Tom, it's Mike. Tony and I are up in Maryland—"

"What are you doing up there?"

"There's no time to explain," Devlin shot back. "Packard isn't the Freedom Killer—it's another ex-cadet, named Rockland Tubbs. He made it look like Packard, and right now he's in Washington getting ready to carry out his comply-or-else threat."

"Exactly where are you?"

"We're in his house. Tony got into his computer. It's all in there—everything."

"What does it say he's going to do?"

"That's the one thing it didn't tell us. We're going to review everything and see what we can figure out."

"Okay, I'll head to the office. Call me as soon as you get anything." O'Hare hung up.

Bonelli asked, "Do we even know what Tubbs looks like?"

"Good point. While you're finishing, I'll look for a photo of him."

As Bonelli turned his attention back to the computer, Devlin went to the bedroom he had checked briefly when he first entered the house.

There was nothing hanging on the walls and no photos on top of the dressers. He searched the drawers. In the closet, he checked some shoeboxes on the floor and another on the shelf.

Nothing. Then he noticed a dark blue work uniform hanging between two suits. Hoping it might have a patch naming an employer on it, he pulled it out. Clipped to a front pocket was a work badge, complete with a photo ID. It was for the Army ordnance depot outside of Baltimore—the same one where they had interviewed and eliminated William Blake as a suspect. The photo showed a blond man in his late twenties with intense but amused eyes. The name on the badge was Walter Lessing. But was he Tubbs?

Devlin quickly searched the rest of the house for pictures. The only one he could find was on the living room wall above some sort of worktable. It was of a man who had the same coloring and bone structure as the man in the picture on the ID. He was smiling with the same condescending smirk Lessing wore in his ID.

Bonelli yelled from the study. "I'm done, Mike."

Devlin came back into the study. "The only thing I could find was this." He held up the badge.

"Lessing? Do you think that's Tubbs?"

"Remember William Blake?"

"The guy at the ordinance depot?"

"That's where this badge is from. Tubbs set it up so if we did get onto his Blake alias, we would go out there and he'd hear about the FBI grabbing one of the employees. It was an early warning device for him. And once we were there, he knew he had to kill his landlord, Lloyd Franklin."

"If you're sure it's him, that's good enough for me."

The face in the photo stared back at Devlin. "I'm sure."

III CHAPTER 54 III

As Devlin raced toward Washington along Highway 50, Bonelli scanned the contents of the disks. "Christ, Mike, there's at least twenty-five files. What am I looking for?"

"I don't know. Read the titles to me."

"Ah, let's see, 'Address,' 'Document,' 'Expenses,' 'Granddad,' 'House'—"

"Look at Granddad," Devlin interrupted. "He said something about his grandfather in that last diary entry."

Bonelli punched up the file. "It looks like a biography or obituary." Scanning the document, he said, "Chapman L. Tubbs, born July 31, 1918, died August 1, 1985. Captain U.S. Army during World War II, stationed in London, England, 1944 and 1945. Convicted of spying for the Germans in 1946. According to court-martial documents, Captain Tubbs had acted as a forward observer for the enemy during the V1 and V2 rocket attacks on England, secretly radioing back to the German launching sites in northern France the accuracy and devastation of the 'buzz bombs' so adjustments to the targets could be made. He was sentenced to twenty-five years but was released in 1957 after serving eleven years. He is survived by his son and grandson, Roland and Rockland Tubbs, of Chevy Chase, Maryland."

Bonelli paused, then read out, " 'And so my grandfather's life was abbreviated in the dark mortuary font of journalistic back pages. One last time, we "survivors" had to stand up and face the guilt of bloodline. One last time Roland had to set his resolve. And to prove his patriotism, he would sacrifice a son—Rockland—to make him a hero, the ultimate hero, a United States Naval Academy graduate. It was to be the final cleansing for clan Tubbs. But the background investigation revealed who my grandfather had been, and the third generation was asked to continue payment on a debt a half century old.

" 'But, dear Father, as you obsessively drove me toward Annapolis, you failed to realize that genes cannot be altered by someone else's desire. It was unfortunate you never were able to appreciate, in your case, that their biologically induced behavior had mercifully skipped a generation.

" 'Finally I have given you rest, Father. And, Grandfather, I have taken up the torch. We have come full circle, from Vergeltungswaffe to Brushfire.' "

Bonelli looked up from his computer. "What the hell is Vergeltungswaffe?"

"The only thing I know from old war movies is that *Waffe*, as in Luftwaffe, means weapon, so I'm going to guess it's the V in V1 and V2. I have no idea what Brushfire is." Devlin dialed the cellular phone.

"FBI Baltimore."

"This is Mike Devlin out of headquarters. Are you the duty agent?"

"Yes I am."

"Do you know who I am?"

"Yes, I saw you on the news."

"Good, I need an indices check on two names: Rockland Tubbs and Walter Lessing."

"Stand by."

Bonelli glanced over at the speedometer. They were doing

eighty. He asked Devlin, "What did he mean, 'Finally I have given you rest, Father'?"

"He killed his father."

"How do you know—is that what you were doing in the basement?"

Devlin nodded. The Baltimore duty agent came back on the line. "No record on Tubbs, but there is a 52B reference on a Walter Lessing dated last month."

"A 52B—that's theft of government property?"

"Let's see, I've got a violation card right here. Yeah, theft of government property valued over five thousand dollars or weapons or explosives are involved."

"Can you pull up the reference?"

"Sure, hold on."

Devlin said, "Tony, run Lessing and the father, Roland Tubbs. See if we have them."

The Baltimore agent said, "It looks like Lessing is a maintenance employee at the Army ordnance depot and was one of about three dozen employees who were interviewed concerning a theft there."

"What was stolen?"

"Uh, it looks like—can this be right?—a surface-to-surface missile called a Brushfire."

"Can you read me what Lessing had to say?"

"That's easy. The interview is only one short paragraph. Lessing said he didn't know anything about a missile and had no idea who had stolen it."

Devlin thought for a moment, "Are there any specifications for the missile in the file?"

"Hold on while I scan through it."

Bonelli said, "I've got a hit on Roland Tubbs. He was one of the registered owners from the Raintree Hotel."

"What kind of vehicle?"

"A white Chrysler van. Maryland tag XX3184."

The duty agent said, "Here it is. The Brushfire is a tripod-launched laser-guided surface-to-surface missile. It was developed after the Gulf War to use for firing into buildings. Its fuse can be set on delay so it will penetrate the outer shell of the building and then explode inside for maximum casualties."

"What's its effective range?"

"Ah, one thousand meters."

"What about the warhead?"

"Let's see. Oh, the advanced design of the warhead gives it approximately twice the killing radius as those used in the Gulf."

"Anything else?"

"Just that it has a night-sight capability and can be launched from an enclosed firing position such as a bunker."

"Call Tom O'Hare at Bureau headquarters and tell him that Tubbs is using the name Walter Lessing and has that missile. And tell him he's driving a white Chrysler van, Maryland plate XX3184. O'Hare won't be there for a while, so keep trying. He'll know what to do."

"Do you know where this guy is headed?"

"Someplace with a lot of people."

||| CHAPTER 55 |||

"Where are we going to look?" Bonelli held his hand on the dashboard as the car swerved through traffic.

"This is your town. Where will there be a lot of people in a building on a Tuesday night?"

"Do you mean like a sporting event or concert? I don't know. Being trapped in that room with you for two weeks, I'm not sure what year it is," Bonelli said. "But there's something I don't understand. Why wasn't Tubbs's father interviewed by the Bureau for having his car at the Raintree?"

"It's those quick-kill leads again. The only people who were immediately interviewed were the ones who fit the race and age profile. Everyone else was put on the back burner. And we don't know how long the father has been dead. The agent who has the lead could have been looking for him all this time. It also makes sense that Tubbs would be using a van. He would have been taking a chance trying to transport that research tech and a wheelchair in a car. I should have thought of that." Devlin could see the Washington Monument now. He handed the phone to Bonelli. "Call the newspaper. See if they know where we can find a lot of people in a building tonight."

"For just the city of Washington?"

"I don't know."

As Bonelli started pushing the cellular's buttons, he felt the car brake hard. The cars ahead of them were at a standstill. "What the hell is this?" Devlin asked.

"Probably an accident," Bonelli said, and he reached over to turn on the radio. "Maybe there's a traffic report."

"Is there an arena or concert hall around here that might be causing this?"

"Not that I'm aware of. But, I think—" Bonelli's voice stopped abruptly. Both men were unprepared for what was coming from the radio. Instead of the usual music, commercial, or talk show rhythms, there was a low murmur of people talking. It was a live broadcast, and the sounds were identical to those that would precede a press conference.

Bonelli offered, "Maybe O'Hare called the press and they're going to warn everyone."

"It's too soon," Devlin answered absentmindedly, concentrating on the broadcast.

The announcer said, "As you may or may not know, ladies and gentlemen, this annual event is mandated by the Constitution and normally takes place on the fourth Tuesday in January. Present will be not only the President and Vice-President, but the entire Congress, the cabinet, the Supreme Court, and the Joint Chiefs of Staff. That is why security here is impenetrable—"

Devlin said, "The State of the Union Address."

"Mike, it would be impossible. They had some of us in Records Management doing computer checks for it last year. Like the announcer said, it's impenetrable. There's a two-block security cordon all the way around the Capitol. No one can get through it without ID and an actual engraved invitation."

"Two blocks is roughly five hundred meters, which means Tubbs can stand four blocks off if he has that Brushfire. What time was the first message sent to *The Real Deal*?"

"I'll have to look it up on that chronology we were working on." Bonelli typed in the query. "Eight P.M."

Devlin looked at his watch. "We've got ten minutes." He cut the wheel hard, got onto the shoulder, and stomped the accelerator. He took the phone from Bonelli and dialed the FBI switchboard. After being put through to the night supervisor, he said, "This is Devlin. Did Baltimore call you?"

"Yes, they did, Mike. We're scrambling every available agent."

"Did you call the Director?"

"No, he's at the State of the Union Address."

"That's the target. You'd better call over there and get them to evacuate the building."

"But everyone is already there. Are you sure about this?"

Devlin looked at the dashboard clock. "You've got eight

minutes," he said, and disconnected the phone. The dome of the Capitol, illuminated by dozens of exterior floodlights, appeared through the windshield.

Bonelli, the tone of his voice indicating he already knew the answer, asked, "Think they'll evacuate?"

"Within those walls are some of the biggest egos in the world. Do you think they'll listen to a street agent from Detroit and a computer clerk?"

Bonelli said, "Take a left here—it's shorter."

Now they were on a surface street, the dome becoming larger. "Tell me what you know about the security here."

"The speech is held in the House chamber, which is on the north—no, the south side of the dome. The chamber's on the second floor."

"I assume there's some sort of hallway between the outer walls of the building and the actual room where they are?"

"I don't know. I've never been up there."

"There has to be. It would be too big a security risk otherwise. Tubbs wouldn't need that delayed fuse if there weren't a couple of walls to shoot through." Devlin thought for a moment. "That's got to be it. His target would probably be a window on the exterior of the second floor. The missile could pass through it easily, and then the delay fuse will carry it through the inner wall before detonating in the chamber. We have to look for vantage points for that kind of shot."

As Devlin continued to weave through traffic, both men listened to the radio, hoping the announcer would suddenly report that the House chamber was being cleared for an unknown reason.

"Turn down Second," Bonelli ordered. "That's probably going to be the eastern security perimeter."

Devlin made the turn, honked twice at a slow car, and then passed it in the oncoming traffic lane. "When we get close, you watch the right side. I'll take the left."

They crossed D Street and could see the barricades on their right. Beyond them, the second floor of the Capitol seemed very close.

Now the radio revealed an increase in the undercurrent coming from the House floor. The announcer said, "The next voice you hear will be that of the Sergeant-at-Arms of the House of Representatives."

"Mike! There, in the middle of the second floor—a window."

"Okay, now help me on my side. Just look for a white van. Wherever he's parked, it won't be conspicuous."

The Sergeant-at-Arms's voice strained with drama to quiet the crowd, "Mr. Speaker—the President's cabinet."

As the announcer named the members of the cabinet, who were filing in, Devlin slowed down to a crawl and drove on the centerline, forcing cars traveling in both directions to go around him.

Finally the applause died down as everyone in the chamber waited for the most anticipated moment of the evening. The Sergeant-at-Arms said, "Mr. Speaker—the President of the United States."

||| CHAPTER 56 |||

"Mr. Speaker—the President of the United States," Rockland Tubbs repeated with amused contempt. He clapped mockingly, matching the rising applause coming from the radio in his van. He checked the missile's target designator again. It was locked on the second floor window on the east side of the House chamber. "Yes, Mr. Speaker, please do introduce the President of the United States. And when he speaks his first word, it will be his last."

The blue decals on the door of the white van identified it as belonging to the Potomac Electric Power Company, allowing it to park unchallenged almost anywhere. It sat at the curb on East Capitol Street, just across from the barricades on Second. The only thing unusual about it, as it sat with its rear doors open and emergency blinkers going, was the opaque black cloth that hung across the gaping rear doorway, cloaking the interior. At the bottom of the cloth, a thick necessary-looking cable ran from the vehicle down into an open manhole, which was guarded by a small, collapsible yellow fence.

Immediately inside the surveillance curtain sat the Brushfire missile, delicately positioned on top of its tripod. Tubbs had cut a tiny circular hole in the fabric covering the rear of the van so the laser sight could be zeroed in.

The applause on the radio died down to accommodate the next increment of protocol. The Speaker of the House stepped up to the microphone. "Members of Congress, I have the high privilege and honor to present the President of the United States." A thundering ovation swelled.

Tubbs lifted the curtain and sat down quickly on a small stool behind the missile and checked his target one last time. "No, *I* have the high privilege and honor to present the President of the United States—and the rest of you—with death." The applause continued. "Hurry up, you bastards. He isn't that good a President."

Finally, the clapping started to lose its enthusiasm. "Come on, just one word." Now there was a shuffling of feet and hundreds of small thuds as the leadership of America seated itself.

Tubbs's hand went to the trigger. He was ecstatic with the

inevitability of it all. The great hall was now silent. "Just one word, Mr. President," he begged impatiently.

Without warning, an explosion of sound and movement threw Tubbs into the wall of the van. The missile was knocked from the tripod and fell toward the rear of the van. It bounced once and skidded out the back door, coming to rest with its nose on the street.

Devlin threw his car in reverse and backed away from the van. He got out and was met by a five-round burst from Tubbs's automatic. Devlin ran across the street to draw any subsequent fire away from Bonelli, who was exposed in the front seat.

Tubbs disappeared into the back of the van and pulled down the curtain. Off at an angle, Devlin took up a good firing position and waited for Tubbs's next volley.

Instead, he heard the van's engine roar and then its tires squeal as it took off, heading east.

Devlin ran back to the car. "You all right, Tony?"

In an angry voice, Bonelli said, "Fine, fine. Let's go get the son of a bitch!"

Devlin thought about making Bonelli get out, but he knew it would take an argument. When he looked down Capitol Street and saw Tubbs take a right and disappear, he knew they didn't have the time. He jumped behind the wheel and took off after the van.

As their car reached the intersection Tubbs had turned at, Devlin could see him a block ahead, taking another turn.

Gaining on him, Devlin realized the neighborhood was becoming residential. They turned onto another street. Ahead, two young black girls were crossing the street. The van swerved, trying to hit them. The message was clear: Give up the chase, or cause innocent people to die. Devlin fired a couple of shots to warn the girls, and they jumped out of the way. "I've got to end this."

Bonelli looked at him, his apprehension apparent. "How?" It was more a protest than a question.

Devlin's car was close behind now. "Next turn, I'll bump him on the opposite side he's turning. It should flip him."

"Flip him! What does it do to us?"

"I don't know. I've never done it before."

Tubbs made a left turn. Devlin accelerated as he followed him, and tapped the unbalanced van in the right rear. It was just enough. The top-heavy vehicle flipped over on its left side, then onto its roof, and finally came to rest on its right side.

Because Devlin's car had been going faster than the van at the time of impact, it started skidding counterclockwise, almost completing a full circle before it slammed broadside into a utility pole. Devlin opened the door. "Find the cellular and call the switchboard. Let them know where we are."

First Devlin heard the explosion of Tubbs's automatic and then, a split second later, the thud as the round slammed into the rear door of his car. He fired four quick shots in the general direction of the van and saw Tubbs, his head bloody, vanish into an abandoned building.

Bonelli yelled, "Wait for some help, Mike!"

Devlin ran toward the building.

III CHAPTER 57 III

Devlin, standing off to the side, threw the door open, trying to draw Tubbs's fire. When none came, he took a quick look inside. Some scattered light from the street lamps outside came through the broken window frames. The building appeared to be the remains of a small manufacturing plant. Waist-high brick walls halfheartedly divided the interior into the areas where the different phases of production had once been performed. The rear door was boarded up. There was no other way out.

Tubbs could have been hiding in a half a dozen places, so Devlin took a deep breath and stepped into the doorway, allowing himself to be outlined in light. He counted, "One thousand," and then dove forward. Just as he did, Tubbs's .45 flashed violently from behind a low wall to the right.

Devlin was on his feet, sprinting in a low silhouette toward the rear of the structure. As he readied himself to dive over one of the walls, his foot caught an old electrical box and he fell short, causing him to land on his already injured right hand. As he hit the ground, he told himself not to let go of his weapon, but the shock ran up his arm and momentarily shut down the muscles that controlled his hand. The gun slid into the darkness ahead of him.

Tubbs was on his feet tracking Devlin through the sights of his weapon. He fired a three-round burst, which forced Devlin

297

to leave his weapon for the safety of the wall. He dove over it and for the third time in less than a minute landed on the hard concrete floor. His hand burned with pain. He flexed it, trying to determine whether it was broken. Everything seemed to work, but with swelling reluctance.

Did Tubbs know he had lost his gun? If so, why wasn't he coming? Maybe he thought Devlin had a backup. But he had given it to Bonelli.

Tubbs's voice came up over the wall. "Devlin, is that you again?"

"Funny how we keep running into each other."

"How did you find me?"

"Your *granddad* told me."

Tubbs thought for a moment. "You broke into my house?"

"Your father didn't seem to mind."

"It's difficult for me to decide who I hate more right now, him or you."

"Isn't it a little late for compliments?"

Tubbs barked a short laugh. "Before we end this, tell me something. How did you know it wasn't Packard?"

"If he was the Freedom Killer, he would have anticipated the phone trace."

"You have to admit he was a logical choice. According to your profiling techniques, he was perfect."

"Now, tell me something," Devlin said. "Was the MMI list part of your plan?"

"No. After the Department of Justice bombing, Packard was going to conveniently commit suicide, and when the FBI investigated him, everything else, including MMI, would fall into place. How *did* you get on to MMI?"

"It was LoFranco. He got on to it because of all the phony addresses around the Naval Academy. And then, of course MMI's motto in your last message."

"I guess I was a little too clever planting that."

"I think LoFranco was the clever one."

Tubbs laughed again. "Yeah, right up until he stumbled onto me."

Devlin remembered LoFranco's last words and seethed at the impudence of the man who had killed him. But he knew he had to stall for time. "Was Packard involved at all?"

"He was so desperate for friendship, he would do anything for me, but he had no idea what was going on. Even when I put the gun to his temple, he seemed appreciative." Tubbs stood up and faced the wall Devlin was behind. "Well, I suppose you've got help coming, so we'd better get this over with."

"What did you have in mind?"

"I think you'll agree this life isn't big enough for both of us, so how about pistols at ten paces?"

Devlin wondered if Tubbs knew that he was unarmed and was trying to lure him into the open. If he was and Devlin refused, he would probably figure it out, walk over, and execute him. "Why would I want to do that? You're the one who needs to get out of here."

Tubbs grunted his pained laugh. "Come on, it's your chance to be a hero forever. With the risks I've seen you take, that's really what you want, isn't it?" When Devlin didn't answer, he said, "Do I have to come over there?"

Devlin had to try a bluff. "Okay, but first I have to know how much ammunition you have left."

"Two magazines. Why should that matter?"

"I don't know how many rounds are left in this clip. I dropped a full one when I fell. The way we kept shooting at and missing each other at the Convention Center, I really don't think this would be fair unless you let me get it and reload."

Tubbs stepped out in front of the brick barrier. "Fair enough. I just want one more chance to go even up with you. Our final and deciding match. That's not asking too much considering you've already taken my life. I just want an equal opportunity to take yours."

Devlin knew he had to step out and face Tubbs, but suddenly a nauseating fear seized him. If Tubbs had seen through his bluff, Devlin knew he was about to die.

"Come on, Mike, you're not going to make me do something as melodramatic as count to three, are you?"

Devlin thought about running until he heard, "One," followed by a single footstep coming closer. There were no other options. He stood up, keeping his right hand behind his thigh as if hiding a weapon.

Without taking his eyes off Tubbs, he walked around to the front of the wall. He decided there were not going to be any *High Noon* heroics for either man. As soon as his gun was in his hand, he would go for a killing shot. As he bent over to retrieve it from the darkness, Tubbs raised his gun and said, "Well, I guess you don't have a second gun. That's poor planning. Did you really think I couldn't tell the difference between your gun and a magazine hitting the floor?" He glared at Devlin, but when he didn't see fear, he said, "You know, snapping LoFranco's finger off with those pruning shears was sweet. Nice and crisp. And shoving that knife up into the base of his brain was an extremely satisfying way to kill him. But it's nothing compared to what I'm feeling now. I've got fourteen rounds in these two clips, and only the last bullet is going to kill you. I'm going to start at your ankles and stitch you all the way up to your thyroid gland." Tubbs grinned and lowered his gun.

Devlin had two choices: He could go for the gun at his feet and most certainly be killed, or dive back over the wall and at the very least be wounded. He decided to go for the gun. He dove to the floor.

A gunshot ripped through the air. Confusion melted the arrogance on Tubbs's face. Rockland Tubbs, a man who wanted to steal a country's freedom, gave up his own as he fell dead on the abandoned factory floor.

Directly behind him, slumped against the doorjamb, with the snub-nose still aimed at where Tubbs had stood, was Tony Bonelli.

||| CHAPTER 58 |||

It was almost 4:00 A.M. when Devlin finally swore to and signed his official statement. The two agents from the Office of Professional Responsibility had been interviewing him in detail since 11:00 P.M. Predictably, they had raised their eyebrows in dissatisfaction when he admitted not only to having taken Bonelli, a disabled clerk, on a dangerous assignment but to having given him a gun as well.

When they asked him why, he told them he didn't have a good answer. He knew he would not be judged at that moment, by the logic and compassion of the two men before him, but rather weeks or months later, against the inflexibility of Bureau policy. And, by the book, he was guilty. But he also knew that the Freedom Killer was dead and no one else had been hurt, so his infractions would be seen as relatively inconsequential and eventually, after some compulsory management head-shaking, waived.

Tom O'Hare was waiting outside the interview room. "How'd it go?"

"They were giving me a pretty hard ride until I gave you up."

"I wish you had. I could use the time off."

"Where's Tony?" Devlin asked.

"They finished with him over an hour ago. I had him driven home."

"How'd he do?"

"He did fine. Hell, he's a hero."

"You don't have to tell me; I was gone until he dropped the hammer on Tubbs."

"He said he'd see you tomorrow at the memorial service."

"I'm going to bed."

"You've got one more stop. The Director wants to see you."

The door to the Director's office was open. Bob August sat at his desk, initialing paperwork. Devlin knocked on the frame as he walked in. "You wanted to see me, sir?"

August stood up. "How's the hand?"

"It's good."

August came around his desk and they both sat down in armchairs. "I asked that you come up here because I wanted to personally thank you for what you did last night. When someone joins this organization, they do it with the hope of someday being able to solve an important case like this. So few of us ever do. If Tubbs had been successful, this country would be in chaos right now."

"It seems like we should both be saying this to Tony Bonelli."

"I couldn't agree with you more. And I have already thanked him, but I wanted to talk to you separately, because I have a proposition for you."

"Four o'clock in the morning, called to the Director's office. How illegal is it?"

August laughed. "It's legal. A little unorthodox, but legal. Through this investigation you have demonstrated an ability to work independently and accomplish a great deal beyond the normal FBI channels and procedures. You have a history of not being able—or perhaps simply refusing, to recognize boundaries. Some people would think that makes you a problem, but I see it as the reason you're successful, while others become bogged down with procedure."

"Sounds like you need a *big* favor."

"I've discussed this with Tom O'Hare, and we both feel there's something reassuring about knowing that you're wandering around out there securing the Bureau's interests. So if you agree, we would like to be able to send you out to use your instincts on selected specials. Much like you did here. You would be responsible only to Tom and me." Devlin said nothing. "And I realize if something like this became too demanding, it could become a hardship for your family, so each assignment would be left to your discretion. If you thought it would be too demanding, you could pass without prejudice. The bottom line is I need you out there."

"I'd like to discuss it with my wife."

"Good. I'll be optimistic then, because I know you didn't get this far without her. Now, what can I do to show my appreciation?"

"Tell me to go home."

August smiled. "I wish I could, but the White House has taken a beating over this case and now they want some mileage in return. Prepare for the mother of all dog-and-pony shows."

"They've got you and the attorney general plus a couple of dozen spokesmen, who live for something like this. They don't need me."

"They think you have a certain, ah—"

"Chevrolet quality?"

"Exactly. What you see is what you get—you're honest, and you work hard for the money. And these people want a heroic ending to a terrifying story."

"In that case, I've got an idea that should make everyone happy."

||| CHAPTER 59 |||

The gray sedan pulled to the curb in front of the Northwest Airlines terminal at National Airport. Tom O'Hare was driving; next to him sat Bill Hagstrom. In the back were Devlin and Bonelli. O'Hare turned around and said, "I still don't understand how you got the Director to let you out of these news conferences."

"I just told him some of the lines I had been rehearsing. Most of them had erection references in them."

Hagstrom said, "And that scared him off? He evidently doesn't realize that the people most likely to talk about that phenomenon are the least likely to experience it."

"Then that would make you the expert."

Hagstrom turned to O'Hare. "What ever happened to loyalty in this outfit? There was a time when you'd make someone a star and they would be grateful enough to let you insult them. Let's get this ingrate's bags out of the trunk before he misses his plane."

As they got out, Bonelli offered his hand to Devlin. "Thanks, Mike."

"I'm the one who needs to say thanks."

"It was a helluva ride. I appreciate the seat up front."

"I enjoyed the company."

Devlin got out and let his smile say good-bye. It was

another smile Bonelli had never seen before: Devlin had a secret.

As he stared out the window, she came up behind him and put her arms around his waist. "You must be tired," Knox said.

Mike Devlin continued to look out the hotel window, watching all the reassuring colors lighting the streets and rides of Disney World below. "Kids asleep?"

"Sound asleep. They had a great time today."

He turned and put his arms around her. "Me, too."

Knox looked at the clock. "Put on the TV. I want to see if it's on again."

Devlin turned the set on and sat down in a chair, pulling her onto his lap. The announcer said, "Today, during a ceremony at the White House, FBI employee Anthony Bonelli was honored by the President, who described him as being doubly courageous—not only for overcoming his disability, but for his involvement in a shoot-out earlier this week that left the infamous Freedom Killer dead. Also on hand was FBI Director Robert August with a special presentation."

The Director stepped to the podium. "By order of the President of the United States and with the full concurrence of both the Congress and the attorney general, I have been empowered to promote support employee Anthony Bonelli to the position of Special Agent."

Bonelli struggled forward on his canes. Amid a thundering storm of camera flashes, he accepted his badge and shook the Director's hand. A reporter yelled to him, "How does it feel, Tony?"

He looked down at the badge for an instant and then back at the reporter. "When you're disabled, you spend a lot of time remembering what it was like when you were young, before the disease, and you realize the best part about being a kid is thinking that all your dreams can come true. The worst thing about muscular dystrophy is believing that none of your dreams will ever come true. I guess I now feel free to dream again."

Knox turned off the television. "I'm really happy for him," she said. "How about you, Mike, do you still dream?"

Pulling her back into his arms, Devlin stared down at his wife. He kissed her softly and tasted the heat in her mouth. "What would I dream for?"

Don't miss this gripping
novel of the FBI!

CODE NAME:
GENTKILL

by Paul Lindsay

Agent Mike Devlin is known for
getting things done—by any means
necessary. And with two FBI agents
executed in cold blood and a
million-dollar extortion case blowing
up in the agency's face, the
beleaguered Detroit Bureau needs
Devlin's brand of insubordination.
But once Devlin is in deep, there's
only one way out—the hardest way
of all. . . .

Published by Fawcett Books.
Available in bookstores everywhere.

WITNESS TO THE TRUTH
by Paul Lindsay

Special Agent Mike Devlin is a walking exception to the FBI rule book. In a Bureau full of G-men who act more like corporate-ladder-climbing yuppies, he's still dedicated to cracking crime—by any means necessary. Exiled to the dead-end of wiretap duty, Devlin gets an explosive earful: someone is planning to expose the Bureau's reservoir of mob informants. Then, even closer to home, a fellow agent's daughter is kidnapped.

Determined to crack both cases, Devlin rounds up a gallery of the best rogue agents to do the jobs right. It means putting his career on the line, and his life in the crosshairs of the Mafia and a maniac. But Devlin wouldn't have it any other way. . . .

Published by Fawcett Books.
Available wherever books are sold.